Seth felt closer to Rebecca than he'd ever felt to another woman.

But he knew that he wouldn't put any woman through the dangers and loss of being married to a lawman. It had cost Clare her life, and that was before they'd even wed. Looking into Rebecca's eyes, Seth knew her love would be true and strong.

"You are turning out to be a good friend, Seth," Rebecca said.

Her gentle smile created a longing in him to take back her hand and never let it go. He told himself that this was a simple reaction from learning that Rebecca had suffered losses much like him.

He hated the thought that his actions had caused her even more loss. Jesse Cole would have been a good husband to her.

Once Rebecca learned the truth of the circumstances of Jesse's death, would she still want to be friends with him?

RHONDA GIBSON

lives in New Mexico with her husband, James. She has two children and two beautiful grandchildren. Reading is something she has enjoyed her whole life, and writing stemmed from that love. When she isn't writing or reading, she enjoys gardening, beading and playing with her dog, Sheba. She speaks at conferences and local writing groups. You can visit her at www.rhondagibson.com, where she enjoys chatting with readers and friends online. Rhonda hopes her writing will entertain, encourage and bring others closer to God.

The Marshal's Promise

RHONDA GIBSON

Love Inspired

Recycling programs
for this product may
not exist in your area.

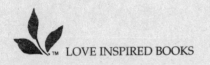 LOVE INSPIRED BOOKS

ISBN-13: 978-0-373-82918-7

THE MARSHAL'S PROMISE

Copyright © 2012 by Rhonda Gibson

www.LoveInspiredBooks.com

Printed in U.S.A.

Many are the plans in a person's heart,
but it is the Lord's plan that prevails.
—*Proverbs* 19:21

Books are never written alone—friends and family
are always supporting the author in various ways.
This book is for Kathryn Velarde Baharmi
and Janet Lee Barton. Thank you both
for all that you do for me. You are true sisters—
maybe not blood, but definitely sisters.

James Gibson—
without you my idea well would surely run dry.
I love you more than words can express.

And above all to my Lord and Savior.

Chapter One

Cottonwood Springs, New Mexico Territory, 1885

"Please don't cry, Miss Rebecca."

"I'm not crying," Rebecca Ramsey said, brushing at the tears that had caught her by surprise. "I— I've got something in my eye."

Grace Miller's young eyes chided her less-than-honest answer.

"Yes, I am crying. I shouldn't have fibbed about it. Please forgive me?" At the child's smile and nod, Rebecca continued, "It's just that, I never expected Mr. Cole to be dead." She'd never met the man she'd been engaged to marry in person, so the tears were more for her and what she'd lost than for Jesse Cole.

Rebecca tried to ignore the presence of U.S. Marshal Seth Billings, who stood beside the door. He had been the bearer of the bad news that her intended groom had been killed. Did he know she'd answered a mail-order-bride ad? Probably not.

He held his hat in his hands, waiting for her reaction. His broad shoulders seemed slumped under the tan shirt and brown vest he wore. There was a U.S. Marshal's star on his chest. Her gaze moved upward to where his sorrowful brown eyes bored into hers.

The rich texture of his voice drifted across the short space between them. "I'll be happy to pay your train ticket back to…" He stopped and looked at her.

The question in his eyes prompted her to say, "Maryland?"

"Maryland." He nodded his head.

What did she have to go back to Maryland for? Her stepmother had made it clear she was no longer needed or welcome in her father's house. The only job available to her, a woman of twenty, was personal maid to the daughter of one of the wealthiest men in Ellicott City.

Rebecca didn't like the job or the daughter. No, Rebecca Ramsey would not be returning to Maryland anytime soon. She squared her shoulders and stood. "Thank you, Marshal, but that won't be necessary."

Seth Billings gritted his teeth; the muscles worked in his jaw. "What will you do, then?" His harsh words cut through her tattered emotions.

Fresh tears threatened to spill over. Rebecca cleared her throat. She wouldn't let it close up on her now. "I will think of something, Marshal. Thank you for coming by and telling me about…" She couldn't finish the sentence and the words hung in the tense room like the scent of burned bread. Rebecca focused on Grace's small back as the child went into the kitchen.

"Well," he said, turning back to the door, "if I can do anything to help you settle here in Cottonwood Springs, you let me know. Ya hear?"

Rebecca nodded, aware that the brown-eyed marshal no longer looked at her and really didn't expect an answer. The door shut behind him. She blew her nose on the white handkerchief she kept tucked into her sleeve for just such occasions.

Mrs. Miller came into the room, wiping her hands on her apron. The aroma of freshly baked apple pies drifted into the room with her. "Is he gone?"

Nine-year-old Grace followed her mother back into the room. The little girl bit into a green apple and chewed, her gaze never leaving Rebecca's face.

"Yes, he's gone."

The older woman eased into one of the overstuffed chairs. "So, now what are you going to do?"

Rebecca sighed. "I'm not sure." The Millers had housed her since she'd arrived five days earlier. They'd given her a room and three square meals and allowed her to sit with them during church on Sunday. How was she going to repay them?

Her plans had been to have Jesse take care of those expenses when he returned to town. Now she knew he wasn't coming. And she had no idea how to repay the debts she'd unknowingly accumulated.

Her temples began to ache. Silently she vowed to stay in New Mexico and not return to a family who didn't want her around. "I suppose I'll look for employment." She rubbed the sides of her head as she paced the floor.

"I don't think you have to make any rash decisions today, Rebecca. You've had a shock. Why don't you go lie down until supper?" Mrs. Miller smiled at her. Pity laced her eyes and filled her oversize face.

Rebecca hated that look. She'd seen it in the eyes of her father's friends many times after he'd remarried, and it wasn't a look she ever wanted to see again. "I think I'd rather have a breath of fresh air, if you don't mind. I would like to go for a walk." She pulled her wool shawl from the peg by the door and looked to Mrs. Miller.

"Go on, child. You have much to think about." Mrs. Miller pushed her immense body out of the chair and headed toward the kitchen. "Grace, come with me. You can peel potatoes for supper."

Rebecca slipped out the door and gently closed it behind her. Butterflies fluttered in her stomach. Her thoughts twisted in her mind as worry and doubt left her feeling faint. She sank into the chair beside the door.

She lowered her head and hid her face in her hands. She and Jesse had been planning to buy a small farm, raise fruit trees and chickens once they were married. Rebecca sighed, but now Jesse was gone and thanks to her stepmother, she couldn't go home.

Before her mother died, Rebecca's life had been one of ease and love. Her father, a businessman, enjoyed the warmth of their home as much as she and her sister had, so it had been no surprise that he'd remarried shortly after her mother's death.

After that day, life had changed for Rebecca. Her jealous stepmother had kept her busy and away from her only living parent. She'd made her feel uncomfortable in the only home she'd ever known. The woman had been sweet in the presence of her husband and vinegar in his absence.

By the time her stepmother had forced her to answer the mail-order-bride ad that Jesse had placed, she'd been ready to leave. She was ready to get away and start a family of her own.

Rebecca desired someone to love her, to make her feel safe and wanted again. She'd thought Jesse Cole was the answer to her prayers. He'd seemed to be stable and to know what he wanted out of life. His letters had promised security and love. Now she knew that wasn't to be, at least not with Jesse.

She missed her father and longed to go home, if only he would stand up to her stepmother. Rebecca knew that would never happen. No, she had to figure out what to do, on her own and with no help from her father.

Lord, what am I going to do now? I don't want to go home and I'm not sure how I will be able to stay here. Why did Jesse have to die?

Seth hated days like today. The shattered look in her eyes had revealed that Rebecca Ramsey felt as if all were lost. Why hadn't Jesse just surrendered? He would have been in jail, but at least he would have been alive.

Jesse had begged Seth as he bled out from his gut wound, "Please watch for Rebecca Ramsey, Marshal. She was to be my bride." Their last conversation continued to play in his mind. "She didn't do anything to deserve this. I really wanted to start a fresh life with her. Please take care of her. Please!"

The easy gait of the horse allowed Seth to recall his answer. "I'll see that she's taken care of, Jesse."

Jesse clutched his shirt and pulled him closer. "Don't let Maxwell or any of the Evans gang near her. They'll try to take her."

Jesse's fear for Rebecca was real and Seth found himself saying the words he knew the dying man wanted to hear. "I'll protect her, Jesse. That's a promise."

With Seth's words, peace entered the young man's eyes and then Jesse Cole took his final breath. Twenty-two was too young to die. Jesse had only been three years younger than himself. Seth shook his head at the sadness of the past week.

Memories of Jesse flooded his mind. Jesse had arrived in Cottonwood Springs six years ago. Nobody knew anything about him, just that he worked hard at the livery where old man Rodgers had given him a job. Then he'd taken up with Maxwell Evans and his brother. For four years he'd run with Maxwell, his brother Clod and Horace Nance.

The four men made up the Evans gang. They had been more a nuisance than a real gang. They'd stolen small things and the men of Cottonwood Springs didn't feel the need to press charges against them. Boys will be boys, as the old saying goes. Old man Rodgers died one night and Jesse moved in with Maxwell.

And then one night Jesse ran into Reverend James Griffin and found the Lord. Jesse turned his life around that night; he started working on the Vaughan farm just a couple of miles out of town. The other Evans gang members hadn't been thrilled with the turnabout and they'd given the Vaughan family plenty of trouble.

Over the next two years the Evans gang had grown and become braver. Their crimes had developed into more serious transgressions. With each passing year, Maxwell had become more dangerous.

Seth hadn't been surprised when they'd robbed the bank in Durango. What had surprised him was when the smoke cleared, Jesse had been the one left to die on the bank floor. He shook his head again. Jesse hadn't even carried a gun. What had he been doing robbing a bank with no gun?

Guilt slammed into Seth's gut. He'd shot down an unarmed man. Never had he felt the gravity of being a U.S. Marshal as strongly as he did now. The law was behind him, but he still felt as if a small part of his own soul had been ripped from his body the day Jesse Cole died. No matter how many times he played the events of that day in his mind, it came out the same. He'd killed an unarmed man, he'd killed Jesse Cole.

Thankfully the Vaughan orchard came into view. He shook his head and muttered, "I need to stop dwelling on it. Jesse is gone and there's nothing I can do about it now." Seth gave a little kick of his boots against the horse's sides and sent it into a trot. It was time to go tell Mr. Vaughan that his hired hand wasn't coming home.

He rode into the front yard. Two big hounds came to greet him with loud barks and yips. Mrs. Vaughan waved from the front porch and Mr. Vaughan walked out of the barn to meet him.

"Afternoon, Marshal. What brings you out this way?"

Seth slid from his mount. "Bad news, I'm afraid. Jesse Cole got himself shot up last week. Didn't make it. He won't be returning to work."

Mr. Vaughan took his hat off and wiped at the sweat on his brow. "I'm sorry to hear that. He was a good man."

"So it would seem," Seth agreed.

"Mind telling me what happened?" The old man slapped the hat back on his gray head and indicated Seth should follow him to the bunkhouse.

Seth fell into step with him. "He was present during a bank robbery over in Durango last week. One of the Evans gang took a shot at me and things got out of hand. Jesse got caught in the cross fire."

Mr. Vaughan pulled the door open and walked to one of three bunks in the one-room building. "I see."

Seth pressed on, trying to explain away his own feelings of guilt for having shot Jesse. "I'm afraid he was running with the Evans boys again. They were the ones hightailing it out of Durango with a bag full of money." He didn't feel the need to tell Mr. Vaughan that Jesse hadn't been carrying a gun when he was shot. That fact still bothered him. Instead Seth asked, "Did Jesse say where he was going when he left here?"

"No, just said he had some unfinished business and that he'd be back in a couple of days." He pulled a suitcase out from under a bunk that Seth assumed was Jesse's. "I thought he'd gone into town to see about buying the Porters' place. Had no idea he was running with the Evanses again." He grunted as he lifted the case for Seth to take. "These are his belongings. Feels like this thing is filled with rocks. He also has some clothes lying around here, too. Do you want those?"

Seth shook his head.

"Do you know if he has any family we can give this to?"

Seth took the heavy case and shook his head again. He frowned at the weight of the container. "I don't think he does, but there is a young woman in town that might. I'll ask her."

Mr. Vaughan nodded and followed Seth from the bunkhouse. "It's too bad." He muttered more to himself than to Seth. "I really liked that boy. He was real excited when that gal answered his mail-order-bride ad, too."

They walked back to where Seth's horse waited. Seth set the suitcase onto the saddle and then swung up behind it. So Rebecca Ramsey was a mail-order bride. He'd heard of women answering those ads, just never figured he'd meet one way out here in the New Mexico Territory.

Seth arranged the case in front of him, before saying, "I'd like to keep this as private as we can. His mail-order bride arrived last week and, well, I'd just as soon she not be told what happened to him." He paused and shook his head. "Honestly, I'm not sure I know what happened. I'd like to think Jesse was there against his will."

Mr. Vaughan took his hat off and twisted the brim. "All I know, Marshal, is the poor boy seemed to have got caught in some cross fire and was shot in Durango." He shook his head and looked at the ground. "Poor boy was at the wrong place, at the wrong time." He looked back up.

Seth nodded. "Thanks."

"Do you know if his lady will be staying in Cottonwood Springs or moving on?" He shielded his face from the sun as he looked up at Seth.

Seth had wondered the same thing. "Don't know yet." He waved and headed back to town. His thoughts turned to what Mr. Vaughan had said.

Had Jesse been heading to town to buy a place and get married? Or had he met up with the Evanses with the purpose of robbing the bank to secure a better future for his new bride? Seth could still see the fear and concern in Jesse's face for Rebecca's safety.

As the horse lumbered back to town, his thoughts turned to the pretty young woman who had come to town to marry Jesse. Her eyes had done something to his heart that only one other woman's eyes had ever done.

Remember she was killed because of your job, Billings. How could he forget? He couldn't. And because of Clare's death, Seth vowed never to love another again. His job and her meekness had gotten her killed. Nope, he wasn't going to fall in love again, at least not until he was done with marshaling. He doubted any woman would wait for him that long.

Rebecca Ramsey's heart-shaped face filled his mind's eye. No, Seth Billings had no intentions of hurting or being hurt by another woman because of his career. A career he felt sure God approved of. *Lord, please help me to fulfill my last promise to Jesse and help me to overcome this pressing guilt of killing an unarmed man. And if it be Your will, keep Rebecca Ramsey far from me. I don't want to see her hurt.*

Chapter Two

Rebecca stepped into her favorite blue dress and buttoned up the front. She pulled on her shoes and hurried to get her hair fixed just right. Her fingers worked the hair into a French braid and she eased small strands forward to frame her face.

Today she would look for employment. The night before, she'd talked to the Millers and assured them she would pay for the days she'd stayed with them. They'd been kind and offered to let her stay as long as she needed. For this, Rebecca was thankful to the Lord.

She walked to the dining room and stopped just inside the doorway. The fragrance of eggs, bacon and hot biscuits greeted her. Rebecca ignored the sound of her stomach as she made her way into the room. Mrs. Miller and the marshal were seated at the table. He held a cup of fresh coffee in his hand. When Mrs. Miller saw her, she motioned for Rebecca to join them.

"Good morning, Rebecca. The marshal has come to see you."

Rebecca acknowledged them with a nod of her head. "Good morning."

Mrs. Miller indicated that Rebecca sit with a sweep

of her hand. The heavyset woman braced her hands on the table to push back her chair and stand. "Would you like some coffee and eggs?"

Rebecca slipped into the wooden chair. "Just coffee this morning, thank you." She had decided the night before not to eat any more than she had to until she could repay the Millers what she owed them.

"I'll be right back. You two carry on with your business." Mrs. Miller lumbered out of the room.

What business did the marshal have with her? Had she done something wrong? Rebecca shook the thought away. No. It couldn't be that. Then what? Sensing his brown eyes upon her, she folded her shaking hands on the tabletop. "What did you want to see me about this morning, Marshal?"

He lowered his cup and took a deep breath. "Yesterday I went out to where Jesse had been living and let his boss know he wouldn't be returning to work." His gaze studied her face.

She still didn't understand why he was there. "I see." She met his look head-on. Marshal Seth Billings was a nice-looking man. His light brown hair curved above his collar, chocolate-colored eyes looked back at her and when he spoke, a dimple winked in his left cheek.

In a soft voice, he said, "I wasn't finished."

Mrs. Miller returned with Rebecca's cup of coffee. "Here you go, dear. It's hot." She set the cup on the table in front of her along with a small sugar bowl.

"Thank you, Mrs. Miller." Rebecca pulled both the coffee and sugar toward her. "Please go on, Marshal." She scooped two teaspoons of sugar into her cup.

"If you two will excuse me, I've work to do in the kitchen." Mrs. Miller left without waiting for their answers.

"As I was saying, while I was out there, Mr. Vaughan gave me some of Jesse's personal belongings. The sheriff and I have gone through them and there are a couple of things we thought you might like to have, Miss Ramsey." He picked up his coffee and took a sip.

The marshal continued to study her over the rim of the cup. His eyes bored into her as if searching for something. Rebecca ignored his look. She focused on her coffee instead as her mind raced.

What could he possess of Jesse's that she might like to have? His letters from her? Maybe. A family Bible? But wouldn't that go to his family? The Bible, not the letters, she mentally corrected herself.

When it became apparent he was waiting for a reaction from her, heat began to fill Rebecca's face. She set her cup down and asked, "What sort of belongings?"

The marshal reached inside his jacket pocket and pulled out a small bundle of letters. When he handed them to her, Rebecca recognized her handwriting on the outside of the envelopes.

Had he read them? She searched his eyes for the answer. He held her gaze, but she couldn't read their expression. Now her face felt on fire. She prayed he hadn't read them. "Thank you." She laid the bundle on the table and reached for her drink.

"There's more." The marshal reached into the other side of his jacket and pulled out another envelope. He handed it to her.

She didn't recognize this one. Rebecca turned the plain white envelope over in her hands. "Are you sure? I didn't send this one to him."

The marshal raised his head and nodded. "Yes. I think you should have it."

Rebecca ran her fingertips over the seal. "What about his family?"

"Jesse moved here six years ago. During that time he never mentioned family, so since you were to be his wife, the sheriff and I decided you should receive that, as well." He nodded his head in the direction of her hands and grinned.

He'd discussed this with the local sheriff? "What's in here?" Her hands trembled. Was she really ready to take whatever was inside the envelope? Was it a deed to the farm he had talked about in his last letter?

A warm chuckle brought her attention back to the marshal's face. A woman could get used to the sound of his easy laugh and handsome features; she jerked her mind away from such foolish thoughts.

His eyes twinkled. "Why don't you open it and find out?"

Rebecca's mouth dried, she picked up her coffee and sipped the bitter sweetness, allowing it to wash over her tongue. Then she took a deep breath and slid her fingernail under the envelope flap.

Within the depths of the envelope lay a letter. She pulled it out and carefully unfolded what she saw to be a blank piece of paper. Hidden within the paper were money notes. She counted the money and realized there was enough there to pay the Millers for the time she'd spent with them and she'd have a little left over to stay for maybe a month longer. Rebecca silently thanked the Lord for meeting her needs.

"Are you sure it's all right for me to keep this?" She searched his features once more. His eyes were serious; the chocolate color that had just twinkled with amusement now seemed almost to caramelize as he stared back at her.

He nodded and then finished his coffee. "That money was in his possessions. I'm sure he'd want you to have it. I'd say there is enough money there to take you home, Miss Ramsey."

Rebecca shook her head. "No, it's enough to pay the Millers what I owe them. And, I've already told you, I'm not going back."

He stood. "So you are determined to stay here?"

How many ways did she have to say she was staying? She looked up from the money. Then she felt it. Something wasn't quite right, but she couldn't put her finger on what it was. Did the marshal suspect her of some wrongdoing? Or was this just his normal way of dealing with what he might consider a grieving fiancée?

Rebecca stared at the handsome man before her. His jawline tightened and his eyes narrowed. She raised her chin and returned his stare. "Yes, Marshal, I am. You needn't worry about me. I am an upstanding citizen and, God willing, I will find a job today."

Rebecca Ramsey hadn't reacted the way he'd thought she would when she opened the envelope. Maybe she didn't know about the rest of the money he'd found in that suitcase. And then again, maybe she did and was sticking around town to find it. What had Jesse been doing with so much money in money notes, diamonds and gold?

Was that the reason Jesse had begged him to keep watch over her? Did the Evans gang know about the stashed treasure in Jesse's possession? Would they come after her, thinking she had it? The questions swirled through his mind like a Texas twister.

What if she really was just an innocent and had no

clue Jesse had been an outlaw? Or that he was far richer than he'd let anyone know. Seth's protective instincts surged through his stomach.

Seth admitted to himself that he found Jesse's girl attractive. She seemed young and naive. What kind of woman ventured alone to answer a mail-order-bride ad that would take her to an isolated place like the New Mexico Territory?

He'd read her letters. They were simple letters telling Jesse her age, what she looked like and when she would arrive. She'd asked no questions of Jesse Cole. From what he'd read, it seemed as if Rebecca Ramsey had simply come with no knowledge of anything about her soon-to-be husband.

His first promise to Jesse echoed in Seth's ears. *I'll take care of her.* He tilted his head sideways and studied her. If she really was just a girl looking for work, he should help her. He'd promised, and Seth Billings never broke a promise. "What kind of work are you looking for?"

"I'm not picky, Marshal, and I'm a hard worker, so it really doesn't matter." She shrugged her shoulders, picked up her morning coffee and took another sip.

The blue in her dress brought out the blue shades within her eyes. Small ringlets of blond hair drifted about her face as she bent to the hot beverage. Miss Ramsey smiled as she savored the drink. Seth stared at her soft lips and then shook himself mentally. The young woman in front of him was quite attractive, but no lady liked to be stared at.

"Why? Do you know of a position?" Her question pulled him from his musings.

She gazed into his eyes as if she were looking into his soul. What did she see there? He didn't want to know.

"I might. The sheriff and I were talking this morning and I've come to the conclusion that I need a house here in Cottonwood Springs." Those cornflower eyes continued to study him. "If I find one, I'll need someone to clean, do laundry and cook for me when I'm in town. Would you be interested in something like that?"

"When will you know if you are going to take up residence here?" Her gaze moved to his left hand.

The urge to tuck it into his pocket proved mighty powerful. He didn't want her looking to him as a replacement for Jesse. "I'll let you know by this afternoon. How does that sound?"

Her small smile turned into a big grin. "It sounds like something I wouldn't mind doing."

Seth nodded and then headed for the front door. He had a lot of work to do if he planned on having a home in Cottonwood Springs by this afternoon. The soft swish of her skirts informed him that she had followed him. "I'll see you later," he promised and then left.

He shook his head as he climbed into the saddle. *Seth Billings, you are going to have to stop making promises.*

Chapter Three

Rebecca pulled her wool shawl over her dress, picked up the money and then carried her coffee cup into the kitchen. "Mrs. Miller, I am leaving now to look for employment." She placed the empty cup beside the older woman.

Mrs. Miller's hands were up to her elbows in hot soapy water. A pile of dirty dishes was stacked to her left. "Your business with the marshal is finished?" She looked over at Rebecca. Mrs. Miller's gaze moved to the envelopes in her hand.

Rebecca tucked the letters she'd sent to Jesse under her arm and then opened the packet that held the money. She turned her body so that Mrs. Miller couldn't see the full contents of the envelope. "I'm not sure. He's offered me a job."

Mrs. Miller dried her wet hands on a dish towel and rested a hip against the counter. "Then why are you looking for another one?" Her brows arched as she watched Rebecca count out the money.

"Well, it's not a for-sure job and I can't continue living here if I can't pay for my stay." Rebecca knew Mrs. Miller wanted to ask her about the money. The older woman opened her mouth and then closed it again. Almost as if she realized it was none of her business.

Rebecca handed her what was owed. The other woman took the money and dropped it into her apron pocket.

"Will you be back in time for lunch?" Mrs. Miller returned to the dishpan full of dirty dishes.

Cottonwood Springs wasn't that big of a town and Rebecca could return in plenty of time before lunch, but she wasn't sure she wanted to. Mrs. Miller was nice enough, but Rebecca sensed the other woman would like to have some time to herself and, to be honest, Rebecca felt the same. "Probably not."

"Have a good day, dear. I'll see you at supper." And just like that, Mrs. Miller dismissed her.

Rebecca walked to the front door, stood in the doorway and looked both ways down Main Street. The town's dirt street and light breeze had sand drifting in the air. She focused her mind on the business in town and not the fact that she hated flying dirt.

Across the street from the Millers' general store was the newspaper office; next to that stood Mrs. Kelly's hat and dress shop. She studied the false fronts of both businesses. The newspaper office wouldn't offer much employment, but maybe Mrs. Kelly could use another seamstress. She'd start with these two businesses and then make her way around town, should she not acquire employment at either establishment.

As she crossed the street, Rebecca lifted her skirts to keep them from getting dusty. A light breeze picked up from the direction of the river and she shivered. Early spring in New Mexico seemed to be rather cold. Truth be told, Rebecca preferred the heat of summer, at least she had in Maryland. Who knew what New Mexico summers would hold for her?

When she arrived at the door of Mrs. Kelly's hat and dress shop, Rebecca hesitated. She took a deep breath, smoothed out her skirt and slowly exhaled before she entered. A little bell over the door announced her arrival.

A female voice called from the back, "I'll be right with you. Feel free to browse around."

Rebecca walked farther into the room. Sunlight shone through the big plate-glass window, creating a cheerful and warm environment. Colorful dresses, shawls, coats and hats took up most of the room. Toward the back, where the mysterious voice had come from, was a curtained-off doorway.

She noticed an area for sewing in the far corner. A long table and two sewing machines occupied the space. The two machines gave her hope that the other woman might need help.

A brown dress caught her eye. She walked over to it and touched the soft fabric. Its color reminded her of the marshal's eyes. Rebecca admired the way the waist seemed to tuck inward. She took it off the hanger and held it up against her front.

"I like that dress, too, but brown doesn't seem to be your color."

Rebecca glanced up and found a woman who looked to be a little older than she, standing off to the side shifting though a rack of dresses. Soft brown hair peeked out from under a stylish green hat that matched the dress she wore. Straight strands of hair escaped the stylish hat and now rested on each side of her heart-shaped face. She stared at Rebecca with interest.

She pulled a light yellow dress off a hanger beside

her. It looked to be the same style, just a different color and with a soft print of small blue flowers. "The flowers in this one will accent your eyes beautifully." The woman held it out to Rebecca.

Rebecca handed the brown over and took the yellow. Again she held the soft fabric up to her front. It had been a long time since she had a new dress, and this one flowed about her ankles and looked as if it would cinch in her waist. What was she doing? She couldn't afford a new dress. "Thank you, but I can't buy a dress right now."

The woman smiled at her. "That's quite all right." She took the dress back and hung it on its hanger. "So if you aren't here to buy a dress, what can I help you with? A hat perhaps?"

Rebecca shook her head. "No, not today. My name is Rebecca Ramsey and I need to speak with the owner of this shop." She thought that sounded like a good way to start business.

"It is nice to meet you, Miss Ramsey. I am Eliza Kelly and I am the owner." She smiled broadly.

Rebecca hadn't expected Mrs. Kelly to be so young. She'd pictured an elderly woman running the dress shop. "It's nice to meet you, Mrs. Kelly. I wondered if you had a position I might fill."

Her eyes saddened. "I'm afraid not. This is a one-woman show for the time being." She tugged at a strand of her hair.

"I see. Thank you, Mrs. Kelly." Disappointment filled her voice and Rebecca wished she could take it back. She offered a smile to show she wasn't upset and then turned to leave the shop.

The other woman followed her. "Aren't you Jesse's

girl? I mean… I was just about to make a pot of tea. Would you be interested in having a cup with me?"

Rebecca started to refuse, and then saw Mrs. Kelly's cheeks had turned pink and her eyes held warmth. She hadn't meant her inquiry to sound as rude as it had. Did the whole town think of her as Jesse's girl? Rebecca hoped not.

The thought of a nice cup of tea swayed her decision to stay. It had been weeks since she'd had a sip of her favorite beverage. "Yes, I am, or I was, Jesse's girl, and I'd love a cup of tea, Mrs. Kelly."

"Oh, thank you. I was so worried I'd overstepped my bounds. And you must call me Eliza." She turned to walk into the sitting room. "I hope you can find employment, Rebecca, but I'm afraid if the other merchants are having as hard a time as I am they won't be open to offering you a job. Have you tried the other shops?"

She followed Eliza into the sitting room, through the dining area and into the kitchen. "No, I came to you first."

Eliza picked up the teapot and filled it with water. "That is so sweet. I really wish I could afford to hire you. It would be wonderful to have another lady to talk to during the day."

The statement sounded odd to Rebecca. "Don't you talk to women all day? I mean, this is a dress shop."

"Well, yes, I guess I do, but not real talk. You know, my customers are here to talk about dresses and they share gossip, but I want something more, you know?"

Rebecca did understand. "I believe I do."

Eliza smiled. "I just had a feeling you and I would understand each other. It's strange how that works.

Hannah is fun to talk to, but she only comes to visit once a week. You know Hannah, don't you?"

At a shake of Rebecca's head, Eliza pressed on as she made the tea. "Hannah Young. She's the schoolteacher. She's about our age and has no husband. But she is devoted to her work as a teacher and only allows herself to visit on Saturdays, and then of course Sunday is full of church."

Rebecca remembered someone introducing the schoolteacher last Sunday. If memory served her right, Hannah Young was a small woman maybe four feet eleven with black hair and she walked with a slight limp. She'd also seemed very shy and hadn't spoken much. A flash of humor tugged at the corners of Rebecca's mouth. Eliza's fast talking must be the reason Miss Young kept to herself.

The morning flew by as Rebecca enjoyed her visit with Eliza. It didn't take long to learn that Eliza was lonely. She'd lost her husband two years ago; he'd died when they lived in Silverton, Colorado. According to Eliza, her Charley had been killed in an avalanche during one of the worst snowstorms she'd ever seen. Thankfully, they'd saved enough money for Eliza to get to Cottonwood Springs and purchase this house to start up her hat-and-dress business.

The sound of the bell ringing in the shop had Eliza up and hurrying to take care of her next customer. Rebecca knew it was time to go. She needed employment if she wanted to stay in Cottonwood Springs and get to know her new friend better.

Eliza came back into the room. "That was Mrs. Pierce. She picked up her dress and matching hat."

Rebecca stood to leave. "I best be going, Eliza. It's almost lunchtime and I haven't inquired about employment anywhere but here." She slipped her shawl over her shoulders and headed for the door.

"Oh, I wish you didn't have to go." Eliza followed her. "Do come back when you are done and let me know if you found a job."

Rebecca smiled. "I will and thanks for the tea."

Eliza had been right. An hour later, Rebecca walked out of the general store still jobless. Everyone wanted to give her employment, but none of them had the funds to do so—everyone, that was, except Mrs. Walker, the owner of the general store. Rebecca had the impression that Mrs. Walker had taken an instant disliking to her.

Her thoughts went to the marshal. Maybe he'd had better luck in finding a house to buy. She hoped so. If nothing else good came of the day, thanks to Eliza, Rebecca now felt she had a friend close to her age in Cottonwood Springs.

Rebecca's gaze moved over the town. It was pleasant enough and sat back against a mountain. The mountain resembled a sand rock, but trees lined the river below and, because smaller streams ran across the back side of the town, cottonwood trees shaded the majority of the businesses and homes. A beautiful spot if ever she'd seen one.

The marshal's voice pulled her from her musings. "Any luck finding work?"

Rebecca searched the shadows of the buildings to locate him. He stood propped against the blacksmith shop. His arms crossed and his eyes narrowed.

His tone indicated he wasn't a happy man. So she answered in a short, crisp reply of, "No."

"I thought we had an understanding." He pushed away from the wall and walked over to her.

Rebecca didn't like his tone and hardened her voice to match his. "What kind of understanding?"

He crossed his arms again, spread his legs and glared down at her. "That you now work for me."

"But, that is only going to happen if you find a house. Did you buy a house, Marshal?" She crossed her arms to match his stance.

He relaxed and grinned. "As a matter of fact I did. And, I have already moved in." The sudden pleasure in his voice surprised her.

Rebecca really hadn't expected him to follow through with his offer of a job. Her spirits lifted, knowing she now held a position and would be able to stay in Cottonwood Springs. She silently thanked the Lord for yet another blessing and smiled. "That's wonderful."

The dimple in his cheek winked. "Would you like to see it?"

"I'd love to, Marshal, and while we walk you can tell me what this job entails."

He tucked her hand into the crook of his arm and began walking. Her heart did a little flutter as tingles climbed up her hand and into her hairline. Seth Billings made her feel alive.

With Jesse Cole dead, could this be the man God sent her to the New Mexico Territory for?

Chapter Four

Seth led Rebecca toward his new home. He hoped she liked it as much as he did. The front was white and had a small porch that led off the right-hand side. Two windows faced forward with dark brown shutters on each side. It was small but could be added on to, should he ever decide to marry and have a family.

He liked the fact that it was on a side street and that there weren't many other houses close by. Cottonwood trees surrounded the house, giving it plenty of shade. He stopped in the yard and waited for her reaction.

Her eyes seemed to drink in the front of the little house. She sighed and pulled her shawl closer about her shoulders. "It's wonderful, Marshal." Rebecca turned to look up at him. She tilted her head sideways and smiled up into his face.

Seth felt as if he would drown in the blue pools of her eyes. "Thank you. I'm glad you like it. I'm thinking of adding a couple of rosebushes to the front, under the windows. What do you think of that?"

She stared at the windows as if she could picture the flowers already in full bloom. "They will look and smell wonderful. What color roses?"

He reached up and gently brushed aside a way-ward curl from her cheek. Seth was surprised when she turned to face him. Her cheeks flushed a soft pink. "Pink, I think."

Rebecca stepped away from him and nodded. "I'm sure they will be lovely."

Seth realized he had embarrassed her with his ac-tions, and moved forward to open the door. She fol-lowed him up the steps and waited. His boot heels clicked against the hardwood floor as he stepped inside the doorway and allowed her to pass.

His gaze swept the sitting room trying to visualize how the space must look to Rebecca. It was small with a couch and end table. A bookshelf rested against one wall, empty of books at the moment.

It felt empty, but Seth had been blessed that the Wil-sons were willing to sell it at such a low price and were willing to leave some furniture behind. Granted, he had plenty of money sitting in the bank, but he had hoped not to have to touch the money until his days of mar-shaling were over.

"This is beautiful, Marshal. I love that the living area is open to the kitchen." She spun around the room, touching the furniture. "It needs a thorough dusting and the floors require a good sweeping, but other than that it is great."

He leaned against the door frame and watched as she flittered from room to room. It wasn't a big house—two small bedrooms, a sitting room, kitchen with a dining area. Each room opened off of the sitting room. With her gasps and excited squeaks, you would think it was a mansion on a hill.

Seth couldn't stop the smile that lifted the corners

of his mouth. For some odd reason he felt pleasure at her excitement. "Thank you, Miss Ramsey."

Her skirts swirled about her ankles as she hurried to the kitchen. "How did you get moved in so quickly?"

Seth pushed away from the frame work and followed her. "It came fully furnished and I don't have that many clothes."

Her gaze moved about the rooms. "That was very fortunate for you."

He nodded. Her eyes sparkled as she ran her hands over the shelves and stove. If he didn't know better, he'd think she was envisioning the kitchen as her own. Maybe she was, it was easy to do.

Seth decided right then and there to continue taking his meals over at the diner. The last thing he needed was to have Rebecca Ramsey getting too comfortable in his kitchen. Women and marshaling didn't mix. He couldn't live through another woman's death caused by his job.

Rebecca looked about the area and spread her hands. "You will need a few kitchen things."

"Kitchen things?"

Rebecca grinned. "Yes, kitchen things."

Seth crossed his arms. He'd just decided on eating over at the diner like normal. He didn't need kitchen things. He set his jaw and started to tell her that he didn't need another thing in the kitchen.

"Wouldn't you like to have a fresh pot of coffee first thing in the morning?" she asked, once again mimicking his stance and arms.

How did she know what he'd been thinking? A fresh pot of coffee first thing in the morning did sound nice. He nodded and grunted his agreement. All right, he'd give in on the coffee, but other than that, Seth refused to give in any further.

And then she walked over to the stove. A wistful longing sound entered her voice. "I can cook some marvelous dinners at this stove. Just think, a hot meal at the end of the day."

The last part seemed to be more a thought to herself than a statement for him. He stepped closer to her. The hopeful sound in her voice pulled at his heartstrings. "Sounds like you miss cooking."

Rebecca tilted her head to the side and studied him. "I do. Cooking was one of the few things I enjoyed back home."

The desire to make her feel at home, in his house, overwhelmed him. "It's a good thing, then, that I said I'd need a cook, too."

As if she'd forgotten, joy filled her face. "That's right, you did."

Seth crossed his arms to restrain himself from reaching out and hugging her. So much for taking his meals at the diner, his inner voice taunted. Rebecca was getting too close and he couldn't afford to allow that to happen.

He took a step away from her. "I need to get back to work. You go and get the things needed for cooking and cleaning from the Millers' store." His boots pounded across the wood floors as he hurried to leave.

"Have Mrs. Miller charge whatever you feel is needed to my account." Seth rushed out the door and across to his horse. He needed to put some space between himself and Miss Ramsey.

Rebecca wrapped her shawl around her shoulders and followed him out the door. She pulled the door shut behind her. What had happened? One moment he'd been smiling and seemed happy she'd taken an interest in his home and her new job, the next he'd exited the house like a cat that had been threatened with a bath. She shook her head. The marshal was turning out to be one complex man.

He mounted his horse and rode out of town. His wide shoulders swayed in the saddle. He was attractive, and for a few minutes earlier, she'd thought he might kiss her. His touch on her cheek had been warm. She shook her head. *Get those thoughts out of your mind, Rebecca Ramsey,* she reprimanded. Now that Jesse was gone, Rebecca knew she could only rely on herself. Her own father had deserted her. No man could be trusted not to cast her aside.

She focused instead on what having a job and money coming in would mean for her. If she saved enough, maybe the bank would allow her to buy a house. She'd need a down payment. Rebecca thought about writing to her father and asking for money, but just as quickly tossed the thought aside. No, it was time she depended on herself.

A few minutes later, she entered Eliza's hat-and-dress shop. The bell announced her arrival. Within seconds Eliza arrived to greet her.

"Oh, Rebecca, you're back!" She grabbed Rebecca's hand and pulled her into the sitting room. "How did the job hunting go? Did anyone hire you? Did you try the druggist? What did he say?"

Rebecca laughed. "If you will stop asking so many questions, I'll tell you." She noticed that Hannah Young sat at the table sipping from a small china cup. "Hello."

The schoolteacher answered in a very soft voice. "Hello." Her blue eyes sparkled with amusement.

"Well, tell us," Eliza demanded. "Rebecca has been looking for employment," she informed Hannah, as if she'd not told her of Rebecca's earlier visit, and then she filled another teacup.

Rebecca eased onto the soft cushion of the kitchen chair. "Thank you." She took the tea that Eliza held out to her.

"Did you?"

"Did I what?" Rebecca teased, setting the cup down.

Exasperated, Eliza huffed, "Get a job?"

"I did."

Eliza squealed and then demanded, "Really? Where?" She put the sugar bowl in front of Rebecca.

Hannah set her cup down and folded her hands in her lap. She didn't say anything, but simply waited.

Rebecca spooned two teaspoons of sugar into her hot tea. She glanced at Hannah and they shared a grin. At a snail's pace she stirred her tea.

Eliza burst. "Oh! Come on, tell us."

At the same time, the little bell over the door jingled the arrival of a new customer.

Eliza groaned. She leaned forward on the table and whispered, "Don't say a word until I get back." Her brown eyes drilled into Rebecca. "Especially you." She shook her finger in Rebecca's direction.

"I promise, I won't say a word about the job until you get back." Rebecca took a sip of her tea.

Hannah stifled a giggle but not before Eliza pinned her with her brown gaze.

"I promise," Hannah said, still grinning.

Satisfied they wouldn't discuss Rebecca's new job without her, Eliza left the room in a swirl of skirts. They heard her call out a greeting to the lady who'd entered.

Rebecca leaned toward Hannah and asked in a soft voice, "Is she always like that?"

Another giggle escaped Hannah before she answered, "Always."

They sipped their tea in comfortable silence. Rebecca's thoughts were on the trip she planned to make to the Millers' store. She intended on stocking the marshal's kitchen with a big coffeepot, lanterns, crockery, pots and pans, iron skillets, a Dutch oven, cooking utensils, knives and dishes. Then there were the food staples she'd need, like coffee beans, spices, baking powder, oatmeal, flour, sugar, eggs, milk, butter, fruit and vegetables, honey and molasses, crackers, cheese, syrup and dried beans. Her mind swirled with what she'd buy and cook in the cozy kitchen.

"She didn't tell you, did she?" Eliza asked as she hurried back into the room.

At Hannah's negative shake of the head, Eliza pressed on. "That was Mrs. McClain and Isabel. Her daughter is getting married in Aztec next week and we had to do a final fitting." Eliza laughed. "I think that's the fastest final fitting I've ever done." She refilled her teacup. "Now, Rebecca, where will you be working?"

Rebecca could only imagine the look on Mrs. McClain's face as Eliza rushed her daughter through the fitting. She set her cup down and answered, "I'll be keeping house, cooking meals and doing the marshal's laundry."

Eliza's jaw dropped. Her brown eyes resembled those of a hoot owl. When her friend had nothing to say, Rebecca looked to Hannah.

The schoolteacher's cheeks were flushed and her eyes bright.

"What is wrong?" Rebecca asked, looking from one of them to the other.

Hannah recovered first. "Nothing is wrong, Rebecca. It's just that we didn't know the marshal had decided to stay here in Cottonwoods Springs."

That seemed like a reasonable excuse for the women's shocked reactions to her news, but Rebecca sensed there was more. "And?"

Rebecca waited. She expected that at any moment Eliza would find her tongue.

Eliza took a big gulp of tea. Hannah followed suit.

The hatmaker shook her head. "Oh, I dread to think what the older ladies will have to say about this. They will chop you up and have you for breakfast, Rebecca. You're going to have to tell the marshal you can't do it."

Rebecca looked from one woman to the other. Hannah was nodding her agreement with Eliza. "No, I accepted the position and I don't care what a bunch of old ladies have to say about it."

"But Rebecca, I thought you were a Christian." Hannah reached across to pat her hand.

Anger boiled to the surface. "I am a Christian, Hannah. But I don't see what that has to do with this."

Eliza jumped to her friend's rescue. "You are a single woman, he's a single man. It wouldn't be decent."

Rebecca sat back in her chair. "It's not like that," she said in a soft voice.

"We know that, but the tongues will begin wagging as soon as the gossips hear this." She pressed on before Rebecca could react. "You haven't been here long. This is a small town with very little for the local gossips to do."

Rebecca took a deep breath and said a silent prayer. Had she made the right decision? Was this something

God approved of? She searched her heart and had peace about the decision. The concerned look on both her new friends' faces had Rebecca reasoning with them. "Eliza, did those same women speak out against you when you bought this house and changed it into a hat shop?"

"Well, yes, but that was different."

Before she could add more, Rebecca jumped in with a question for Hannah. "Have they ever spread rumors or said mean things about you, Hannah?"

The young schoolteacher looked down at her hands and nodded. "Yes."

Rebecca nodded. "So they are going to talk, no matter what I do. Right?"

Eliza answered. "Yes, but living with a man without marriage, that's not right, Rebecca. Surely even you can see that." Again she gulped her tea.

It was Rebecca's turn to become speechless. Who said she would be living with the marshal? Her cheeks began to heat up as she realized what her new friends thought of her. She gritted her teeth and prayed for patience and wisdom before speaking.

"Please don't be angry," Eliza said. "We don't want you to go against…"

Rebecca held up her hand to stop Eliza's tirade of words that was sure to follow. "First off, I'm not moving in with the marshal. I will be going to work and returning to the Millers' place each evening, at least until I can afford my own place."

Eliza opened her mouth to interrupt. But this time Hannah stopped her. "Wait, Eliza. Let her speak."

Rebecca nodded to thank Hannah and then continued, "Second, I'm willing to forgive you both since you really don't know me, and third, I need to go, I have shopping to do." She stood to leave.

Hannah's firm voice stopped her. "Please sit back down, Rebecca."

So that was the way to handle students—firm voice and constant eye contact. Rebecca eased back onto her seat.

"Thank you. Eliza and I didn't mean to upset you or hurt your feelings. You're right, we don't know you very well, but I know we both want to know and help you. Please forgive us for jumping to the wrong conclusion."

It was the most words she'd ever heard Hannah speak. Were these ladies to become lifelong friends who would love her no matter what? Rebecca feared to believe it, and yet, deep down prayed it would be so.

"Yes, please forgive us. I'm not sure why we jumped to the wrong conclusion." Eliza's cheeks held pink coloring and her neck had turned red.

Humbled by their sincerity, Rebecca blushed. "Thank you both. Maybe I should have told you I will be going to his house in the mornings, fixing his breakfast, and while he is away during the day, I will be cleaning his house, doing his laundry and then cooking his dinner. Once he arrives back home in the evening, I will be returning to the Millers'. Yes, that's how I should have told you."

Silence filled the room.

Then Eliza came alive again. "Do you have to stay at the Millers'? Or can you live wherever you want? Because, I'd love it if you would move in with me. Where is his house? Is it close to here?"

Hannah shook her head and then picked up her tea. Did Hannah wonder how Eliza could rush from one thought to the next, like she did?

"Well?"

Rebecca laughed. "No, I don't have to live with the Millers. Yes, I can live wherever I desire. And, yes, the marshal's house is one street over and back from here."

"Then you can live here with me! I have two bedrooms. Yours would be small, but you would have your own space. Come on, I'll show you." Eliza was out of her chair and through the door before either Rebecca or Hannah realized that she planned on leaving.

Hannah stood first. "You might as well humor her." She followed Eliza from the room.

Rebecca took a deep breath before standing. *Lord, will everyone judge my decision to work with the marshal like Hannah and Eliza just did? And, Lord, You better step in quick if I'm not meant to move in here with Eliza.*

Chapter Five

Seth strolled out of the Millers' store with a frown on his face. Mrs. Miller had been happy to inform him that Rebecca had moved from their residence and into Mrs. Kelly's. She'd also given him the bill for the supplies Rebecca had had delivered to his house two hours earlier. He shook his head. Miss Ramsey had been busy, but what had he expected?

His boots kicked up dust as he walked toward his new home. *That she'd be looking for the remainder of the stolen money and diamonds?* He pushed the thought of stolen money and diamonds from his mind.

Would she be waiting for him when he got there? Seth's emotions warred with his reasoning. He wanted her to be there waiting with a hot meal, and then again he didn't want her to be there. The thought of her cooking at his stove, setting his table and smiling across it at him tugged at his heart. He reminded himself that he couldn't get romantically involved with her. Besides, he'd killed Jesse and when she learned that she'd never forgive him.

In a quiet, firm voice, Seth spoke to himself. "I am a U.S. Marshal. I have no business thinking about her that way." Maybe speaking the words out loud would convince his heart it was true.

He slowly climbed the steps to his house. Seth took a deep breath and opened the door. The smell of green chili stew filled his nostrils and his stomach growled its appreciation of the welcoming aroma. Expecting to find Rebecca at the stove, he squared his shoulders and entered the kitchen. Only, she wasn't there.

Disappointment and relief washed through him. He released the air in his lungs and turned to look in the bedrooms for her. After a quick inspection, Seth realized he was alone in the small house. He followed his nose back to the kitchen.

His gaze moved around the room. She'd moved things around. A white cabinet with two drawers now sat beside the stove. A washtub sat on top of it. She'd hung a small shelf above the cabinet and several bottles containing spices set on top of that. The large cupboard now stood against the wall and held all his new dishes. The kitchen table and four chairs sat in the center of the room and in front of the cupboard. The potato bin stood beside the window on the other side of the room. Sheer curtains covered the window and the table had a crisp, clean cloth draped over the dark wood that matched the curtains. How had she done it? In just a few short hours she'd turned his kitchen into a cozy place to eat.

He picked up a bowl and walked to the stove, where a pot of stew, a skillet with a stack of homemade tortillas and a coffeepot were warming. Instinctively Seth reached to the closest drawer in the white cabinet and pulled it open. His gaze landed on a large ladle. He grabbed its handle and dipped the cupped end into the stew. The aroma of meat and green chili teased his nose. Seth located more utensils in the cabinet and then carried his meal back to the table. He pulled out a chair and was almost seated when a knock sounded on the front door. His gaze went to the door and then back to his bowl. The desire to ignore the summons tugged at him. The knock came again. He sighed and walked to the door.

"I'm sorry to disturb you, Seth, but I was wondering if I might have a few minutes of your time."

He pulled the door open wider. "Well, sure, Reverend Griffin. Please do come in." Seth stepped farther back into the room. It was amazing how fast the reverend had located him. "I didn't realize you were in town."

"Only been here a few hours." The reverend smoothed his mustache over his top lip.

"Would you like some supper?" Seth asked, leading the way to the kitchen.

"No, thank you. I just ate over at the diner."

Seth stopped and turned to face him. "Oh, would you rather sit in the sitting room to talk?"

"No, I don't want to keep you from your supper. We can chat at the table."

Seth nodded and continued on to the kitchen. He poured each of them a cup of coffee and then sat. "What brings you here?"

Reverend Griffin pulled out a chair across from him. He cleared his throat. "Why don't you tell me about you and Miss Ramsey?" He picked up his cup and held it his hands.

"There's nothing to tell. She needed a job and I gave her one."

The reverend looked him straight in the eyes and demanded, "Doing what?"

He took a deep breath and folded a tortilla in half. If

it were any other man, he'd tell him it was none of his business, but since James Griffin was a man of God, Seth decided it would be best just to answer. "She cooks and cleans for me."

"That's all?" He arched an eyebrow and studied Seth over the rim of his cup.

Savory stew and spicy flavors coated Seth's tongue. He had to swallow before answering the minister. "No, she also agreed to do my laundry once a week. Why all the questions, Reverend?"

James set his cup down. "It's like this, son. The ladies think it isn't decent for a young woman to be here with you alone."

Seth sighed. "Reverend, Miss Ramsey isn't living here with me. She's coming in every morning, while I'm working, to cook and clean. She wasn't here this evening when I came home. So I don't see what they are upset about. And, if it bothers them so much, why didn't one of them offer to be her chaperone?"

James laughed. "You better be careful what you ask for, Marshal. I can just see Mrs. Walker and her group of friends doing just that. Now, let me get this straight. You won't be home when she's here?"

Seth pushed his bowl back. All his interest in food was gone. "I can't guarantee that, Reverend. There may be times we are both here."

James frowned. "I see."

"But I give you my word, on those occasions Miss Ramsey will be safe with me."

The two men studied each other. Finally the minister smiled and pushed back his chair. "Then that's good enough for me." He walked to the door and Seth followed.

"I'll see you on Sunday, Reverend." Seth stopped in the doorway.

They shook hands and then the minister left.

Seth closed the door and looked about. The sitting room had been dusted and swept. Thanks to his promises, Rebecca now worked for him and the town gossips had started to spread their poison.

Rebecca gathered her basket of applesauce-oatmeal muffins and headed out the door. She stopped on the sidewalk and enjoyed the crisp morning breeze. Mr. Watson entered the newspaper office. He waved at her before shutting the door.

The sound of skipping feet caught her attention and she turned to see Grace Miller skipping toward her. "Hi, Miss Rebecca."

"Well, good morning, Grace. Off to school this morning?" she asked.

Grace held a lunch pail in one hand and a book in another. "Yeah, Ma makes me leave early every morning. I end up there way before the other kids. Where are you going?" She tugged at the long brown braid that had landed on her shoulder when she'd stopped skipping.

Rebecca tried to remember if Grace had left early the mornings she'd been staying at the Millers' house. After a few moments, she gave up. "I am headed to work." Rebecca started to walk down the sidewalk. She liked the idea that she had a job now and didn't have to rely on someone else to take care of her.

"At the marshal's house?"

"Yes, at the marshal's house."

Grace walked along beside her. "Mama says you are

lucky he needed someone 'cause there isn't no work here."

"Because there isn't any work here," she automatically corrected.

Grace frowned up at her. "That is what I said."

Rebecca laughed and continued walking. She was in too good a mood to press the matter further. Grace skipped along beside her.

"Your mother is right. I feel very blessed." Rebecca tucked a wayward curl behind her ear. If it hadn't been for the marshal, she'd have had to go home. The last place she wanted to go.

"Can I go with you to the marshal's house? I don't want to go to school yet." Grace stopped in front of the diner and looked up the hill at the school.

The smell of bacon and eggs drifted to them as the town banker opened the diner door and walked out. "Excuse me, ladies." He tipped his hat at them and then continued on down the sidewalk.

"Yes, as long as you're sure your mother doesn't mind."

Grace smiled. "She said she doesn't mind as long as I get to school on time."

Rebecca frowned. Had Mrs. Miller planned on Grace going with her to Seth's house? That's the way it sounded, but then again, children often maneuvered things around to fit what they wanted to do. Besides, what difference would it make as long as Grace got to school on time? "Well, then, let's go."

They arrived and Rebecca knocked on the door. Grace shifted from foot to foot as they waited. Seth opened the door. He stood before them with wet hair and stocking feet. The brown curls coiled about his white collar and Rebecca itched to reach out and touch the damp strands.

"Good morning," she said in a soft voice.

Grace looked up at her. The young girl tilted her head as if to study Rebecca's face further. The expression in her eyes said she knew something was wrong but wasn't sure what.

Rebecca cleared her throat and said a little more forcefully, "Good morning, Marshal."

He smiled at Grace. "I see you brought a chaperone this morning."

"I'm not a chaperone. I'm Grace Miller." The nine-year-old stood up taller as if to remind him of who she was.

"So you are." He tugged her braid.

Rebecca pulled her shawl closer around her shoulders. "May we come in?"

Seth opened the door farther and Grace slid around him. He looked into Rebecca's eyes and smiled. The dimple in his left cheek winked. "Sure, come on in."

He inhaled as she walked past. "What's in the basket?"

"Applesauce-oatmeal muffins. My mother's recipe." Rebecca walked past him and headed for the kitchen. "I thought you might like them with a hot cup of coffee for breakfast."

"Sounds wonderful," he answered, following close behind.

Her mother used to say that the way to a man's heart is through his stomach. Rebecca hadn't thought of that in a long time. She made the coffee and listened to Grace and Seth talk about school and the spelling test that Grace was dreading.

She put the muffins on the table and got down three

small plates. Next, she poured herself and Seth coffee. "Would you like a glass of milk, Grace?"

"If you have it," the little girl answered politely.

"I do. I'll be right back." Rebecca went out to the well and pulled on a long rope. The evening before, she'd tied a mason jar filled with milk to one end of the rope and lowered it into the cold water below.

She returned a few minutes later to find both Grace and Seth munching on the muffins.

"These are very good." Seth indicated the muffin in his hand and then sipped his coffee.

Rebecca smiled. "Thank you. I never think they taste as good as when Mother made them." She poured the milk for Grace and set the glass down beside her.

"Thanks, Miss Rebecca." She picked it up and gulped it down. "Oh, it's so cold!"

"That's because it just came out of the well." Rebecca sat down and picked up one of the muffins. She bit into the sweetness and sighed. They were good, but like she'd said earlier, not as good as her mother's. The brown sugar and oatmeal topping didn't taste as sweet.

"May I have another one, Miss Rebecca?" Grace was already reaching toward the bowl.

"Of course you can." Rebecca licked the sugary sweetness from her lips. She looked up to see Seth watching her. Tingling heat filled her face.

He pushed his chair back. "If you ladies will excuse me, I need to get to work."

Rebecca followed him to the door. "Is there anything special you want me to do today?" she asked as he stepped out onto the porch.

"Just do what I'm paying you to do, and don't expect anything more from me." He stomped off around the house. Rebecca knew the barn was behind the house and figured he was going after his horse.

Grace came to stand beside her. "What did he mean by that?"

Rebecca shook her head. "I have no idea." The man seemed as skittish as a mother deer with a new fawn, another good reason to stay away from him. She knew opening her heart to a man like him would only lead to heartbreak.

Chapter Six

The sound of the school bell had both Rebecca and Grace hurrying back inside. Grace to get her book and lunch pail, Rebecca to get the breakfast and the previous night's dinner dishes washed. She'd noticed earlier that Seth had piled his dinner dishes into the new dishpan.

"See you after school, Miss Rebecca!" Grace yelled as she raced back out the front door, the sound of the slamming door a sure sign of her departure.

Rebecca grabbed the water bucket and walked out the kitchen door to the well. What had Seth meant by "don't expect any more from me"? Did he think she'd expected him to give her this job? Surely not. He'd been the one to suggest it and had even seemed angry when he'd realized she'd been out seeking employment elsewhere. She carried the water to the stove to heat.

Then she made her way to the bedrooms. The guest room looked the same as when she'd left it the day before. Seth's bed looked as if he'd wrestled a bear during the night. Rebecca stripped the sheets and quilts off it and then remade the bed.

Next she returned to the kitchen and poured the hot

water into the dishpan. After the dishes were washed, Rebecca swept and mopped the kitchen floor. While it dried, she stepped outside and looked at the backyard. To the left someone had hung a clothesline between two boards and to the right an overgrown garden spot had been fenced off. At the back of the lot stood a big red barn.

"Lovely day, isn't it?"

Rebecca turned toward the sound of the male voice. The speaker stood beside the corner of the house, under a large Cottonwood tree. He looked to be about her age. A hat covered his dark hair and hid his eyes. "Yes, it is."

He pressed away from the tree and moved closer to her. "I haven't seen you around here before." His voice dripped of sweetness.

Unease warned her not to allow him to get too close. She took a step back.

The stranger bent down and plucked a piece of grass, he chewed the end of it. His gaze never left her.

"I'm new to Cottonwood Springs." She walked backward toward the door. "If you will excuse me, I have work to do."

He stood and started toward her again. "Aw, why don't you stay outside for a bit? We could get to know each other." A crooked-toothed grin inched across his face.

The hair on the back of Rebecca's neck prickled. She continued walking backward. "I don't even know your name, sir. Now if you will excuse me." Rebecca turned and opened the door.

"Hello! Is anyone home?" The voice came from the other side of the house.

Rebecca looked to find a short man with a mustache and thinning light brown hair walking around the corner of the house. Where were these men coming from? Were they together? Panic crept up her spine. Rebecca's head spun back to where the other stranger had been, but he was gone. Where had he gone?

She jerked her head back in the direction of the shorter man. He'd come a short distance in a fairly fast time. He extended his hand out as he walked toward her. "Miss Ramsey? I'm Reverend Griffin, the circuit-riding preacher for this area. I don't believe we've met. I hope you don't mind my stopping by this morning."

She grabbed his hand within hers and pulled him inside. "I am so glad to see you. There was a man here. He frightened me," Rebecca explained once they were both within the kitchen.

"What man?" Reverend Griffin looked back out the door.

"I don't know who he was. He didn't give me his name, but everything about him made me nervous." Rebecca placed her hand over her pounding heart.

"I'll go see if he's still hanging around." Reverend Griffin barged out the door like a mama bear after her wayward cub. The look in his eye said he was in a no-nonsense sort of mood.

Rebecca stood up and poured herself and the reverend cups of coffee. She waited at the table for him to return. Sipping the rich beverage, Rebecca allowed her mind to go over the events of the past few minutes. Maybe she had overreacted. By the time the preacher returned, her heart rate had slowed its terrified rhythm and her hands had ceased shaking.

The reverend stopped in the open doorway. "I'm sorry, Miss Ramsey. He's gone."

"Please come in and sit down, Reverend. I'm glad

he's gone." She took a drink of her coffee and then continued, "I might have been a bit excessive in my reaction to him."

He entered the kitchen, shutting the door behind him. "Never underestimate your first gut reaction to a person, Miss Ramsey. It's better to be cautious than to be sorry." He picked up the coffee cup and took a sip. "You make very good coffee, young lady."

"Thank you. Would you like a muffin?" She took the cloth off the basket of muffins she'd made that morning.

He waved a hand. "No, thank you. I appreciate the coffee but I need to be on my way. I only stopped by to introduce myself and invite you to church on Sunday." Gulping the last of his drink, he stood.

Rebecca stood, also. "Thank you for stopping by. I'll be sure to attend Sunday morning."

"Very good. Services start at ten." He opened the kitchen door and left the way he'd entered.

She gathered their cups and took them to the full dish basin. Had the strange man been innocent of wrongdoing? Had she overreacted like she'd told the traveling preacher she might have? The hair rose on Rebecca's arms. No, she'd been right in staying away from him.

Rebecca washed and rinsed the dishes. She pushed thoughts of the stranger away and focused them on Seth and his parting words. She didn't know why he'd snarled at her, but she was determined not to give him a reason to fire her. The rest of the day was spent scrubbing his house and cooking dinner.

Grace arrived shortly after school let out. "Hi, Rebecca!" she called as she came through the front door. "Oh, something smells delicious."

"I'm in the kitchen," Rebecca called back to her. "I baked chocolate-chip cookies."

The nine-year-old tossed her lunch pail on the table. "May I have one?"

Rebecca smiled. "Yes, you can tell me if they are any good."

Grace grabbed a warm cookie from the plate on the cupboard and took a big bite. "Mmm, these are great," she mumbled around a mouthful of cookie.

"I'm glad." Rebecca finished wiping off the table. Grace reminded Rebecca of her sister back home. Joy would be ten in a few months. Joy loved her sweets, and her little round body was proof that their mother had been the best baker in all of Maryland. Tears filled her eyes as she thought about Joy and their mother. She blinked hard and reached for the pan of dishwater. Thankfully their stepmother had taken a liking to Joy. Probably because Joy looked so much like her father. Rebecca, on the other hand, looked like Mother, which didn't sit well with her stepmother at all.

"Do you want to walk home with me today, Miss Rebecca?" Grace asked as Rebecca tossed the dishwater out the kitchen door.

Rebecca looked to the roast and potatoes she'd cooked for Seth's dinner. They were finished and would stay warm until he came home. She looked about the house. There really was no reason for her to stay longer today. "I would like that, Grace. Thank you."

The little girl smiled her pleasure. "I can't wait to tell Ma how well I did on the spelling bee." She picked up her lunch pail. "May I have another cookie?"

Rebecca handed her two and then covered the dish with a clean cloth. She placed it in the center of the table for Seth to find when he got home.

"Thanks!" Grace skipped to the front door.

She followed and pulled her shawl from a row of nails she'd hung earlier in the day. As she put it on, Rebecca looked about the house once more. The smell of fresh baked cookies was inviting, the house was clean and dinner was on the stove.

Thanks to her hard work, Seth Billings would have no reason to fire her. She pulled the door closed behind them and followed a skipping Grace home.

The hair prickled on Rebecca's neck. She looked about nervously. Was it her imagination? Or was someone watching them? Seeing no one, Rebecca hurried after Grace. She prayed the stranger from earlier in the day wasn't around.

Seth glanced over his shoulder at the man tied to the horse behind him. He stifled the yawn that threatened to reveal just how tired he truly felt. It had taken all night to track the man, but he'd done it. Thanks to the reverend's quick thinking, Seth had been on his trail fairly fast.

Thankfully the reverend had seen the stranger running from his house. He'd watched to see which direction he'd been going before returning to Rebecca. It hadn't taken the preacher long to find Seth at the jail and give him the man's description and details he needed to track the villain.

A yawn over took him and he winced as the cut on his lip stretched with the motion. The prisoner had put up quite a fight and had gotten several good hits in before Seth had knocked him out. Once subdued, Seth had learned the man's name was Jacob O'Malley and that he was the newest member of the Evans gang.

Seth frowned; he hadn't gotten much out of the prisoner. Jacob was willing to admit that the Evans gang had grown in the past few months. He'd even confessed he was supposed to be watching Jesse's girl, but other than that his lips were sealed. Seth didn't like it; he didn't like it at all. Rebecca Ramsey was in danger. He'd put her there. Guilt over Jesse's death and his failure to keep her safe ate at him.

What would have happened if the reverend hadn't arrived when he did? Would Jacob have kidnapped her? Hurt her in some way? Taken her to Maxwell, the gang leader?

The reverend had said she'd been frightened. Had her blue eyes shown that fear? He wanted to hurry back to his house and pull her into his embrace. The thought of holding her and stroking her soft hair, inhaling the sweet fragrance of sweet vanilla that was her scent alone, pulled at him.

He gently kicked his mount's sides and put both horses into a gallop. The sooner he got Jacob back to Durango, the sooner he could return to Cottonwood Springs and Rebecca. He told himself he only wanted to be by her side to protect her, but knew it wasn't true.

Seth pulled the animal back and forced himself to remember why he and Rebecca could never be a couple. *You are a U.S. Marshal and people who get too close to you die.*

Chapter Seven

Rebecca frowned. Nothing had changed. The roast and potatoes still sat on the stove, now ruined. When Seth hadn't answered the door, she and Grace had let themselves in. Now, seeing he hadn't been home, Rebecca found herself chewing on her bottom lip.

"May I have a few cookies to take to school?" Grace asked, lifting the cloth from the desert.

She nodded and watched Grace take three. "I don't think the marshal came home last night," Grace said around a mouthful of cookie.

"No, I don't think he did either." Rebecca moved to the stove. She removed the pan from the stove and set it on the white cabinet. They hadn't talked about what she should do, should he not come home.

Grace looked up at her. "What are you going to do?"

"I'm not sure."

The bell at the school rang. Grace started for the front door. "I have to go. Should I come by after school?"

"No, I think I'll head home and when the marshal gets back, I'll find out what I need to do in circumstances like this one." Rebecca pulled her shawl closer about her shoulder and followed Grace outside.

Grace raced up the hill to the school. Hannah stood on the porch. She waved and Rebecca returned the gesture. Her new friend herded the children into the building much like a mother hen shelters its chicks from a spring rainstorm.

Rebecca decided to toss the meat and potatoes. She returned to the house and let herself in. What was she going to do with the ruined meat? Rebecca returned her shawl to the nail and walked into the kitchen. What she needed was a slop bucket. Her gaze moved about the kitchen.

A few moments later, she'd decided on a pan to use as a slop bucket. She dumped the meat and potatoes into it. Then she went outside to get water to wash the pot she'd dirtied the night before. Her gaze darted to the trees. Seeing no one, she hurried to pull the water up and go back inside.

While it heated, her thoughts went to Seth. Being a marshal, he probably didn't come home every night. Why hadn't she thought of that before? She rinsed out the coffeepot and began to make fresh coffee.

Her mind worked on what to do. She didn't want to waste food, but she also didn't want the marshal going hungry or having to eat at the diner in the evenings. If she didn't come up with a solution fast, Rebecca reasoned she'd be out of a job.

Simple food, that's what she needed to make. She needed to create easy meals so that no matter what time he came home, Seth Billings would have something good to eat. She poured herself a cup of coffee and sat down at the table. What had her mother fixed? Fresh bread came to mind.

Rebecca stood and began work. She'd make bread and see about buying a smoked ham. He'd be able to have a sandwich, if he came home too late. *What else can I do?* she asked herself as she worked.

As soon as the dough was rising, Rebecca headed to the general store for the ham she intended to buy. Normally she would have gone to the Millers', but she knew that Mrs. Miller always purchased her meats from the general store.

Hot from the heat of the stove, she left her shawl hanging by the door and walked up the street. A light breeze lifted the hair off her damp neck.

Her gaze moved about as she thought of the man who'd visited with her the day before. She didn't have the feeling he was around or watching her, and she relaxed. Maybe she'd been right in her assumption that she'd overreacted.

A small brass bell jingled overhead as she stepped inside. The delightful scents of cinnamon and fresh-baked banana bread greeted her. Her eyes widened as she looked around. Unlike the Millers' store, this one was packed with sellable goods. Shelves filled with every kind food and household item she could imagine covered the walls. Glass jars holding lemon drops, peppermint sticks and other colorful candies stood next to the cash register. Baskets of apples, walnuts, potatoes and onions sat on the floor in front of the sales counter. Bolts of cloth and baskets of thread and notions covered the far wall. Rebecca made her way to the counter. She prayed Mrs. Walker, a round woman with black hair piled high and hazel eyes, would have a ham for sale.

"What can I help you with, Miss Ramsey?" Mrs. Walker asked without looking up from the ledger she was writing in.

Rebecca hadn't expected Mrs. Walker to sound so frosty. She cleared her throat. "Do you have a ham that I can buy?"

The cool hazel eyes looked up at her. "There might be one in the smoke house, but it won't be cheap," she warned.

"Good. I'll want it placed on the Marshal's account."

Mrs. Walker straightened. "I'm sorry, Miss Ramsey, but I can't do that."

"Why not?" Rebecca asked, also pulling herself up to her full five feet two inches.

"The marshal has not approved you to make purchases on his behalf." Her icy voice should have sent chills down Rebecca's spine but had the opposite effect. Heat filled her face, neck and body. Anger boiled. The woman was treating her as if she was a criminal.

She took a deep breath. "Then I shall be making all future purchases from the Millers." Rebecca turned, held her head high and walked from the store.

Out on the sidewalk she sighed. "Why did Mrs. Walker have to be so rude?" Rebecca marched down to the Millers' store.

She squared her shoulders as she entered. It looked and smelled much like the general store, just not as crowded. Rebecca smiled as Mrs. Miller entered from the sitting room. "Hello, Mrs. Miller. How are you today?" she asked.

"Very well, thank you, Rebecca. What brings you in today?"

Rebecca took a deep breath. She really didn't want to tell the other woman about her encounter with Mrs. Walker, but she didn't see any way around it. "I went to see Mrs. Walker about acquiring a ham for the marshal and she refused to sell it to me." The heat rose in her cheeks once more, this time from embarrassment more than anger.

"That old gossip! What excuse did she use?" Mrs. Miller placed her hands on her hips and waited.

"Gossip?" Rebecca didn't understand what Mrs. Walker being a gossip had to do with her.

Mrs. Miller waved her hands as if it weren't important. "That doesn't matter, Rebecca. Why didn't she sell you a ham?"

It did matter, but Rebecca knew no more information about Mrs. Walker would be coming from Mrs. Miller. "She said the marshal hasn't given me permission to put anything on his account. She treated me like a criminal."

Mrs. Miller yelled, "Josiah! Come here."

Mr. and Mrs. Miller's oldest son hurried into the room. "Yes, Ma?"

"Go to the general store and tell Mrs. Walker I need a ham."

He nodded and hurried out the door.

"I'll add the price of the ham to Seth's account." She wrote in her ledger and then turned back to Rebecca. "Would you like a cup of coffee while we wait, Rebecca?"

Rebecca shook her head no. "I had two cups already this morning. But thank you."

Mrs. Miller nodded. "Well, then in that case, go sit down in the parlor and look at the new mail-order catalogue. It's on the table by the window. I have a chocolate cake to check on." She led the way into the parlor without giving Rebecca a chance to reply.

She sniffed the air appreciatively. The smell of baking chocolate cake caused her tummy to rumble. Rebecca sat down and wondered if Mrs. Walker would give the ham to Josiah. She had to know that the Millers were getting it for her. And, what had Mrs. Miller meant by calling Mrs. Walker a gossip? Had the local gossips been talking about her?

Seth rode into town by the light of the moon. His body ached from being in the saddle for almost two days straight. Had the Evans gang tried to contact Rebecca again during his absence? He didn't think so, and even if they had, the reverend had promised to keep an eye on her.

Reverend James Griffin was a small man with a big attitude. He wouldn't have allowed the gang to get within ten feet of Rebecca, of that Seth was sure. He had seen the little traveling preacher stand up to some pretty tough guys and not back down. He thought about riding over to the church but decided against it. The hour was late and he was bushed. Tomorrow would be soon enough to talk to James.

He rode his horse back to the barn and bedded him down. The stallion nudged him gently when he gave him fresh water and oats, as if to say thank-you. Seth finished up and then continued to the house. He opened the door and immediately became aware of the delicious scent of fresh bread and coffee.

With a will of their own, his tired legs carried him to the kitchen. His eyes widened when he saw Rebecca sitting in a chair but slumped over the table. One arm was stretched out and her head rested on it. Fear welled in his chest. Was she hurt? Had the Evans gang left her there as a warning?

He hurried to her side. *Oh, Lord, please let her be all right.* Seth sent the silent prayer heavenward and then reached out and touched her cheek. It felt soft and warm.

Rebecca jerked away from him. Her sleep-filled eyes resembled an owl. She stood so fast that her chair slid backward and hit the wall with a loud thud.

Seth held up both hands. "Easy, it's just me."

Her gaze darted to him and then about the room. A shaky hand came up to her throat. "You scared me," she accused.

"I'm sorry. I didn't mean to." He moved to pick up the chair and she skittered away from him to the other side of the room.

Seth searched her face and saw that her eyes still seemed glazed over with sleep. "Rebecca, are you awake?" he asked softly.

She looked at him once more. Rebecca's voice came out soft, velvety. "Seth?"

"Yes, it's me." He sat down and laid his hands on the table. The last thing he wanted to do was frighten her more.

She yawned and pulled out the seat across from him. "When did you get home?"

Home. Seth looked about the clean room. A pot of coffee and a fresh loaf of bread rested on the stove. What would it be like to come home to Rebecca every night?

"Marshal?"

Seth looked back at her eyes. She was alert now. Did she even realize she'd called him by his first name? He cleared his throat. "Just a little while ago. What are you still doing here?"

She stood and poured them both a cup of the aromatic coffee. "I have been staying late so that if you came home, you'd have a hot meal." Rebecca set a cup in front of him. "I must have fallen asleep tonight." She sipped at the hot beverage.

"You stayed all night?" he asked, praying the local gossips didn't know if she had.

Rebecca shook her head. "No, I've been going home and would have been gone tonight, but as you know, I fell asleep."

He studied her. She'd waited for him, like a wife waits up for her husband. The thought touched a part of his heart that he hoped to keep locked away from her. Her blond hair had come down and brushed the sides of her face, giving her a vulnerable look. Normally clear sharp eyes now were clouded with the remains of sleep, giving her the look of someone who yearned for tenderness and love. He wanted to reach out and hug her to him, to absorb the softness that her sleep-filled eyes promised. But he knew that would never happen. He couldn't allow it to.

A light pink flush filled her cheeks. "Are you hungry? Would you like for me to fix you something to eat?"

"No, I think we'd better get you home before the gossips find out how late you were here tonight." He pushed back his chair and walked toward her, surprised when she didn't move. He held out his hand and waited until she took it. Then he helped her from the chair.

"Thank you." She looked up into his eyes and a small smile tilted the edge of her mouth. "I probably should have gone on home, but I was starting to worry about you. Where have you been?"

Seth liked the idea that someone worried about him. He pushed the warm feeling away and released her hand. He'd had that kind of love three years ago, but Clare had paid the ultimate price for their love. "I picked up a prisoner and took him to Durango. I'm sorry I worried you."

Rebecca walked to the front door and pulled her shawl from the nail. "It's all right. I know your job is a dangerous one—that's the only reason I worried." She opened the door.

The night had grown colder and he wondered if her shawl would be enough to keep her warm. Pulling the door closed behind him, Seth took her elbow and helped her down the three short steps. "I think we'd better talk about your hours. The thought of you walking home this late doesn't sit well with me."

She looked over at him. Under the moon's light, her hair created the illusion that she had a halo over the crown of her head. "You might be right."

"You can continue to come in the mornings at the same time, but I really think you should return home before dark." Seth stepped up on the wooden sidewalk and helped her to do the same.

The hem of her skirt brushed the wood and snagged on a nail. Rebecca bent to work the cloth free. Her words floated up to him. "I did the first night you were gone and my roast and potatoes were ruined." She stood. "I'm surprised you didn't stop by to tell me you were going."

Seth pulled his shoulders up straighter. The accusing sound of her voice struck a chord in him. Who did she think she was? His mother? Wife? Fiancée? Fresh, painful thoughts of Clare filled him once more. No, Rebecca Ramsey wasn't his fiancée. That position had been Clare's alone. He didn't owe Rebecca an explanation. "I didn't think about it."

They stopped in front of the hat shop. Rebecca turned to look at him. "Well, maybe from now on, when you have to leave town you can let me know."

He studied her features. She was serious. His jaw

clenched. What if he was on the trail of a killer? He wouldn't have time to stop and return home so he could tell her where he was going. Didn't she see that? No, from the look on her face, she didn't, and that was the problem. It had always been a problem, at least for him. This very conversation was one of the reasons he'd decided not to get married, at least not until his marshaling days were over. "Let's talk about it in the morning. I'm tired and I know you are, too."

Rebecca nodded. "All right." She reached for the door. "Thank you for walking me home, Marshal. I'll see you in the morning." And with those final words Rebecca Ramsey shut the door in his face.

Seth turned to go home. "Lord, please keep her far enough away from me that the thoughts of marriage and loving will not return anytime soon," he mumbled, and kicked a pebble.

Chapter Eight

Rebecca woke the next morning with a headache.

Her first thoughts of the day were on Seth Billings. Why did he have to be so stubborn? All she'd done was ask him to let her know when he'd be leaving town. She'd seen the way his chin lifted and his jaw hardened. The tenseness in his voice had also warned her that he had no intention of telling her when he wouldn't be returning for the evening.

She buttoned the front of her dress and then moved to the dressing table. Sitting down, Rebecca pulled a brush through her hair. How would she know whether to fix dinner or not? Tears filled her eyes. What if he decided to have his meals fixed at the diner? Then he wouldn't need her. She'd have to find another way to stay in Cottonwood Springs.

"Rebecca? Are you awake?" Eliza called through the bedroom door.

"Yes, come on in." She laid the brush down and turned to face her friend.

Eliza entered, looking fresh and alert. "You're running a little late. I was worried you might have overslept." She dropped onto the bed and smiled.

"No, I didn't sleep too well last night and woke up before Mr. Daniel's rooster. Then, when sleep did return, I woke with a headache." Rebecca worked her hair into a knot and fastened it at the back of her head. She didn't care if it did make her look like an old maid today.

Her friend made tsking noises and then asked, "What kept you up?"

Should she mention her problem to Eliza? Would her new friend be able to help? Rebecca placed two combs in her hair and then decided she had nothing to lose by asking for Eliza's advice. "The marshal came home last night."

"Oh, that's wonderful. I really was starting to worry about him. Until you came along, I didn't really give his job much thought, but now, well, I find myself praying for his safety. Since he was missing, well, not really missing, but you know what I mean." She waved her hand and then covered her mouth. "Oh, I'm sorry. I just kind of went off there for a second. Please, continue."

"I asked him to let me know when he'll be leaving town like that again, so that next time I'll know not to fix big meals, and he locked up on me like a snapping turtle on a wooden stick."

Tears stung the back of her eyes again.

Eliza laughed. "I've never heard that saying before."

Seeing the mirth on her friend's face made Rebecca smile, too. "I think I made it up. Anyway, my point is, if he won't tell me when he's going to be home and when he's not, how will I know how to cook for him?"

"How about we go have a cinnamon roll and think on that for a few minutes?" Eliza stood up and walked to the door. "I do my best thinking with sweet stickiness coating my tongue." Her skirts fluttered about her ankles as she hurried to the kitchen.

Rebecca followed. Eliza wore a brown hat with a little brown bird nestled into ruffles on the side. The feathers on the bird's head stuck straight up and were light brown in color, matching her dress and scarf beautifully. "That is a cute hat you are wearing this morning."

Eliza reached up and touched the brim. "Do you like it? I was concerned the bird might be a bit much."

"I do and it isn't." The smell of cinnamon and sugar filled her senses as she entered Eliza's kitchen. It was much cozier than Seth's, with a colorful tablecloth and matching curtains on the bay window that looked out over her backyard. "I'll get the coffee."

Eliza placed a pot holder on the table and then set the pan of sweet rolls on top of it. "Thank you. Use the teacups, I'm feeling girlish this morning." She giggled. "Probably because of this hat." Her hand fluttered up to the brim again.

She poured the coffee and joined Eliza at the table. "These smell wonderful."

"Why don't you take a couple over to the marshal? You should probably take one for Grace, too. That girl is growing again. Her mother will have her in here any day now for a new dress. I don't know why Mrs. Miller doesn't just ask me for the pattern and measurements. She thinks I don't know that she tears my dresses up and makes her own patterns. But how else would Grace come up with several dresses just like the one I made her?" Eliza stopped talking long enough to bite into the still-warm pastry.

Rebecca smiled across at her friend. "Thank you, I'm sure they will enjoy them."

For a moment Eliza looked confused as if she'd forgotten her original statement, and then she grinned and licked the sugar from her fingers. "Oh, good. Now for your problem. The way I see it you have two choices. One, you can make him dinner anyway, and if he doesn't come home you can bring it here and we'll put it in my icebox, or option two, you can go to Farmington and buy him an icebox."

"Oh, I'd hate to put you out. I wonder if Mrs. Miller or Mrs. Walker can order one and have it delivered to his house?" Rebecca savored the taste of sweetness as she sunk her teeth into the cinnamon roll.

Eliza stood. "Maybe, but really it wouldn't be a problem, if you want to bring the meals back here. You are a good cook, you know." She smiled mischievously and licked her lips.

"Thank you. But all the same, I think I'll ask Mrs. Miller after I get the marshal off to work with these cinnamon rolls in his stomach. You aren't a bad cook yourself, you know." Rebecca stood, too. She retrieved a plate from the cupboard and placed several rolls onto it.

"Thank you." The bell rang over the door in the hat shop. "That will be Miss Grace coming to get you."

Rebecca looked about and realized she'd left her shawl in her bedroom. "Would you mind telling her I'll be right there? I need to fetch my wrap."

Eliza nodded and Rebecca hurried back to her bedroom. She grabbed the shawl and took one last look about. The bed was made and covered with a log-cabin quilt done in soft blues and yellows. It matched the curtain over her window. Everything was in its place, just as it should be, she thought. Her heart swelled. She said a silent prayer of thanks to the Lord for her comfortable home and then hurried out to greet her young friend.

"Good morning, Miss Rebecca." Grace held the plate of rolls in her hands. Her lunch pail sat on the floor beside her.

Rebecca slipped her shawl about her shoulders and then extended her hands to take the plate. "I'll take those, so you can carry your lunch pail."

Grace handed it over, but the look on her face said she wasn't pleased. Rebecca tried to hide her grin as she turned to Eliza and said, "I'll be back this afternoon."

Eliza nodded. "Good, I'll put on a pot of tea. And maybe make some finger sandwiches. I've always wanted to do that. I wonder if Hannah would like to come, too? We could make it into a regular tea party."

"I'll ask her," Grace said, walking toward the door. "Hurry, Miss Rebecca, I want to try one of those before I have to be at school. They smell wonderful."

"Thanks, Grace!" Eliza called after her as the young girl slipped out the door.

Rebecca closed the door behind them and walked to where Grace waited for her at the end of the sidewalk.

"Miss Eliza can sure talk fast, can't she?" Grace jumped off the sidewalk and headed across the back of the lot to the next street.

Rebecca followed. When the little girl stopped for her to catch up, she answered, "Yes, she can. But she has a heart of gold and is my best friend."

Grace's bottom lip popped out. "I thought I was your best friend," she complained.

She reached out and hugged the girl's shoulders to her. "You are a good friend, and I'm very happy to have you in my life." Rebecca released her and Grace grinned. "Besides, how would Anna Harper feel if she heard you say I was your best friend?"

Grace kicked at a rock in the road. "I imagine her feelings would get hurt."

"I think so, too."

They walked in silence for a few moments. Grace was so much like Joy. Rebecca knew her feelings were still stinging. "You know, I can honestly say that of all my younger friends, you are my favorite."

Her brown head came up and hazel eyes looked into hers. "Really?"

"Yes, really. I like that you walk to work with me every day and then walk home with me again after school. It's nice having a friend to talk to about my day." Rebecca smiled. Grace usually did most of the talking, but it didn't seem to matter to the little girl who did the talking, as long as they were together.

"Me, too," Grace answered and then skipped ahead to knock on the front door.

Rebecca held her breath as she waited for him to answer. What kind of mood would he be in this morning? Last night, he'd seemed annoyed, but he hadn't really said anything to indicate he was angry.

Clenched jaw and balled-up fists might have indicated that he was, but then again, maybe he was overly tired. *Yeah, and maybe you are the biggest dreamer this side of the Rocky Mountains.*

Chapter Nine

"Good morning, Grace. How are you this morning?" Seth spoke to the child, but his gaze moved to the woman behind her.

Rebecca wore a soft yellow dress with little blue flowers on it. She'd pulled her hair back into a knot at the base of her neck; he imagined it was easier to work with it up like that, even if it wasn't the prettiest style. Who was he kidding? The curve of her exposed neck, her sparkling blue eyes and her gentle smile made Rebecca Ramsey the most beautiful woman in this small town.

"I'm good, Marshal. I'll be even better when you let us in so we can eat those sticky buns Miss Rebecca is holding," Grace replied.

Heat consumed his neck. Seth stepped back and let Grace pass. "By all means, let's get to whatever smells so good." He continued to hold the door open for Rebecca.

She passed him and said, "Good morning to you, too, Marshal."

What was wrong with him? Hadn't he addressed

her? Or had he simply stared at her like a schoolboy at a church social?

He felt like a child who had just been chastised. "Sorry, good morning." And now he sounded like one, too.

Grace pranced out the back door declaring she'd bring in the milk from the well.

Seth took his seat and looked at the cinnamon rolls that Rebecca had placed on the table. His mind wouldn't stay focused this morning as he watched her pour steaming coffee into a mug.

Rebecca handed the cup to him and their fingers touched. Did she feel the same sensation in her hand as he did? His gaze moved to look into her blue eyes. She held his gaze for a moment, still holding the mug, still touching his hand.

The back door slammed as Grace reentered the house. Rebecca's gaze moved to the table and her hand released the cup. A soft pink stain filled her cheeks before she turned away.

Lord, please help me this morning, I seem to have lost my senses.

An hour later, Seth stood in the sheriff's office. His gaze looked out the window, but his mind stayed on Rebecca Ramsey. She'd been quiet during breakfast, with Grace doing most of the talking. At one point she'd looked as if she wanted to ask him something, but then she'd jerked her head to the side and avoided eye contact with him.

What had gotten into him this morning? He'd acted like a schoolboy looking at his pretty new teacher. Why did Rebecca have that effect on him? Seth shook his head and returned to the stove for a fresh cup of coffee.

He sipped the fragrant brew. It didn't taste nearly as good as Rebecca's.

"You're pacing again, Marshal."

Seth stopped and looked at the sheriff. His head was bent over the papers on his old desk. He wasn't a young man, but Seth wasn't sure of his exact age. The man's gray eyes rose to meet his. "What is troubling you, Seth?"

"Who said something is troubling me?" Seth asked, moving to sit on the corner of his desk.

"The pacing, the constant gulping of coffee and the furrow between your eyes as you look out the window with unfocused eyes tell me all I need to know." He returned his attention to his papers.

Had he been that obvious? Seth glanced down into his half-empty cup. The sheriff was right; he was gulping the hot liquid and hadn't even been aware of it.

"If you ask me, I think it's that Ramsey woman." The sheriff didn't look up but continued working.

Seth exhaled the pent-up air in his lungs. "No one asked you, Bob."

"No, I don't guess so." He looked up and grinned. "But, I'm pretty sure I'm right."

Now would be a good time to change the subject. Seth looked down at the Wanted papers on Bob's desk. He didn't recognize any of the men, but he hadn't really expected to. "How long did you say you were going to be gone?"

The sheriff scooted his chair back and turned around. He tacked the posters behind his desk. "Most of the summer. Is that what's troubling you?" He turned back around and rested both his hands on the desk.

"No, I was just thinking that my life will be a little different over the next few months. As a marshal I go all over the territory. Being acting sheriff will keep me closer to home." Seth pushed off the desk and walked back to the window.

Cottonwood Springs was a quiet little town that saw very little trouble and for that he was grateful. Of all the towns in the territory, he preferred this one, and the main reason was that it never saw the kind of trouble that, say, Farmington or Durango did. They were bigger towns with bigger problems. Cottonwood Springs didn't have more than two hundred people in and around it.

"And closer to Miss Ramsey." Bob slapped him on the back. "She's a pretty little thing, isn't she?"

Seth mentally pictured Rebecca. He didn't think she was merely pretty. Her beauty drew his eye, like honey pulled at the bears. "Yes. I've been worried about the Evans gang getting too close to her. Jesse thought that she was in danger."

Bob leaned against the wall. "And he proved right, if Jacob O'Malley can be trusted."

From the corner of his eye, he saw that Bob studied his profile. The man evaluated him much like he would a prisoner. "Yes, he did."

"Do you want me to see if I can put Sarah Beth off for a few weeks?"

A smile tugged at Seth's lips for the first time that morning. "No, your wife would shoot us both if you postpone taking her home to her family." He laid a hand on the sheriff's shoulder. "But I appreciate the offer."

Bob laughed. "Yeah, she'd hang us both from the highest tree if I went home and told her I couldn't go." He sobered. "I am worried about the Evans gang, though."

"Don't give them a second thought. I can take care

of them." Seth wished he felt as self-assured as he sounded.

Bob nodded. "I believe you can. And other than the Evans gang messing around, nothing ever happens here." He walked back to his desk and sat down.

"What time are you leaving?" Seth asked.

"First thing in the morning." He looked at the clean surface and sighed. "I think everything is done here."

Seth opened the door. "You should probably head home to pack." He motioned for Bob to leave.

The sherriff stood. "I'm being kicked out of my own office." The complaint didn't sound too unhappy.

"Yep." As soon as the sheriff crossed the threshold, Seth followed and shut the door behind him.

The two men shook hands. "Have a safe trip, Bob. Cottonwood Springs will be here when you get back." Seth knew it was another promise he intended to keep.

"She's in good hands. I expect by the time I get back you will either be a married man or well on your way to being there." Bob slapped him on the shoulder once more and then turned away. Seth heard him whistling "Here Comes the Bride" as he walked home.

Seth had no intention of being married by summer's end. Marshals didn't get married. At least this marshal didn't. He wouldn't leave a woman alone to fend for herself or, worse, put her in danger, like he had Clare. Bob might not mind taking the chance that his Sarah Beth could become a widow because some criminal cut his life short, but Seth couldn't see himself doing that to a woman.

Rebecca pinned her hat on. She didn't think Seth would approve, but she was determined to go to Farmington and get an icebox. Mrs. Miller didn't have one in her store. Farmington had an icehouse so Rebecca felt confident that she'd find a box there, as well.

She looked at herself in the mirror. Her dark blue traveling dress, blue hat with an orange flower in its band and her best traveling boots didn't ease the feeling of nervousness that filled her stomach. Going alone wasn't the greatest plan she'd had, but no one else had the time to go with her and she wouldn't ask Seth Billings.

Rebecca took a deep breath, squared her shoulders and asked God for His protection on this trip. With God's protection, the wagon she'd found in Seth's barn and the horse she'd rented for the day, it shouldn't take more than a couple of hours to get to Farmington. She pulled on soft, leather riding gloves. Then if it took a couple of hours to find the icebox and a couple more to return to Cottonwood Springs, she'd be home before supper and Seth would be none the wiser.

Not that she needed his permission, but Rebecca knew Seth would probably tell her she couldn't buy the icebox or, even worse, if he approved, he would not want her traveling alone. And then if he insisted on going with her, she'd have to spend the better part of her day with him.

For a moment she stopped and thought about that. What would be so bad about spending the day with a handsome man? And Seth Billings was handsome. She liked the way his dark brown eyes crinkled at the edges when he smiled and that dimple winked at the same time. Rebecca shook herself. She didn't like his high-handed manner and the last thing she needed was to get too close to him.

Her idea of a husband was a man who was stable in his moods, was willing to talk about what was bothering him and would love her deeply. So far Seth Billings was none of those things.

She'd agreed to marry Jesse for two reasons. One, he helped her escape her stepmother, and two, he'd offered her a chance at love. His letters had promised she'd be equal to him and he'd seemed to be an even-natured man.

Rebecca sighed. She wanted a marriage like her mother and father had had, one of love and mutual respect for each other. Jesse's letters had promised such a union.

She had to admit, though, Seth Billings did something to her system no other man ever had. Those feelings brought on thoughts, thoughts of love and marriage. Thoughts of what it would be like to be married to the handsome marshal.

Rebecca wanted a family more than ever but didn't think the marshal was the man for her. His moods changed too rapidly for her liking. One moment he was warm and friendly, the next he growled and became hard. At times he seemed to care about her well-being, and then he acted as if he couldn't stand to be in the same room with her. She shook her head. Even if he were warm, friendly and caring all the time, she didn't need a man. What would stop him from loving her? If her own father could desert her, what more could she expect from Seth?

But then again, she hadn't really known Jesse at all. The thought of Jesse and the hopes and dreams she'd held for them brought her full circle.

Rebecca took one last look at her reflection in the mirror and then headed into the dress shop, determined to get to Farmington before the morning was up. She waved to Eliza, who was with a customer. Rebecca saw a man sitting beside the door with his hat in his hands. He looked as if he'd rather be in the field plowing than sitting here waiting. She didn't recognize the couple and wondered if they were visitors to Cottonwood Springs.

When Eliza looked up, she waved at her.

"Excuse me," Eliza to her customer, and then she walked across to Rebecca, the big yellow feather in her hat sweeping in front of her with each step.

As soon as she was close, Rebecca said in a low voice, "I'm leaving now. I'll be back before supper."

"I really wish you'd wait. I could go with you on Sunday." The look in her eyes begged Rebecca to listen.

She reached out and hugged her friend. "Eliza, I'll be fine. So don't worry."

"You know I will, but since you are bent on going I made you a lunch basket to take." She dashed into the other room and returned with a glance in her customer's direction. "There are sandwiches, pickles, a couple of apples, a jar of chilled apple juice, and I made you some tea." Eliza gave her the basket and another quick hug.

"You packed enough for a small army, Eliza." The sensation of tears prickled her eyes. Rebecca hurried to leave. Eliza had turned out to be the best friend she'd ever had. The woman cared about her and that was more than she could say for her family.

"Be careful," Eliza called after her.

"Thank you. I will."

She pushed the bitter thoughts of her family back down deep where they belonged and climbed onto the seat of the wagon.

A queasy feeling hit her stomach as she rode past the sheriff's office and saw Seth Billings staring in her direction. What would it be like to have a man like him really care about her? She slapped the reins over the horse's back and told herself she didn't want to know.

Chapter Ten

"Now where does that woman think she's going?" Seth pushed himself upright. He'd been reclining against the wall of the jail house when Rebecca drove past him in his wagon.

Her back was ramrod straight and her head was held high. The orange flower in her hat bobbed with each turn of the wagon's wheels. She didn't look to the left or the right and so therefore hadn't seen him watching her. Surely she wasn't leaving town.

His eyes narrowed as she did just that. He stomped toward Eliza's hat and dress shop. Eliza would know where Rebecca was going and he'd soon go after her.

Seth slowed down. Should he go after her? She was a full-grown woman who could do whatever she wanted. She'd obviously been planning on going and hadn't mentioned it to him. He stepped onto the sidewalk a few doors down from the hat and dress shop.

A man and woman exited the store. He felt a little sorry for the stranger, who was burdened down with packages. His lips tugged into a smile. That must be what it's like to be married and in a strange town. The woman chattered happily with Eliza and her hand moved to the oversize hat on her head. A bird's nest peeked from the top and lace trailed behind.

Seth moved a little closer and watched as the man turned and offered his hand to his wife. From this distance he could see them much better. The man's nostrils flared and his eyes softened as he took his wife's hand and assisted her onto the wagon seat. She patted his shoulder and smiled her thanks.

What would it be like to have a woman look at him like that? He shoved the thought aside and turned to Eliza.

"They are a sweet couple, aren't they?" she asked.

He stood a little taller. "I didn't notice." The lie tasted bitter on his tongue.

Her eyebrows lifted. "No? I could have sworn you were looking straight at them. How could you not have noticed?"

Time to confess. He swallowed before answering. "All right. I noticed." Seth felt better confessing he'd lied.

Eliza's soft laugh caught his attention. She had a nice smile and her laughter was pretty, but he found himself comparing it to Rebecca's. "I thought so. What can I do for you, Marshal?" She pulled a broom from inside the door and began sweeping off her section of the sidewalk.

Seth watched the couple head on out of town. Their wagon followed the same road that Rebecca had used a few minutes earlier. "I noticed Miss Ramsey heading out of town." He waited for her to say something.

The stubborn woman clamped her lips shut forcing him to ask. He continued to wait. Given enough time, silence often forced a woman to talk. But it seemed

Eliza knew that trick and continued to sweep, forcing him to ask. "Do you know where she is headed?"

"She mentioned it in passing."

The swish of the broom filled the tense silence.

He blew out frustrated air. "Can you tell me?"

"I can, but I'd rather not." She walked back to the door and stepped inside.

Seth frowned. He could follow Eliza and ask her point blank to tell him, something he didn't relish doing. She'd had a mischievous sparkle in her eyes that didn't sit well with him. He leaned against the building and watched the quiet town.

The sheriff stepped out of the general store. He made eye contact with Seth and then walked across the dirt street. The bag in his arms looked heavy. When he got close enough, Seth asked, "Last minute shopping?"

Bob nodded. "Sarah Beth suggested I pick up a few things. Did I just see Miss Ramsey ride out of here?"

It was Seth's turn to nod. "Sure did."

"Where she going?"

Seth tightened his jaw muscles. What made the sheriff think he'd know? "No idea."

He shifted the bag. "Are you going after her?"

"Haven't decided yet."

"Sam mentioned that Horace Nance was in the store this morning."

Seth stood up straighter. Horace was Maxwell Evans's number one sidekick. His voice came out hard and demanding. "Why didn't he tell one of us?"

"He did. He just told me."

"Where is Nance now?" Seth's eyes darted up and down the street. His hand went to his gun.

Bob used his boot to kick a dirt clod off the sidewalk. "Don't know. Sam said he took what he wanted and hightailed it out the back door about two and a half hours ago. Horace said if Sam or the missus stepped foot outside, it would be their last steps. They listened and didn't move until I walked in."

Seth didn't need to ask if the sheriff had checked around. He shook his head. The Evans gang were slicker than mud on a wet pig. They moved in and out of town like shadows and he didn't like it.

"You know. If they are after the Ramsey girl…" The thought hung in the air for a split second. "Maybe we should go after her."

Seth shook his head. "You have to get home to your wife. I'll do it."

The sherriff shifted the bag from one arm to the next. "If you aren't back by morning, I'm cancelling my trip."

He nodded. "Fair enough. I'll check in with you before you leave town, Sheriff." Seth headed to his house at a fast clip. As soon as he was sure no one would see him he ran for the barn and his horse. Rebecca Ramsey might not like his company, but he thought she'd like the Evans gang's even less.

Rebecca tried to ignore the tingling sensation on her neck. The desire to turn and see if someone was following pulled at her. But she refused to do it again. The past two times nothing had been there. Even the wagon that followed earlier had turned off down a small path. She was just being silly.

She raised her head and looked up into the clear blue sky. *Lord, I trust You to take care of me. I will not give in to fear. Amen.* Rebecca brushed at the goose bumps on her neck with a hand.

A tall tree marked the halfway point. Her stomach

growled. Rebecca frowned. Should she stop for lunch here? It was a common resting place. The grove of trees created a perfect picnicking spot. She saw a canvas-covered wagon pulled off to the side, but there were no horses attached to it. She searched the area for its owners.

A baby's cry filled her ears and she guided her horse up beside the wagon. Her hands shook as she set the brake. Rebecca climbed down and then heard the baby again. The sound seemed to be coming from the woods. She followed the sound and prayed the little one was safe.

The grass grew taller as Rebecca walked deeper into the wooded area. The infant's cries became louder, and then she saw a basket that looked much like the one Eliza had given her. The wicker container wiggled with each outburst of sobs.

Rebecca looked around to see if the parents were close by. Not seeing anyone she knelt beside the covered basket. "It's all right, sweetie. I'm here." She pulled the lightweight blanket off and looked inside.

A red-faced baby girl let out another weak cry. The child's fists beat the air.

"Oh, you poor baby." Rebecca scooped the infant up. Moisture filled the hand that covered her little diapered bottom. She cuddled the baby in one arm and scooped up the basket with the other.

With her head bent over the infant, Rebecca cooed at her. Soft black ringlets curled about the baby's face. Watery blue eyes stared up at Rebecca. She'd stopped crying but now whimpered, sounding much like a lost kitten. "It's all right, little one. We'll find your mother and she'll take care of you." Even as she said the words, Rebecca knew it wasn't true.

Something had happened to the baby's parents. Why else would the child be all alone in the woods? She hurried back toward the wagons. Goose bumps jumped up on her arms and neck. Rebecca ducked down behind a tree and studied the two wagons in front of her. Her rented horse stomped its hooves on the ground. She searched the ground under them. Maybe the baby's parents were hiding under their wagon.

She didn't see them. Rebecca tipped her head to the side and listened. Birds chirped in the trees, a small animal scurried through the leaves off to her left and the mare neighed as it, too, heard the soft clip-clop of a horse. She searched the bend in the road, praying the new arrival would be friendly.

Breath she hadn't realized she'd held whooshed from her at the sight of Seth Billings. He sat tall in his saddle. His brown vest stretched across his chest over a tan-colored shirt. The badge on his chest twinkled in the sunlight.

Her gaze moved to his serious eyes as they took in the two wagons and lack of people. Rebecca stood and moved from around the tree. Had he been following her? Was he who she'd sensed earlier? She willed the questions away. In a low voice, she called, "Marshal."

Seth dropped from the horse and walked to her. His gaze swept the area and he listened, much as she'd done earlier. When he got close enough, she whispered, "Something isn't right here. I found this baby alone over there in the woods."

He placed his hands on her arms and walked her backward behind the tree. He whispered, "Stay down and keep the baby quiet. I'll go see what has happened to its parents."

She looked down at the whimpering infant. Her little

face was blotchy and it looked as if at any moment she might squeal her anger again. When Rebecca glanced back to where Seth had been, he was gone. How did he fade into the surroundings like that? And if he could do it, were there other men close by who could do it, too?

The baby sniffled. Rebecca turned her attention back to the child. She looked into the basket and found a small pile of white diapers. The bed of grass would have to do for a place to change her. Rebecca spread the little blanket out and laid the baby down.

She diapered the child and then scooped her up again, minus the damp blanket and soiled diaper. Rebecca patted the baby's back and waited for Seth. Where was he? It seemed as if he'd been gone forever. She wanted to know what was happening.

Seth came from the opposite side of the campsite. "You can come out," he called.

Rebecca gathered up the soiled clothes, basket and baby, and hurried to join him. "What did you find?"

His large hand came up to rest on the baby's back. "She's an orphan now." Seth's dark sorrow-filled eyes searched out Rebecca's.

She wanted to reach out to Seth and hug him. The sadness in his eyes pulled at her heart. Rebecca drew the baby tighter to herself. The little girl giggled and dug her tiny hand up under Rebecca's hat and grabbed a fistful of hair. "What will happen to her?"

"She'll probably end up in an orphanage." He ran his hand over the sweet baby's black curls.

The little girl continued to tug at Rebecca's hair, unaware she was as alone as Rebecca had felt all morning. The baby had no family, just as Rebecca had no family. Perhaps together they could become a family. The thought of the baby girl ending up in an orphanage tore at Rebecca's heart. Would the baby grow up unloved?

Words sprang from Rebecca's heart and through her lips. "Oh, Seth, please can I have her?" Heat flooded her cheeks. She'd called him by his given name. "Um, I mean, Marshal. I want her."

The dimple in his cheek winked at her as a smile tugged his lips into a small grin. "I have to see if I can find her family, if she has any in the area. Until then, you can keep her."

"Thank you." Rebecca tugged the baby's hand out of her hair. Her hat fell to the side and Seth caught it. For now, the baby was hers. They would be a family. Rebecca would make it happen. Neither of them would ever be alone again.

He nodded at her and carried the hat to his wagon. Rebecca followed. She enjoyed the way his wide shoulders swayed as he walked. The baby gurgled and blew bubbles. Her little blue gaze focused on Seth, also.

"Why don't you look in the other wagon and see if there is anything that will identify her and her family?" He pulled a shovel out from under the seat of the wagon. "I'll be back in a while." Seth walked away, rolling up his sleeves as he went.

Rebecca knew the job ahead of him wasn't one that he would enjoy. "Lord, please give Seth the strength he needs to do the task at hand. In Jesus' name. Amen."

She patted the baby's back and then gently laid her down on a thick blanket just inside the wagon bed. "Neither of us will ever be alone again, little one. If Seth can't find your family, I will be your family." Rebecca kissed the baby's soft cheek, as she said her earlier thoughts aloud.

For the next two hours Rebecca kept busy while she

waited for Seth. First, she gathered things that the baby would need and transferred them to the other wagon. When the baby started to fuss again, Rebecca decided she must be hungry, but since she didn't have any milk to feed her with she improvised and dribbled apple juice into the baby's mouth. After a little while the baby quieted down again.

For now the baby's needs were basic. How would she raise the little girl on her own? Maybe she could take in laundry and ironing to help supplement her income. She'd find a way. Rebecca refused to let her grow up feeling unloved.

She patted the baby's tummy. "I can do all things through Christ, who strengthens me. And that includes taking care of you, little one. If it's God's will for you to stay with me, He will provide a way." She picked the baby up, knowing she had to believe what she'd just said was true.

Rebecca changed and dressed the little girl. There was nothing to identify the baby or her parents in the covered wagon. Just clothes, a few baby toys, household items and tools. How would Seth be able to find the baby's family?

Chapter Eleven

Seth asked himself the same question as he buried the couple. The woman had been several feet from her man, but neither of them had had an easy death. There were no clues as to who had murdered them or why.

Lord, how can people do this sort of thing to one another? He fought down the bile that threatened to choke him once more. His stomach had already lost its contents once today; he really didn't want to do that again.

He focused on finding out who would have killed them and why. He didn't think it was an Indian attack. The local tribes had been peaceful over the past few years. His gaze moved about the tramped-down grass around him. Seth figured this was the job of one, maybe two men, but he had no clues as to who those men might be. He sighed as he tossed the last shovelful of dirt on the husband's grave.

Seth bowed his head and prayed. "Lord, I pray that this man and this woman be with You today. I'm not sure who they were or what their lives were like, but Father, I ask You to welcome them home today. And, Lord, please help that baby girl grow up to be a fine young woman someday. Amen." He lifted the shovel off the ground and carried it back to the wagon.

He stood in the tree line and watched Rebecca cuddle the baby close to her. What if she had gotten there a little earlier and been with the family when they were attacked? His heart lurched at the thought. There would now be three graves instead of two. He didn't like that thought. He didn't like it at all.

She hummed and rocked. Her hat still lay on the side of the wagon; her blond hair glistened like gold in the afternoon sun. They hadn't known each other long, but he felt confident that she would make a good mother to the little girl.

Rebecca looked up. Her gaze met his and she smiled. He stared into her eyes as if he were drowning in a sea of blue. What was it about this woman that pulled at him? He'd asked the question before and still didn't have the answer. She drew him to her with a simple look and Seth found himself closing the space between them.

He stopped and looked at the sleeping baby. Her little heart-shaped mouth sucked at a chubby thumb. Long eyelashes shadowed plump rosy cheeks. His gaze moved back up to Rebecca. Her cheeks were also a light red and her eyes were soft. Her lips were slightly parted and soft-looking.

She puckered them to shush him. Seth couldn't resist the urge to lean forward and touch them with his own lips. They were as soft as they looked and tasted mildly like apples. Warmth filled him and he stepped back. Awe filled his voice. "You taste like apples."

Rebecca's eyes had turned almost purple. She whispered back, "I just ate one." He loved the way her warm, sweet-scented breath caressed his lips.

The baby chose that moment to wake up with a hearty cry. Her little fist beat the air and her fat little legs kicked out. Rebecca picked her up and laid her over one shoulder. She patted the baby's little back until she settled down.

Seth looked on with interest. "How old do you think she is?" he asked.

She rubbed the baby's back with gentle circular motion. "She's small, but I think she's about six months old. When we get back to town, I'll take her over to Doctor Clark's office and see if he can guess any better than I can." She laid the baby down on a pile of blankets.

"That's a good plan." Seth turned to his horse. The sorrel stallion had moved to stand under a tree and munch on the green grass.

After tying his horse to the back of the wagon, he asked, "Do you want to head back to Cottonwood Springs?"

She frowned and then looked down at the infant who was reaching for her bonnet. "I suppose we should go home so that I can take her to the doctor." Rebecca picked up her hat and placed it back upon her head.

Seth nodded. He took the baby in one arm and then helped her up onto the seat of the wagon. The little girl wrapped her hand around his finger and grinned up at him. At six months old did babies really grin? Or did this little tyke simply have gas? He'd heard something about them being gassy. The thought spurred Seth into quickly returning the baby to Rebecca. He didn't relish the idea of changing a stinky diaper. Not that he'd know how to, anyway.

Rebecca shifted about on the seat. She tucked a lightweight blanket around the baby and gently rocked.

"Was there anything in there to identify the family?"

She shook her head. "No, just their clothes, cooking supplies and tools. No books, no Bible, nothing. Not even a letter."

He climbed up and sat down beside her, taking the horse's reins in his hands and turning the beast around. "I'll come back out later and see about getting their wagon back to Cottonwood Springs." He wondered if there might be a hidden compartment in the floor of the wagon. He'd check for that, too, when he returned.

Rebecca didn't know what to say so she didn't say anything. How sad that when those people died they left nothing behind. She would have had her Bible with her if she'd been traveling far. With that thought came another—that maybe they weren't traveling far. Maybe they had family in Farmington and were returning home.

"Where were you going?"

The abrupt question took her by surprise. She didn't want to answer him. "To Farmington."

"I figured you were." He clicked his tongue and set the little mare in motion. "Why were you going to Farmington?"

Rebecca lowered her head and brushed at a lock of black hair that had fallen into the baby's eyes. "I wanted to buy something."

By the look in his eyes, she knew he wanted to know what she had been planning to buy. For the life of her, Rebecca couldn't bring herself to tell him. Heat filled her face. She felt foolish now, putting her life in danger for an icebox.

Rebecca prayed he wouldn't ask her any further

questions. What if she'd been there when the bandits had overtaken the other family? She'd be dead, too. Her hands grew cold and clammy at the thought.

"Promise me that the next time you want to go to Farmington, you'll let me come with you or at least ask someone else to go with you." Seth kept his eyes looking straight ahead, but there was a catch in his voice.

Did he really care that much for her? She relived their kiss. It had been warm and exciting to feel his lips press gently against hers. The thought that she should have pulled away first drifted through her mind. Had she acted indecently by allowing him to kiss her?

He turned hard brown eyes upon her and growled her name. "Rebecca?" This time there was no nonsense in his voice. He wanted her promise and he wanted it now.

"I promise."

Seth nodded and then returned his gaze to the road ahead. The wagon rocked along; every time the baby would drift off to sleep the wagon would hit a rock or a chug hole that would jerk it awake. Rebecca would coo at her and promise that everything was all right.

After several minutes of this, Seth asked, "What are you going to call her?" He looked at the sleepy baby, who returned his stare.

"I'm not sure. I wish there had been something in the wagon that would have told us who they were." Rebecca rubbed the back of the baby's hand.

"How about the name Jane?"

Rebecca looked up at him. "Why Jane?"

"Because, it means 'the Lord is gracious.'"

She tilted her head to the side. "Really? And how do you know that?"

Seth lifted his gaze to her. "My sister's name is Jane. Mother said she'd named her Jane because it meant 'the Lord is gracious.'"

She smiled at him. "I like that. But I hope you don't mind if I call her Janie."

He laughed. "Not at all."

"Good." She turned her attention onto Janie. "Then you shall be named Jane Beatrix Ramsey. What do you think of that, Janie?"

In response the baby reached out and grabbed her finger. A little giggle sounded in her throat and she kicked her tiny feet from the blanket.

"Very nice. I think she likes it." Seth slapped the reins over the mare's back and glanced back to check on the stallion. "I'm not sure you should add your last name just yet."

"I know it's premature but I wanted to see how it sounded." When he didn't say anything, Rebecca added, "I like it."

He chuckled. "So do I. But don't get too attached to it."

Was he warning her not to get too attached to the baby or the name? Rebecca sighed. It didn't matter— for now she was Janie's mother.

How long would it take him to ask about the name Beatrix? She waited and smiled down at Janie.

"Beatrix, huh?"

"Uh-huh." Rebecca tickled the baby's tummy and waited.

It didn't take long for him to add, "That's an unusual name, isn't it?"

"My grandmother didn't think so when she suggested it to my mother."

He pulled the horse to a stop and turned to her. "Your name is Beatrix?" His hand moved to the stray hair that had fallen beside her face and gently tucked it behind her ear.

The breath caught in Rebecca's throat at his touch. "Yes, my full name is Rebecca Beatrix Ramsey. I thought it fitting that my first child should have my name. Don't you?"

Sorrow filled his eyes. "Rebecca, if her family comes for her, you will have to give her up."

"How will we know that they are her real family?" She shook her head and turned from the warmth of his hand. "No, Janie is mine, Seth, and no one is going to take her from me." Rebecca picked up Janie and hugged her close. The sweet scent of baby filled her nostrils; love filled her heart.

He clucked his tongue at the horse and they began moving again. Rebecca released the air in her lungs. What if he was right? Would her family come looking for her? Did she have grandparents who could stake a claim to her?

Even though she'd only been with the baby for a few hours, Rebecca didn't know if she could turn her over to strangers. She glanced over at Seth. His jaw was set and he held his gaze straight ahead. Was he planning on taking the baby from her now that he knew she didn't want to give her up?

She pushed the thought from her tired mind. If Seth entertained those thoughts, he didn't speak of them the rest of the way back to Cottonwood Springs.

He pulled the horse up in front of the doctor's house

and office. "Would you like me to stay with you and Janie while the doctor examines her?"

Rebecca handed the baby, basket and all, to him. "No. I'm sure Janie is fine." She climbed down from the wagon and then extended her arms up for the baby.

Seth held her close and studied the infant. Was he thinking about taking her away?

She cleared her throat to get his attention.

"I'll go put away the wagon. Let me know, if the doctor finds anything wrong with her." He handed the baby down.

A little later, Doctor Clark smiled and handed the baby back to Rebecca. "You're right, Miss Ramsey. She's probably about six months old and I am happy to say she is healthy."

Rebecca took Janie in her arms and hugged her close. "Thank you, Doctor." She inhaled the sweet baby scent.

"So, you are going to be her new mama, huh?"

"Yes, sir."

"Do you know how to take care of a baby, Miss Ramsey?" He wiped down his examination table.

Rebecca smiled. She knew he was only doing what he thought was right by the baby. "Yes, I do. I helped Ma raise my little sister." She placed Janie in her basket and tucked the blankets around her small body.

"Good." He put his rag away and walked to the door. "What has Mrs. Kelly said about you moving a new baby into the house?"

What would Eliza say? Would she tell Rebecca they'd have to find a new home? She didn't think so, but worry still wormed its way into her heart. "I haven't told her yet."

He patted Rebecca on the back. "I'm sure Mrs. Kelly will be fine with the baby."

As she walked to the dress shop, Rebecca prayed the good doctor was right. She opened the door and, not seeing Eliza in the store portion of the house, sighed. Rebecca mentally rebuked herself as a coward. Eliza was a sweet, loving person. Surely she'd fall in love with Janie, too.

She squared her shoulders and walked into the sitting room of the house. Still no Eliza. Maybe the other woman wasn't home. Rebecca continued to the kitchen. She wanted to make Janie a nice warm bottle.

"There you are. I have been worried sick. Did you get the icebox? What's that?" Eliza's statements and questions came at Rebecca faster than sand off the desert on a windy day.

Rebecca set the basket on the kitchen table. Turned to smile at Hannah, who was sitting at the table, and then answered Eliza. "I'm sorry I kept you waiting. No, I didn't get the icebox." A smile pulled up the edges of her lips. "I got something better."

Janie let out a small gurgle.

Hannah's eyes grew round. "Is that what I think it is?"

Eliza rushed to the basket. "What is it? I want to see. Do you mind if I lift the blanket off? Oh, I love surprises!"

Rebecca nodded. She held her breath as Eliza pulled the blanket off. Her mouth shaped into an O and she turned to Rebecca. "There is a baby in here."

"I know." Rebecca would have laughed, but worry concerning her and Janie's future home kept her sober.

Hannah stood and looked into the basket. "Oh, she is beautiful," she breathed.

Again Rebecca answered with, "I know."

Eliza reached inside and picked her up. Janie grabbed one of the strands of hair that hung beside her face and pulled. "Whose is she?" She untangled the baby's fingers.

The moment of truth had come. Rebecca licked her lips before answering. "She's mine."

Hannah jerked her gaze from the baby. "Yours?"

"How is that possible?" Eliza pulled the baby back and searched her face.

Rebecca couldn't help but smile. "Yes, she's mine. I found her and the marshal said I can keep her, if her family doesn't show up for her."

Eliza plopped back into her chair. "I think you have some explaining to do."

Hannah motioned for her to sit down. "Have a cup of tea and tell us what happened. If Eliza wasn't so shocked, I'm sure she'd be asking you a million questions right now."

Eliza was brushing soft black curls off Janie's forehead. Her eyes were focused on the baby's face. She seemed to have forgotten that Hannah and Rebecca were still in the room.

Rebecca picked up a cup and poured warm tea into it. She dropped two teaspoons of sugar into the liquid and stirred. Still Eliza said nothing, simply stared into Janie's eyes. "Eliza, are you all right?"

"I'm fine. Tell us how this baby came to be in your care, Rebecca."

After Rebecca told the whole story, she looked to Eliza. "I was hoping it would be all right for me to move Janie in here with us."

Eliza tickled the baby. "Of course it is all right. Aunt Eliza wouldn't have it any other way."

Relief oozed from Rebecca's shoulders. "I'm so glad. Thank you."

Her gaze ran over her friend and Janie. How long would they be together? Fear knotted her stomach as the thought came to her that Seth might find the baby's family.

Chapter Twelve

Rebecca hung the clothes on the line and yawned. The ever-warming sun beat down on her head. She glanced at the sky and realized it was early afternoon.

Janie rested in her little basket. Even breathing told Rebecca that the baby was asleep. The desire to join the infant in a nap pulled strongly at her. Having a baby was proving to be a tiring job. Over the past week, Rebecca had gotten little rest. Between that and her job, she felt as if her bones were getting heavier by the day.

She scooped up the sleeping baby and the empty clothes basket, then headed back to the house. Her thoughts turned to Seth. He hadn't said any more about Janie's family and they had fallen into a routine. She, Grace and Janie spent breakfast with him. He was gone for the day and returned each evening at supper time. Then he walked her home each evening. Nothing he'd said this morning indicated today would be any different. Rebecca decided to go curl up on the guest bed and take a short nap with Janie.

In the house, she kicked off her shoes, found a light blanket and then lay down. The feather mattress's softness engulfed her.

Later she awoke to the sweet smell of frying bacon. Rebecca yawned and stretched as she came fully awake. She inhaled the delicious scent and her stomach growled. Her gaze moved to the dark window.

The dark window? Rebecca jerked upright. Instinct directed her search for the baby. Seeing only an empty basket she bolted out of the bed and raced to the kitchen.

Seth stood beside the stove, forking bacon and talking to the baby. "I guess your mama is going to sleep all night, too."

Janie cooed up at him. He'd placed her on a blanket on the floor and surrounded her with pillows and toys. Her blue eyes were glued to his face.

Unaware of her presence, Seth continued, "You have worn her out, little girl, but we're going to have to wake her up soon. What would the neighbors say if I let her stay all night?"

"They'd say more than either of us wants to hear." Rebecca walked into the room and held out her hands. She frowned when Seth handed her the fork and moved away, still talking to the baby.

He knelt down in front of Janie. "She's right, you know. I guess it's a good thing she got up on her own." The dimple in his cheek winked at Rebecca when he smiled in her direction.

Janie grabbed his finger and pulled as if to say, *Pay attention to me.*

Rebecca felt her cheeks burn. How long had she slept? Her gaze moved to the dark windows. "I'm sorry, I overslept. What time is it?"

"A little after seven."

Her hands flew to her face. "That late? I'm sure you are starved." She turned back to the stove. "Let me get this bacon done and I'll fry you up an egg. I think there are a few biscuits left over from this morning. I'm so sorry, Marshal. I promise this will never happen again." Rebecca made the promise more to herself than to him.

"It's all right. You are tired. Maybe I should start cooking my own dinner and you can go home when Grace comes by after school."

Rebecca turned to look at him. "That isn't necessary, Marshal."

His brown eyes were filled with warmth and compassion. "I'm not sure you will be able to keep up this pace, Rebecca."

Concern laced those beautiful brown eyes. Every time he said her name, something in her gave way. He'd taken to calling her Rebecca after their shared kiss. Something she couldn't forget and couldn't allow again.

She turned her back on him. "Janie and I are just settling in. She'll sleep the night through soon and I'll be fine. I can't afford not to work, Marshal." She removed the bacon and reached for the bowl of eggs.

"Your pay won't change." He stood so close to her that she felt the hairs on the back of her neck move with his breath.

Rebecca gasped and dropped an egg. They both bent to clean up the mess and bumped their heads.

"Ouch."

Seth stood and rubbed his head. "I'm sorry, I didn't mean to startle you." He took a step back.

She'd had enough. Enough of him being in her way, telling her what to do and making her insides do the wiggles. "Marshal, please go sit down and let me finish your dinner so I can go home." Her voice came out sharp and shrill.

At the sound of her raised voice, Janie gave out a

startled cry. Seth spun on his heels and walked back to the baby. He picked up the little one and placed her against his shoulder. His warm voice soothed the child as he murmured, "It's all right, little Miss Janie."

Rebecca finished the meal and placed his plate on the table. She turned to face him. "I'm sorry. I shouldn't have snapped like that."

He handed the baby to her and nodded. She waited while he said grace and then took his first bite.

"I don't want to give up cooking dinner for you, Marshal. As soon as Janie and I get used to one another, everything will be fine." Rebecca gathered Janie's things. Tears stung her eyes and she wished she'd never lain down. Now Seth didn't think she could handle the workload and Janie. Would he take Janie from her? Could he take the baby? What were her legal rights?

She picked up Janie's bottle and walked into the living room. Rebecca stuffed all of Janie's things into her bag. Rebecca pulled her shawl about her shoulders, and continued to the front door. "I'm leaving," Rebecca called as she pulled it open.

"Wait. I'm going with you."

"But, you haven't finished eating," she protested. "I can walk myself home, Marshal."

He wiped his mouth off with the dish towel he'd carried into the room with him. "No, you can't. It's after dark and I don't want a single woman with a baby walking the streets this late."

She wanted to go now, but she didn't want his dinner to get cold. The last thing Rebecca enjoyed eating were cold eggs. "Then we'll wait until you are finished with your supper before we go."

"Why are you in such a hurry, anyway?" he asked

as he placed both hands on his hips. His brown gaze bored into her eyes.

Heat filled her face. "Marshal, are you going to eat? Or ask me questions?" Rebecca prayed she sounded braver than she felt.

Seth didn't know how to react. One moment she was sugar and spice, the next salt and vinegar. He really wished he knew what was wrong with her. Maybe she hadn't gotten enough rest. Or maybe she was still embarrassed that he'd caught her sleeping on the job. Literally. Either way, this side of Rebecca wasn't where he wanted to be.

"Look, if you want to go home, we can go now. I just don't understand what I did wrong this evening." And he really didn't understand why he was allowing her to get to him. What difference did it make if she was grouchy? Or angry at him?

As far as he could see, he'd done nothing wrong. Seth replayed the events of the day in his mind. The dark circles under her eyes this morning had bothered him and he'd realized that they were there because she hadn't been resting well. He'd thought to send her home early. But when he returned home and found her asleep, he'd taken the fussy baby out of the room, changed her diaper and fed her.

A deep sigh came from Rebecca. "You haven't done anything wrong. It's me. I should have been up when you arrived, I should have had dinner cooked, and I should have been taking care of my own child. I guess I'm being oversensitive tonight. Please, go ahead and eat. I'll wait right here for you." She closed the door and walked to the couch.

Seth nodded. If he lived to be a hundred he would

never understand women. His own mother was much like Rebecca. Strong-willed and unwilling to accept free help. He gulped the remainder of his food, washed it down with coffee and returned to the sitting room.

Rebecca's head was resting against the back of the sofa. Janie played on the floor at her feet. Rebecca's eyes were closed and her breathing even. Had she fallen back to sleep? Was the woman totally exhausted? A soft snort exited her lips. Yes, she had fallen asleep sitting upright. Seth sighed. If only he could leave her like that, but he knew that the gossips of the town would be on it first thing tomorrow morning if he did.

He walked behind the couch and laid a hand on her shoulder. "Rebecca, I'm ready."

She opened her sleep-filled eyes, looked up at him and smiled. "Good. I almost went back to sleep."

Almost? Who did she think she was kidding? The woman had been asleep. She'd snored—in a very dainty manner, but it was still a snore! He fought to keep the corners of his mouth from tilting upward. "Then we should get you home so you can climb into bed."

Chapter Thirteen

Rebecca grinned at Janie. "You are getting so big. Look, your feet are coming out of the basket." She tickled the baby's feet. Much to her satisfaction Janie kicked and smiled. The baby had grown quite a bit in the past month.

Since the house was clean, the laundry done, and dinner simmered on the stove, Rebecca decided to go to the Millers' store. Maybe Mrs. Miller would have a bigger basket or something even better to carry the baby about in.

Then she thought of her hair. She'd told Grace she didn't care who saw her with her hair down, but the truth was she did. "How can I fix my hair so that it's up and respectable?" she asked Janie as she pulled it back into a ponytail and then twisted it to create a knot.

Her gaze looked about for something to hold it into place. If only she'd thought to grab a hat or something this morning, she chided herself. Not seeing anything, she looked out the door and into the backyard. The thought that she could use a stick brought a grin to her face.

Why not? If Eliza could wear birds, flowers and all

kinds of other outdoor things on her hats, then why couldn't she use a stick to hold her hair in place until she could get to the store and buy more pins? Rebecca scooped up the baby and hurried outside. She searched the ground for just the right size stick. It had to be long and pointed.

"Well, well. What have we here?"

The voice came from her right. Rebecca turned to find a dark-haired, thin, foul-smelling man standing beside the well. She clutched the baby to her. His clothes were torn and dirty, and his hair looked as if it hadn't been washed in a month of Sundays. He staggered toward them.

Rebecca took a step back. "You better move on, mister. My man will come if I scream," she warned, praying he'd believe her.

Janie whimpered.

He snorted. "Nope, your man ain't home. I saw him head out hours ago."

She shook her head in denial. *God, please protect Janie and me.* Would he? After she'd just lied? Rebecca forced the questions aside and continued watching the man. "There are houses all around us. All I have to do is scream and someone will come," she threatened.

"But you won't." He moved swiftly and grabbed her by the arm. He spoke low and harsh. "That brat will get hurt, if you so much as squeak."

Janie grabbed handfuls of Rebecca's hair and attempted to get away from the threatening stranger. Her cries filled the air and her little body shook with fear.

Alcohol coated Herman's breath. Body odor clung to him like death. The combined smells gagged her. He wasn't a big man and Rebecca held out hope that she could get away. She twisted her body to free herself but only accomplished hurting her arm. Desperation and anger warred within her as she fought to hold tight to Janie and to free herself from the foul man who held her captive.

Seth climbed off his horse and allowed it to drink from the cool stream. He bent down and splashed cold water in his face. Maybe that would wash away the sight of Rebecca and the way she'd looked this morning. Her hair had been down, and swished across her back with each step she took, reminding him of spun gold. She'd hurried into the house smelling of vanilla and cinnamon. Grace had said they were late because Miss Rebecca almost burned the cinnamon bread.

He smiled. Grace had a way of telling things like they were. She'd gone on to say that Miss Rebecca said, "If the old gossips wanted to talk about her hair, let them talk." Nine-year-old Grace had mimicked Rebecca to a tee.

More ice-cold water splashed into his face, but it wasn't doing the job of washing away his thoughts. Seth pushed up from the creek bank and stood, his horse studying him. "I know. I'm not myself today," he said, as if the animal could understand him.

Back in the saddle again, Seth continued his circle around the town. Everything appeared normal, just the way he liked it. He sat on the hill beside the school and looked down on Main Street. Everything seemed as it should.

His gaze moved to his house. Would Rebecca be fixing lunch for herself? He thought about going down and joining her and Janie for the noon meal. Seth used his knees to set the horse into motion and then pulled back on the reins to stop it.

"No, I'd better head to the diner." He wanted to go home, but in his state of mind he'd probably end up kissing Rebecca silly and that wasn't something he wanted to get into the habit of doing. He licked his lips and then moved the reins to direct the horse back to Main Street when a movement beside his house caught his attention. Seth stood up in the stirrups to get a closer look. There it was again. He couldn't make out a person, just the shadow moving.

The hair on his arms rose, a sure sign that the marshal in him had just kicked in. Seth's thoughts raced to the Evans gang. Had Maxwell Evans decided to make a move toward Rebecca?

A few minutes later, Seth moved in silently behind the drunk and prayed Rebecca wouldn't give him away. His choices on how to separate the man and Rebecca were limited. He could jerk him away, and possibly hurt Rebecca and the baby in the process, or he could hit him over the head with something and knock him out. Seth chose the latter.

Drawing his gun, he gripped the barrel and used the handle as a club. Seth hit the drunk with more force than he intended. A loud crack split the air and the man went down. Seth caught him as he fell and laid him out on the ground. "Are you all right?" he asked Rebecca.

Her big eyes looked to him, and the baby tried to lurch into his arms. Seth hurried to Rebecca's side and pulled her into his arms. He clutched her and the baby to him. What if he hadn't returned to town?

She gasped. "We're fine." Her pain-filled voice caused him to pull away and look into her eyes.

Rebecca jiggled the baby in her left arm. Her right arm hung limp.

"You're hurt," he accused. His mind continued to

play the scene in his head. He'd seen her jerk to the side. That must have been when she'd injured her arm.

"Really, Marshal, I'm fine."

"No, you aren't. We're going to see Doc." He inhaled the soft fragrance of vanilla as he took the baby from her arms.

"But what about him?" Rebecca protested.

"He'll be all right until I get back. I hit him hard enough, I don't think he's going anywhere for a while." Seth tucked Rebecca close to his right side and cradled the baby to his left.

She pushed away from him. "I can walk myself to the doctor's office, Marshal. Why don't you take care of him? I'd hate for that evil man to get away. What if he wakes up while you're gone?"

Seth wanted to refuse, but the determination in her eyes stopped him. A flash of fear also entered those soft blue orbs. He didn't want the man to get away either, so he nodded. "You go straight to see the doctor and I'll drop this one in a cell and be right over." He placed Janie into the crook of Rebecca's left arm.

Rebecca continued to speak in a soft tone to Janie but her gaze never left his face. "I will." Tears filled her eyes.

He raised her chin and lightly ran his lips over hers. "I promise, this man will never hurt you again." Seth released her chin.

She nodded and then turned away and walked toward the doctor's office.

He picked the thin man up and slung him over his shoulder.

His heart rate slowed as he neared the jailhouse. Seth had experienced pure fear back there, and memories from the past had pushed their way to the forefront of his mind. Memories of Clare and the day she'd died. No, she didn't just die. She'd been murdered and Seth knew it had been his fault.

He didn't want the same thing to happen to Rebecca, and yet the events of a few moments ago had been so similar that it choked him. When would he learn? Women were not a part of his future. There would be no wife. No children. No love. At least no real love—not the kind between husband and wife. His job wouldn't allow it. No, *he* wouldn't allow it.

Seth opened the door to the jail and grunted as he tossed the drunk onto one of the hard mattresses. He stared down at the man. How could a man hurt a woman? What did he gain from the experience?

God, I can't fall in love with Rebecca. Please give me the strength to fight the emotions that she brings up within me. You know I am called by You, Lord, to protect others and in doing so I hurt those I love and care for. Now two people have died because of me. Please don't let Rebecca be the third. I have enough blood on my hands.

He locked the door and walked over to the doctor's office. Rebecca would be fine. He knew that now. But his first reaction had been to protect her and get her help. His second had been to kiss her and offer words of comfort. Something he should not have done. Now he wished he didn't have to face her again. Maybe with God's help he'd get over the edgy feelings he had for her and learn to keep his kisses to himself.

Seth took a deep breath and opened the door. His nostrils filled with the scent of disinfectant. The waiting-room chairs sat empty. He wondered if he should sit down, but just then the doctor came out of the examination room. "How is she?" Seth asked.

"Both mother and child are just fine. Miss Ramsey's arm will hurt tomorrow, but she'll be right as rain in a few days." He stopped at the reception desk and looked down at his appointment book. "She'll be out in a few minutes. You might as well sit down. Did you find out why the guy attacked her?"

Seth ignored the good doctor's advice and chose to stand while he waited. "Not yet. He's still out cold. I'm going to walk Miss Ramsey home and then go wait for him to wake up."

The older gentleman looked up and chuckled. "I wouldn't want to be him and face you."

He didn't answer because Rebecca chose that moment to come into the room. She had a white sling on her arm and was carrying Janie in the other. Seth hurried to her side and took the baby.

Janie's bright blue eyes looked up at him. A soft smile touched the baby's lips. With just a look, the little one twisted his heart around hers. He'd protect this child with his life, should he be required to do so. Janie was as much his as she was Rebecca's. When he thought of how close he'd come to losing both this sweet baby and Rebecca, Seth saw red.

"I want you to take these for the pain." The doctor handed Rebecca a small brown bottle.

She took the medicine. "Thank you, Doctor. I'm sure I'll be fine."

"You're still staying with Mrs. Kelly. Is that correct?" At Rebecca's nod he continued, "Good. Make sure she is available to take care of the baby. Those pills might make you sleepy."

Rebecca nodded again. "I will. Thank you, Doctor." Her pain-laced eyes looked to Seth. The air swished

from his lungs and his gut twisted. Whether he liked
it or not, he would protect her until the end of time or
until she returned to where she belonged.

Chapter Fourteen

Rebecca cradled her arm against her stomach. "Marshal, I need to know something."

He patted the baby's back. She curled against his neck and her breath came easily as she relaxed into a nap. "What's that?"

"Who are these men hanging around your house? And who are they after? You or me?" Rebecca knew the answer, but needed him to tell her. Maybe she was wrong in her assumption.

Seth stopped and turned to look at her. "They are a part of the Evans gang. Well, the first man you saw was, but he's locked up now in Durango so he's no threat to you."

She rubbed her arms to ward off the cold chills that had popped up. "I see, and the man today?"

His large tan hand stroked the baby's soft curls. "I'm not sure about him. He might prove to be just a drunk who saw a pretty lady." He reached out and tucked her hair behind her ear. The calluses on his palm scratched her cheek.

"Do you think the Evans gang is after me, or you?"

Seth held her gaze. "You."

Her voice sounded small. "Why?"

His thumb rubbed her cheekbone. She wanted to lean into his palm but held herself straight. Weakness wasn't something Rebecca Ramsey gave in to. She would do what she had to, to protect herself and Janie.

"Do you feel up to going into the diner?"

Was he avoiding her question? She tilted her head to study him closer. "Will you answer my questions, if I say yes?"

Seth dropped his hand and nodded. The serious lines in his face gave her pause. Did she really want to hear the answers?

Rebecca squared her shoulders. Yes, she did. Her gaze moved to a sleeping Janie. Her little thumb was tucked between her lips and her sweet head rested on Seth's shoulder. Rebecca had more than herself to think about now. She had the start of a family.

Her gaze moved up to his chocolate eyes, which studied her face. Was Seth Billings to be a part of that family? Her pulse quickened. The gentle kiss they'd shared earlier had comforted her and awakened feelings within her. But right now wasn't the time to think about such things. "All right."

Seth pushed the door open to the diner. He stepped back and allowed Rebecca to pass before him.

"Well, hello, you two!" Mrs. Velarde, the owner of the diner, hurried toward them.

Janie gave a little start and her big blue eyes looked at Seth. He gently patted her back and she laid her head back down.

Mrs. Velarde lowered her voice. "You are very good with her, Marshal." She led the way to a table at the back of the building. They followed the tall woman. She wore an apron tied about her thin waist and took long steps toward one of the many wooden tables. "I'll put you back here where the little one can sleep in peace."

Seth held out a chair for Rebecca. She noted that he took the side of the table that allowed him to face the door. He continued to pat Janie's back, but his gaze remained on her face.

"What can I get you folks to drink?"

Seth nodded at her to answer first. "I'll have tea, please," Rebecca said.

"Just coffee."

After Mrs. Velarde left, Rebecca turned her full attention on Seth. "Why are they after me, Marshal?"

He stared at her for several moments. "Because you were to be Jesse's wife and he was a part of their gang."

"Jesse was a thief?" Her voice caught in her throat. Did everyone in town know that Jesse had been a thief? Is that why Mrs. Walker didn't want to extend credit to her in Seth's name? She thought Rebecca would steal him blind? After all, you are known by the company you keep.

Seth nodded. "But during the last two years of his life, he'd changed. Left that life behind. Joined the church, was a regular upstanding citizen." He continued to study her face.

"Then why are they after me?"

He shrugged. "Jesse warned me that they might come after you."

She wanted to reject the idea that Jesse had been a thief, that he'd stolen and who knew what else he had done. "But I still don't understand why they want me." Her voice came out stronger than she'd planned. Rebecca looked around the diner to see if anyone had noticed.

Mrs. Velarde crossed the room with a glass of tea

and a steaming cup of coffee. But other than her, no one else seemed to pay any notice to them. Rebecca sighed in relief. It was bad enough her arm was bandaged and Seth carried her daughter as if she were his own.

"Here you go," Mrs. Velarde said, setting the drinks on the table. "Can I get you anything else?"

Seth looked to Rebecca again. "Would you like something?"

"No, thanks." She thought of the beans simmering on the stove and hoped she'd left enough water in them to keep from scorching.

Seth nodded. "Nothing for me right now either."

"If you change your mind, just wave." Mrs. Velarde walked away.

"I'm not sure. I've been trying to find out, but the first man I arrested wouldn't say and the other one is in my jail cell sleeping off too much liquor and a knot on the head." Seth picked up his coffee and took a cautious sip.

Rebecca tugged at a string on her sling. "Oh, no." Had Seth given her stolen money? She looked up to find him studying her again. "The money you gave me?"

"Was money Jesse had earned working for the Vaughans."

Tears pricked the back of her eyes. She'd almost married a criminal. What would her life be like now if she had married Jesse? The outlaw gang would still be after her and Jesse. Now they were only after her. What was she going to do? The thought of leaving town entered and fled her mind in quick sucession.

"You can't leave, Rebecca. They will just follow you." Seth shifted the sleeping baby to his other arm.

She didn't tell him she'd already thought of and dismissed the idea. "Is that why you didn't tell me? You thought I'd leave?" Rebecca held hope in her heart that he was starting to care for her.

"Yes. I promised Jesse I'd watch out for you and I can't do that if you leave town."

"I see." He didn't care about her. She was just another part of his job. Thinking of his job reminded her that he was her boss and that by placing her in his house he could fulfill his promise to Jesse. She picked up her tea and drank deeply.

Janie began to fuss.

Rebecca looked to the baby in his arms. She didn't belong there. Setting her glass down, Rebecca stood. "I'm ready to go." She held out her good arm to take the baby back.

"I'll walk you back to Eliza's." Seth stood and tossed money onto the table for their drinks.

She straightened her back, determined not to spend one more moment in his presence today. "No, thank you. You have beans on the stove that need to be taken off before they burn."

Seth looked down at her and something about her stance must have told him to let her go. He gently placed Janie into the crook of her good arm. His hand reached up and tucked a strand of hair behind her ear.

"Don't. I'm not your responsibility, Marshal, so you don't have the right to do that." She stalked out of the diner as quickly as her legs would carry her. The feeling that everyone was watching her only fueled her legs to move faster.

Janie protested the sudden jerky movements and began to cry in earnest.

How could I have been so stupid? First I answered an ad to marry a man I didn't know. And now, I've fallen for a U.S. Marshal who only thinks of me as his responsibility.

Tears streamed down Rebecca's face as she hurried into the dress shop and passed a surprised Eliza.

Two days later Seth walked among the apple trees behind his house. They belonged to the Shelbys and had become one of his favorite places to think. Today his thoughts were where they always were—on Rebecca Ramsey. She'd not set foot out of the dress shop since the attack.

He'd half expected her to show up for work that morning but then realized it was Sunday, her day off. Seth picked up a smooth pebble and carried it to the river's edge. He skipped the stone across the water and sighed as he counted one, two, three, four, five and six.

The thought that he should be in church came to mind. Maybe Rebecca was there. He'd been pretty hard on her the other day and guilt ate at him. Seth knelt by the water and listened to its soft song as it washed over the rocks and sand.

After several long moments, the hair on the back of his neck began to prickle. Without being told, he knew someone or something was watching him. Very slowly, Seth stood and turned.

Rebecca sat on a quilt a few yards into the tree line. A picnic basket rested beside her. Blue eyes stared back at him. From this distance he couldn't tell if she was still hurt or angry at him.

Throwing caution to the wind, Seth approached her. "May I join you?" he asked.

"I can't stop you, Marshal," she answered, smoothing her dress with her good arm.

"Are you out here alone?" He looked about the clearing. Surely Eliza wouldn't have let her come out into the orchard alone. Especially since he'd made Rebecca aware she was in danger from the Evans gang.

She raised her chin. "Yes, I am."

He stood beside the quilt, not sure what to do. Seth saw a couple of sandwiches, chunks of cheese, sliced pickles, quartered apples and peaches in various containers around her. Was she expecting someone?

"You are welcome to sit down, Marshal. I've plenty of food for both of us." Rebecca waved her hand at the spot across from her.

Seth set down and smiled. "Are you sure I'm not intruding?"

Rebecca sighed. "Not at all. I just needed to get out of the house and took advantage of Eliza's offer to take Janie to church with her this morning."

He offered her a friendly grin. "So Mrs. Kelly has no idea you aren't tucked away safe at home, resting."

She shook her head and looked out across the water. "No, and I'd like to keep it that way."

"Your secret is safe with me." Seth pulled his knees up and wrapped his arms around them.

She grinned at him. "Thank you."

They sat in comfortable silence for several long minutes. The river ran before them and the birds chattered in the trees behind. It really was a peaceful spot to have a picnic.

"Rebecca, can I ask you a personal question?" He didn't look at her, simply waited.

"Only if I can ask one in return," she answered.

He released his legs and turned to face her. "Seems fair enough."

She handed him an egg salad sandwich. "What's your question?"

Seth stretched his legs out in front of him and took the sandwich. "Why did you answer Jesse's ad?"

Pain filled her eyes and she looked away. "My father had remarried and I was no longer needed around the house. Jesse seemed like the answer to my prayers."

He wanted to take her in his arms and offer some sort of comfort. Had her stepmother abused her? Before he could ask her, Rebecca turned those pain-filled eyes on him and changed the subject.

"I've been wondering. Why did you become a U.S. Marshal?"

Seth thoughts turned to his father, Abe Billings. "I guess you could say I'm following in my father's footsteps."

She nibbled on a chunk of cheese. "So your father is a U.S. Marshal, too."

"Not anymore. When I was younger he was ambushed and hung on a lone tree by the same bank robbers he was chasing." The gravel in his voice caused him to clear his throat.

"Oh, Seth, I'm so sorry." Rebecca reached out and touched his arm.

"It's all right, Rebecca. It was a long time ago."

She withdrew her hand, leaving a warm tingly spot on his forearm. He missed her light touch. "What happened to your mother?" he asked, hoping to pull the attention away from himself.

"She caught a bad chest cold that moved into her lungs, and died. That was about five years ago. I still miss her." They sat in silence, each wrapped up in their own sorrows. Rebecca broke the stillness. "Sometimes my heart still feels like it is breaking."

Seth wanted to relieve the sorrow that he heard in her voice but didn't know what he could say or do that would take away the pain of losing a loved one. His brown gaze searched her blue one.

"Do you think someone can really die of a broken heart?" she asked, softly.

He felt as if his chest would burst with pain, remembering the misery from his own losses. "After my father died, people whispered that my mother died of a broken heart. So it might be true."

Her hand reached out to him again. He took hers in his and gave it a little squeeze. For some reason sharing his pain helped him to feel better about it. He felt closer to Rebecca than he'd ever felt to another woman, even Clare.

"She must have loved your father very much. Someday I hope to share that kind of love with another." Rebecca seemed to realize that she'd spoken out loud. A nervous laugh escaped her throat. "Listen to me going on with such romantic notions."

He wished it could be him that she fell that hopelessly in love with. But he knew that he'd not put any woman through the dangers and loss of being married to a lawman. It had cost Clare her life and that was before they'd even wed.

Looking into her eyes, Seth knew Rebecca's love would be true and strong. He found his voice at last. "I'm sure you will, Rebecca, and when you do that man will be the luckiest man alive."

She pulled her hand from his. "Thank you, Seth. You are turning out to be a good friend."

Her gentle smile created a longing in him to take back her hand and never let it go. He told himself that this was a simple reaction from learning that Rebecca had suffered losses, much like him.

He hated the thought that his actions had caused her

even more loss. Jesse Cole would have been a good husband to her.

Once Rebecca learned the truth of the circumstances of Jesse's death, would she still want to be friends with him?

Chapter Fifteen

"I don't know that I should go," Rebecca said, shoving the last safety pin through the fabric of Janie's fresh diaper. She joined Hannah at the table and handed the baby a toy.

Eliza placed both hands on the table. "And why not? You're young, single and could use a night out."

Rebecca laughed. "I am also a mother now. A single mother with no one to watch the baby. So I can't go."

"Already taken care of. I asked Mrs. Brown to look after her for you. It will only be for a couple of hours." Eliza brushed at imaginary crumbs on her dress.

Rebecca frowned. "You asked Mrs. Brown to watch Janie?"

"No, she volunteered when she heard how sad it was that you couldn't go to the social event of the year."

Hannah looked up from her tea. "I wouldn't call it the social event of the year."

Eliza shrugged.

"She didn't mind taking her?" Rebecca caressed Janie's soft curls. Over the past month, she'd not had Janie out of her sight. During the two weeks it took her arm to heal, Eliza, Hannah and Grace had been there to help her with the sweet baby, but even then, Rebecca had made sure she was in the room with them. Could she stand to have the little girl stay with someone else?

Hannah reached over and patted Rebecca's hand. "It's only for a few hours. You need to have a little fun."

"Mrs. Brown offered to take her. She's excited. You really should go." Eliza picked up her teacup and took a sip.

Rebecca knew they were right. She looked from one friend's determined face to the other. Their expressions said she was going, no matter how long it took them to talk her into it. "All right, but I'm not staying long."

Eliza jumped from her chair. "I have just the hat and dress for you. I've been saving them for such an occasion." She hurried from the room and into the store.

Hannah shook her head and smiled. "She picked out my hat and dress, too."

"I guess of the three of us, she does have the most fashion sense." Rebecca waved her hand over the pale yellow house dress she wore. Did she have enough money saved up for the outfit Eliza had for her?

"Here they are!" Eliza swirled into the room. The two-toned blue dress she carried flared out with her movements. "Don't you just love it?" She stopped in front of Rebecca. "The colors will bring out the various shades of blue in your eyes."

"It's beautiful," Hannah sighed.

Rebecca handed Janie to Hannah and reached out to touch the fabric. Its silky smoothness slid over her hand. "It is beautiful, Eliza. How much does it cost?"

"Nothing."

"It has to cost something, Eliza. You can't just give it to me," Rebecca protested. She took the offered dress and held it up to her chest. This was a dress that had cost a lot to make. Its stitching was perfect and the fabric had to be the finest. Never had she owned such an exquisite gown.

Hannah whispered to Janie in a loud enough voice for the other two to hear, "Here it comes."

"You're right. I can't just give it to you. But I don't want money for it either." Eliza pulled a comb from her hair. A small bluebird sat on the edge of the comb among what looked like small diamonds.

"So what do you want?" Rebecca's worried gaze met Hannah's.

"First, I want you to wear this comb in your hair, instead of the promised hat. I got to thinking and this will look so much better in your hair." Eliza tucked the comb into Rebecca's blond locks.

"And second?" What was the catch? Rebecca knew her friend would never hurt her, but she seemed reluctant to tell Rebecca whatever it was she wanted.

Eliza fiddled with the placement of the comb. "When the ladies ask about your dress, I want you to tell them I made it." She dropped her hands to her side and smiled broadly.

Rebecca studied her sparkling eyes. "Is that all?"

"Yes. I want all the ladies in town to start coming here for their party dresses." She returned to her chair and sat down.

Something wasn't right. Why did this matter so much to Eliza? Rebecca looked to Hannah for answers.

In a very soft voice Hannah explained, "The younger ladies had a predance party last week and went to Farmington for all their dresses. Not one of them bought one of Eliza's creations."

Rebecca looked to Eliza. She picked at the flower on the tablecloth. "That's terrible." Rebecca hung the dress over the vacant chair at the table. "Why not? Did they say?"

Eliza shook her head. Her eyes filled with tears and she offered a wobbly smile. "No, but I want them to see that you and Hannah are wearing the prettiest dresses there." Eliza wouldn't look up from the table and meet her gaze.

Rebecca walked to her chair and gave her a hug about her shoulders. "We'll make sure they know who designed them. I promise." She looked to Hannah, who added her nod.

Later as she dressed, Rebecca questioned her own sensibility. Eliza expected her and Hannah to do a lot of dancing, keep her dresses on the dance floor for all to see. She didn't want to be the center of attention. Why had she said she'd do this? Because she cared about Eliza, and Eliza needed her to do this.

She looked at herself in the mirror one more time, then picked up Janie and then headed for the kitchen. Her stomach felt queasy. Maybe a sip of cold milk would ease the sensation. Rebecca entered the room and found Hannah standing by the icebox. Her face pale and her lips surrounded by white milk. "Upset stomach?"

Hannah nodded. "I have this rock in my tummy, Rebecca. I just don't know that I can dance in front of all those people."

Rebecca set the baby on the counter and reached for a glass. Janie grabbed a spoon and banged it against the counter. "I know what you mean, but we have to, for Eliza."

"Did someone mention my name?" Eliza breezed into the kitchen looking like a ray of sunshine. Her yellow-and-gold dress floated about her legs, giving the illusion that she was walking on air. The light blue feather on the top of her hat bobbed in time with her swirling about.

"We were just talking about how we're helping you out tonight." Rebecca gulped the milk from her glass.

Eliza's lip spread in a large smile. "And I sure appreciate that, too." She handed a tea towel to Hannah.

Hannah wiped off her milk mustache and then handed it to Rebecca.

"We'd better get going, if we plan to get there early." Eliza linked her arm into Hannah's. "You won't get cold feet, will you, Rebecca?"

Rebecca picked up Janie and placed her into her basket. "No, I'll be there as soon as I drop off the baby with Mrs. Brown."

"Good." Eliza led Hannah out of the kitchen. "We'll see you there."

The walk to Mrs. Brown's was short, but Janie had fallen asleep along the way. Her thumb was tucked between her little lips and the sound of sucking filled the night air. The smell of irises filled the air surrounding Mrs. Brown's house. The purple flowers created a hedge on both sides of the door.

Rebecca knocked and was surprised when it opened instantly. Mrs. Brown, a sweet lady in her eighties, greeted her with a smile. "I'm so glad you took me up on my offer to watch the little tyke. I miss having children around." She stepped back and let Rebecca pass.

"I'm grateful you are willing to watch her. She will probably sleep the whole time I'm gone." Rebecca set the baby's basket on the floor beside a chair that still rocked gently from Mrs. Brown's recent evacuation. Quilt squares were scattered about the chair, and part of the nine-patch quilt she was working on rested on the hardwood seat.

Mrs. Brown shuffled toward the chair. "That's all right. I don't get around as well as I used to, but I do love babies. I don't think she'll be any trouble at all."

"If she wakes while I'm gone, I've made a bottle for her. I won't be gone long. I promise." Rebecca twisted her hands in the folds of her new dress. She didn't want to leave Janie.

The older woman gently guided her back toward the door. She opened it and smiled. "You have fun. There is no reason to hurry back." And then she shut the door.

The urge to knock and demand her baby back threatened to overpower Rebecca's good sense. She lifted her skirt and walked down the front steps. Her weary feet carried her to the dance of their own accord. Rebecca wondered if the marshal would be present.

Over the past month they'd spent some time together but not as much as they had in the past, and Grace and Janie were always with them. Did Seth regret kissing her? Was that why he'd stayed away as much as possible? They hadn't spoken much since she'd hurt her arm. She fixed his meals, straightened the house—not that much needed to be done—and went home early. Rebecca missed their nightly walks.

Gossip had it that he was out chasing the Evans gang. She worried about him but knew that was his job, and according to the older men that frequented the Millers' store, Seth Billings was the best. She prayed he'd be at the dance. Rebecca hated to admit that she missed him. But she did.

Music poured from the Grand Hotel. She made her way up the stairs and took a deep breath. Built in eighteen eighty-four it was the grandest building in Cottonwood Springs. The ceilings were high, the floors were covered in the finest wood and the ballroom was the place where girls dreamed of dancing with their favorite beaus. Her gaze swept the many dancers and people who stood off to the side.

He wasn't here. Her heart sank, but Rebecca plastered a smile on her face and hurried to Hannah's side.

Seth followed the sound of the music. He'd told himself he wasn't going, but then again knew that as acting sheriff his attendance was required. His gaze searched the dance floor and stopped on the vision in blue. Her eyes sparkled up at her dance partner. She laughed at something he said, tilting her head back and revealing a slender throat.

A growl grew within his chest. He fought to keep it down. Rebecca didn't belong with the cowboy who was holding her too tight. Seth took a step toward the dance floor. But before he could move, another man tapped the cowboy on the shoulder.

Even from this distance, Seth saw the cowboy's scowl of disappointment as he released Rebecca and watched her dance away with the new partner.

"Good to see you back in town, Seth."

Seth turned his attention to the preacher. "Nice to be back, Reverend."

"Having any luck with the Evans gang?"

He nodded. "A little." Seth's focus wasn't on the reverend or the Evans gang tonight. Rebecca held his attention like a spider trapping a fly in its web. He had to know who she was dancing with now.

"Jesse's girl has been dancing the night away ever since she arrived. I don't think there's a man in the place that hasn't circled the floor at least once with her, including me. She's a really sweet gal. Maybe I should mosey over there and see if she needs a rest."

Before the preacher could move, Seth barked, "I'll do it."

Rebecca spun around on the floor with Mr. Miller's oldest son, Josiah. Seth's hand clamped onto the young man's shoulder and stopped him in midstep. "Excuse me, Josiah. I'm cutting in."

The young man nodded and stepped to the side. "Thank you, Miss Rebecca, for the dance."

She curtsied and smiled sweetly at the young man. "You're welcome."

Seth scooped her up into his arms and began the dance. He held her a little closer than he probably should have. Anger fueled his bad behavior.

"When did you get home, Marshal?"

Her soft voice washed over him like warm rain. "This afternoon."

The beat of the music slowed. Seth pulled her closer and inhaled. The scent of vanilla soothed his nerves. And then she laid her head on his shoulder.

"I'm glad you are back. I missed you."

After the way he'd behaved over the past few weeks, how could she be so sweet? Spending as little time as he could with her and growling like a wounded animal every time she'd come too near, he'd expected vinegar to spew from her lips, but instead he had received honey. Why? Seth pulled away from her. He took her hand and led her off the dance floor.

"The reverend said you've been dancing all evening. Would you like a drink?"

Rebecca smiled up at him. "I'd love one and then I need to go home."

Seth nodded. "Be back in a moment."

He weaved his way through the good people of Cottonwood Springs. Seth nodded to each person who welcomed him back. He'd never been a big talker so he hoped no one would take offense to his brief nods and words.

A fruit punch was within his sights when Millie Hamilton stepped into his path. "Hello, Marshal."

"Miss Hamilton." He moved to step around her and found his path blocked by her again.

She twirled her hair onto one finger, cocked her head to the side and gave him a wide grin. "When did you get home, Marshal?"

When Rebecca had asked him that same question his heart had melted with the knowledge that she'd been interested and even cared. When Millie asked, he simply felt annoyed. "Today. If you will excuse me, I must be on my way."

Her smile dropped. "Why? So you can get back to Jesse's girl?"

Why did everyone insist on calling Rebecca Jesse's girl? "I don't believe that is any of your concern, Miss Hamilton." He stepped around her.

The girl was a troublemaker, barely sixteen and on the hunt for a man. He focused on the refreshment table and was almost within reach of the punch bowl when he heard Eliza Kelly's voice rise.

"You spoiled brat!"

Seth stopped and moved closer to the two ladies arguing. "Call me all the names you want to, Mrs. Kelly, but if you continue to let her live with you, we'll continue to take our money elsewhere. We don't care how pretty your dresses and hats are." He recognized the voice of Millie Hamilton's best friend, Charlotte Walker.

Eliza faced the young girl. She stood straight with her shoulders pulled back. "You mean your daddy's money."

The girl snarled back, "That's right, and after Millie and I get done talking to Mama, not a woman in this town will enter your shop."

He admired the steadiness in Eliza's voice. "That's fine, Miss Walker, but I'm curious, why do you care who lives under my roof?"

Venom dripped from the youthful voice. "She's Jesse's girl. We all know that he did horrible things so it stands to reason that she is a bad person, too. We don't want her kind in our town."

Seth clenched his fists. The townspeople hadn't wanted Jesse in their town either. That's why he'd advertised for a mail-order bride. There were some good people who hadn't minded Jesse, but they were very few. Still, the young man had tried to turn his life around. What had happened to put him at that bank on the day of the robbery? He'd asked every Evans gang member he'd caught and none would give him an answer.

Eliza smiled, but the emotion didn't reach her eyes. "I see. So being rude is what good people do?"

When the girl didn't answer, Eliza stood a little taller and pressed on. "And, for your information, Miss Walker, Jesse was a petty thief and nothing more. He'd turned his life around and had become a Christian and a good citizen of Cottonwood Springs." She crossed her arms and stared the younger girl down.

Charlotte raised her chin. "Maybe so, Mrs. Kelly, but no respectable woman would answer a mail-order-bride advertisement. Miss Ramsey shouldn't be here." Before Eliza could respond, the young girl was gone.

Seth watched Eliza's shoulders sag. He moved to the punch bowl and filled three cups. Picking up all three, he turned to find Eliza. She hadn't moved so he walked to her side. "Can I offer you a drink, Mrs. Kelly?"

Watery eyes looked up at him. "Thank you, Marshal." She took the closest cup.

He nodded. While she sipped, he looked toward where Rebecca stood talking to a young man. She didn't deserve the women's scorn. Seth glanced at Eliza. Her eyes were trained on the cup she cradled in her palms. "I overheard. How can we make this right?"

A soft sob escaped her pursed lips. "I don't think we can, Marshal. I won't ask Rebecca to leave my home and those girls won't change their minds either."

"Don't forget, Eliza. These are teenage girls you are dealing with." How could he help this sweet woman who had been through so much?

He'd always had a soft spot for Eliza. They'd connected early on and he felt as if she was the sister he'd never had. He didn't like seeing her hurting and fearful. What could he do to make the young women of Cottonwood Springs buy their dresses from Eliza, befriend Rebecca and treat others as they'd like to be treated? He silently asked the Lord for guidance.

The words came as if on their own. "Mrs. Kelly, wasn't that Mrs. Walker's daughter, Charlotte?"

Eliza wiped her nose on a little white handkerchief. "Yes."

"Isn't Elizabeth Miller also a friend of Charlotte Walker's?"

Eliza nodded. "I believe so. What are you getting at?"

Seth grinned at her. "I was just thinking, if Mrs. Miller gets wind of how her daughter's friends are behaving I think she would take matters into her own hands. As you know, she and Mrs. Walker aren't exactly friends."

Her mouth shaped into an O. "I see. So if a little birdie mentioned this to Mrs. Miller, she might just nip it in the bud."

It was his turn to nod.

"Oh, thank you, Marshal." Eliza smiled.

"My pleasure. Now, if you will excuse me, I need to take this drink to Miss Ramsey before one of those young men whisks her off for another round of dances."

Eliza laid a gloved hand on his forearm. "Would you tell her I have a headache and am going home now?"

He nodded. "Rebecca said she'd be heading home, too, after she finishes this drink."

"Thank you again, Marshal." Eliza seemed to have her old step back as she headed for the exit. Seth thanked the Lord for giving him the right words to help his friend, and then he joined Rebecca and the young man.

Her fingers brushed his when he handed her one of the cups. A deep pink filled her cheeks and she refused to meet his eyes.

Had he interrupted something? Was she interested in this boy? Seth looked the young man over. The kid couldn't be a day over eighteen. Seth scowled.

"Excuse me, I think I'll go ask Miss Hamilton for this dance," the young man said, hurrying away.

Seth grinned into his drink. That had been easy.

"Thank you, Marshal." Rebecca took the cup and sipped.

He nodded once. Seth watched the people dance and laugh. All around him families and young couples enjoyed the evening. Sometimes he wished he could do that, but being the marshal put him in a position where he had to stay alert at all times.

"Miss Ramsey, may I have this dance?"

Seth jerked from his wayward thoughts.

"Yes, that would be nice, Doctor Clark." She set her cup on a small table and held out her hand.

He watched as the doctor swung Rebecca around the floor. His gaze sought out Mrs. Clark. Seth walked over to her and asked, "May I have this dance?"

"You are sweet, Marshal, but I don't do the fast dances anymore. My old knees don't hold up as well as they used to." Her green eyes sparkled up at him.

Seth turned to leave, but at that moment the music changed to a slow waltz. He extended his hand to Mrs. Clark. "I believe they are playing our song."

She took his hand and he led her out to the dance floor. The soft scent of rosewater drifted into his nostrils. He missed Rebecca's sweet vanilla fragrance.

"You are very light on my feet, Marshal."

He grinned. "I don't believe I've crushed your toes yet."

Mrs. Clark laughed. "I know. Doctor Clark isn't as light as you."

A light tap landed on his shoulder. He turned and found Dr. Clark and Rebecca standing behind him.

Doctor Clark asked, "Might I exchange partners with you? I believe the missus and I will be going home after this dance."

Seth gently handed over the good doctor's wife. "Thank you for the dance, Mrs. Clark." Seth pulled Rebecca in his arms.

"It was my pleasure, young man," Mrs. Clark said as Doctor Clark waltzed her away.

Rebecca smiled. "They are a sweet couple."

Seth's gaze followed hers. The older couple danced with ease, their graying heads close together. He wondered if the good doctor was stepping on his wife's feet.

What would it be like to marry Rebecca and grow old with her? During her time in Cottonwood Springs, she'd created a home for him. Her caring personality and loyalty to friends made her special. The flash in her eyes when he angered her brought a spark alive in him, as well.

A spark that needed to be flattened now. He didn't want or need a wife. *U.S. Marshals do not get married,* he reminded himself.

As if she sensed his mood swing, Rebecca looked at him with questioning eyes. Eyes that drew him to her much like a hummingbird to a rose. Seth thought about pulling away from her but his feet refused. How much longer could he stand to hold her and not taste the sweetness of her lips?

Chapter Sixteen

When the music stopped, Rebecca allowed Seth to lead her to the sidelines. He'd been silent both times they'd danced, but to her they were the dances that counted. Seth was home again. She'd missed him.

He bowed to her. "Thank you for the dance."

"You are welcome." Rebecca searched the ballroom for Hannah or Eliza. She wanted to tell them she was leaving.

Seth cleared his throat. "Before I leave you for the evening, Mrs. Kelly asked me to tell you she had a headache and was going home."

Rebecca looked for Hannah once more. "I need to go get Janie and head home, too." Not seeing Hannah, she decided that the schoolteacher must have walked back with Eliza.

He sighed heavily. "I'll walk you back."

She heard the sound and frowned. Once more Seth was pushing her away. "That's not necessary, Marshal."

His voice came out hard and cold. "I believe it is, Miss Ramsey."

Why did he always seem to be growling at her? She inclined her head. "I can't stop you, Marshal."

They left the Grand Hotel together. She turned in the direction of Mrs. Brown's house.

Seth took her arm. "Where are you going?"

Rebecca looked up at him. "To pick up Janie."

He ran a hand through his hair. "I must be really tired, I'd forgotten all about the baby. How is she?"

She took a step forward and he released his hold on her. "She's growing so fast. Can you believe she pushed herself up and rocked back and forth for several seconds before collapsing to the floor yesterday? She'll be crawling before we know it."

From the corner of her eye she watched his lip twitch into a half smile as if he could picture Janie trying to crawl. "Wish I could have seen that."

"Me, too." They walked on in silence for a few more moments. "Seth, did you ever find out what happened to her parents?"

"No."

Rebecca looked up into the star-filled sky. It looked as if she could reach up and touch heaven. Had Janie's parents been believers? She'd wondered that question every day since she'd taken Janie in.

The smell of wood smoke filled the evening air as they passed several houses. Mrs. Brown's house came into sight and Rebecca hurried her footsteps. She'd missed Janie and wanted to cuddle her, inhale her baby scent and kiss her soft cheeks.

Seth walked in time with her. He held the fence gate open so that she could enter Mrs. Brown's front yard. It had felt so right dancing with him tonight. But she didn't like the way his mood changed from moment to moment. There were moments when she'd thought he might kiss her. Would she have allowed him to? Rebecca frowned at the question. She wasn't sure.

* * *

Seth leaned over in the saddle and studied the prints he'd been following for the past two days. Horace Nance and another member of the Evans gang were a few hours ahead of him. He was saddle sore and bone tired.

For two weeks he'd been tracking down the Evans gang. Each member he caught led him to the next. He sat up and yawned.

The only problem was that no one wanted to tell the gang's exact number. When had they grown so large? Every disgruntled outlaw in the New Mexico Territory seemed to have joined them. What he wouldn't give for a good cup of Rebecca's coffee and his warm, soft bed.

He climbed out of the saddle and led the horse to the river's edge. While the horse drank, Seth leaned against a tree. His eyes were heavy so he shut them. The warmth of the sun caused him to relax further.

Shots filled the air. Pain sliced through his right leg and left shoulder, and his side burned. Seth sunk to the ground and grasped his side. He pulled sticky red fingers back and felt the warm blood that coated them. Seth ducked his head just as a bullet grazed his left temple.

Ambushed.

How had he let this happen? Seth flattened his body against the ground and searched for his horse. Tail held high, the stallion raced up the river bank on the other side. Now what? Would the outlaws finish him off? Or take him captive?

Darkness edged into his line of vision. Seth shook his throbbing head. He pulled himself behind the tree he'd been leaning against moments before and prayed for protection as inky blackness shut out the light.

* * *

Rebecca couldn't stand being idle any longer. She scooped up Janie, a basket of dust rags and her shawl. Seth had been by several times to check on her and Janie, but had said she didn't need to come to the house because he wasn't spending much time there. He'd also warned her not to go anywhere alone.

She tickled Janie under the chin. "I'm not alone, am I, sweetie? You're with me." Rebecca walked into the dress store and called to Eliza, "Eliza, I'm heading over to the marshal's house to dust."

"It'll be dark soon. Don't stay over there too long." Eliza turned back to the ironing board.

She knew her friend was thinking about the Evans gang. So far they hadn't approached her again, but still her friend worried about her. "I won't." Rebecca rocked the basket as she walked to Seth's house. She missed him.

Grace came running up to her. "Hi, Miss Rebecca. Where are you going?"

Rebecca smiled at her young friend. "Over to dust the marshal's house. Want to come?"

Grace wrinkled her nose. "Do I have to dust, too?"

"Nope. But if you want to play with Janie for a little while, you're welcome to do that." Rebecca handed Grace the basket.

"All right."

Rebecca stepped inside the musty-smelling house. She left the door open and handed Janie to Grace. Next, she spread out a blanket on the floor for Grace to put the baby on. "This place needs a good airing out." Then she headed into the kitchen to open the back door, too.

"It does smell in here," Grace called from the sitting room.

A light breeze flowed from one door to the other. "That will help." Rebecca came back into the sitting room and pulled a dust rag from the basket. "Don't let her put anything into her mouth," she warned Grace.

"I won't." Grace took a little rattle from the basket and gave it to the baby. She talked to Janie and pulled out another small toy. Rebecca smiled at the two girls before going to work on the dust that had accumulated during her absence.

She dusted the sitting room and the guest room and had just entered Seth's room when she heard a commotion outside.

"Miss Rebecca, hurry!" Grace squealed from the sitting room.

Rebecca ran to the girls. Her heart pounded as she watched two men carry another man into the house. She couldn't see his features but knew it had to be Seth. Blood covered one side of his face. His arm hung limp, and dark color stained his shirt and pants.

They stopped just inside the doorway. "Excuse me, Miss Ramsey. Where is his bedroom?"

Her eyes met the doctor's serious gaze. Her hand shook as she pointed to the room she'd just left. "What can I do?" she asked, following the men into the small room.

Seth groaned as they laid him down.

"I need hot water, a pair of scissors and freshly laundered rags to clean up these bullet wounds." He'd already moved past the other men and was tearing at Seth's shirt.

Rebecca turned to do his bidding and ran into Grace. She caught the girl before she fell and hit the floor. "Grace, please take Janie into the other bedroom and watch her for me."

"Yes, Miss Rebecca." Grace raced back to Janie and picked her up.

She hurried to the kitchen and grabbed the water bucket. Empty. Rebecca ran outside to the well. As she pulled the water up her thoughts went to Seth. What had happened? Was it the Evans gang? Or someone else? Being a lawman was dangerous, but she'd never expected to see Seth covered in dried blood and looking so pale. Tears burned the back of her eyes.

Rebecca put the water on the stove and then built a fire to heat it. She found a pair of scissors and took them to the doctor. The two men who had carried Seth in were gone.

He took the scissors and waved for her to leave the room. The doctor returned to Seth's side and began cutting his shirt off his shoulder. Rebecca looked past him to Seth. His breathing came in shallow gasps.

She whispered, "Is he going to make it?"

The doctor continued to cut away Seth's clothes. "If I have anything to do with it, he will. Now go check on the water, I need to clean up these wounds and dig out the bullets."

Rebecca hurried into the guest room to check on the girls. Grace played with Janie on the bed. "Thank you, Grace. I don't know what I would have done if you weren't here to take care of Janie."

"Is the marshal going to be all right?"

She tugged on Grace's braid. "Doc says he thinks so. Do you mind watching Janie for just a few more minutes?"

Grace smiled at the baby. "No, I don't mind. But she's getting hungry."

"As soon as I get the hot water for the doctor, I'll come back and feed her."

"All right." Grace turned her attention back on Janie.

Rebecca hurried to the kitchen and poured hot water into a big bowl. She found a clean dishcloth and took everything to Seth's bedroom. The doctor took the bowl and rag. "Thank you, Miss Ramsey."

He dismissed her with a wave of his hand. "Don't go far, I may need you to hold him down when I remove these bullets."

She gulped. "I'll be in the next room feeding Janie."

Once more he waved her away with his hand. "Fine, fine."

Rebecca headed back into the kitchen and warmed up a bottle for Janie. Tears pricked her eyes again. What if Seth died? Her heart twisted at the thought. She closed her eyes and silently prayed. *Lord, please don't let him die. In our own way, we've become friends and I don't want to lose him.*

"Miss Rebecca, Janie is crying." Grace stood in the doorway holding the screaming baby.

Rebecca tested the temperature of the milk on her wrist and then turned to Grace. "I'm sorry, Grace. Bring her here and I'll feed her."

Grace handed the baby to Rebecca. As soon as Janie saw the bottle she stopped her thrashing and reached for the milk. "She sure raises a fuss when she's hungry, doesn't she?" Grace said.

Rebecca rocked Janie in her arms. "She sure does." She smiled at Grace. "Thank you again, Grace. If you want to go home before it gets too dark, go ahead. I'm going to feed Janie and then she'll be ready for bed."

Relief washed over the little girl's face. "All right." Grace hurried from the room. The sound of the door slamming into place announced her exit.

She returned to the guest bedroom and sunk into

the rocker that Seth had purchased shortly after they'd found Janie. His thoughtfulness had touched her and now she realized he might not live to see Janie grow into a beautiful young woman. *Stop thinking like that!* she told herself. *Seth is strong—he's going to make it.*

Janie's soft sucking noises filled the silent room. The sound of the doctor moving about the bedroom next door filtered through the wall. Seth groaned. Rebecca's heart twisted. She picked the baby up and gently patted her on the back, then continued rocking until Janie fell asleep.

Rebecca continued to hold the baby long after her soft snores filled the air. She listened to the sound of sloshing water from next door and the occasional moan from Seth. A few moments later, the doctor filled the bedroom doorway.

"Miss Ramsey, can you help me?"

She nodded.

He turned to leave.

Rebecca said a silent prayer for strength. She laid the baby in the center of the bed and placed rolled-up blankets around Janie to keep her from falling off. Then she straightened her shoulders and walked into Seth's bedroom.

The bowl of water she'd given the doctor earlier sat on a small table beside the bed. She gulped at the amount of blood on the dishcloth. "I need fresh water and another dishrag, please," the doctor said as he cut away Seth's pant leg.

Relief washed over her as she scooped up the red water and hurried from the room. She'd thought he wanted her to hold Seth while he dug for bullets. Rebecca tossed the water out the back door and hurried to rinse out the bowl. She refilled it with fresh hot water and grabbed another dishcloth before returning to Seth's bedroom.

She set the bowl down and looked to the doctor. He bent over Seth's thigh and frowned. "That bullet is going to have to come out. The ones in his arm and side went straight through, but this one seems to be buried against the bone."

Rebecca dreaded what he would ask her to do next but squared her shoulders to comply. She knew the doctor would have to cut the bullet out. Did she have the strength to hold Seth down? Tears filled her eyes.

Chapter Seventeen

Rebecca's gaze went to Seth's pale face. The doctor had washed off the blood and placed a bandage around his forehead. She wondered where he'd gotten the cloth to create the dressing and then saw that one of the sheets had been torn into bandages.

"Is the baby sleeping?"

Rebecca nodded.

"Good. Go to the livery and ask Hank to come over here. Then go to the blacksmith shop and see if Dan can come, too. I'll keep an ear open for the babe." He never looked up from his work. His fingers prodded the open wound.

She hurried from the room. Fresh tears filled her eyes when she heard Seth yelp in pain. Within moments both Dan and Hank were rushing to the marshal's house. Rebecca followed them inside. She listened as the doctor gave them instructions on where to stand while he removed the bullet.

Rebecca hurried to the guest room and scooped up a sleeping Janie. She hurried from the house to avoid the sounds of surgery. If Eliza hadn't already left for the pie supper over at the church, Rebecca would have taken Janie home. Tears blinded her as she carried Janie to Mrs. Brown's house. She prayed the older woman wouldn't mind watching her baby.

Mrs. Brown met her at the door. "Hello, dear. What brings you here?"

She cradled the baby to her. "I was wondering if you would mind watching Janie for me. I will be back in a couple of hours to get her."

"I'll be happy to, Miss Ramsey." The older woman extended her arms to Rebecca.

She handed her Janie. The baby continued to sleep and suck her thumb. "She should sleep until I return." Rebecca brushed the hair off the baby's forehead.

"I'll take good care of her. Now hurry back to the marshal, dear."

Rebecca looked deeply into the older woman's eyes. "How did you know I'd be going back to the marshal's?" Did the woman think that she wanted to get rid of Janie to spend time with Seth? The desire to reach out and take her baby back from the woman threatened to overtake her.

"Oh, the old gossips have already been by the house. Is he as shot up as they say he is?" Mrs. Brown tucked a little black curl behind Janie's small ear.

"He's pretty bad off. I'm heading back to see if I can do anything to help the doctor," Rebecca replied. Hadn't she already said that? Rebecca couldn't remember. Her mind wouldn't focus on anything more than getting back to Seth.

The old woman nodded. "I'll take care of the baby, don't worry."

"Thank you," Rebecca said and then turned to leave.

"Rebecca?"

She stopped at the sound of her name. "Yes?"

"If you ever need a friend to talk to, these old ears will listen."

She smiled at Mrs. Brown. "Thank you. I'll keep that in mind."

The crickets began to chirp their happiness at the coming of nightfall. As she hurried back to Seth, Rebecca wondered about Mrs. Brown's words. She thanked the Lord above that she had Eliza and Hannah to talk to when she needed sympathetic friends. Was Mrs. Brown offering friendship because she needed friendship? Rebecca decided she'd explore that thought more, once Seth was feeling well again. Until then, she wanted to be by his side with no distractions.

She hurried through the door just as the men were leaving the bedroom. Their grim faces caused her to think the worst. "Is he…?" Rebecca couldn't finish the question around the large knot in her throat.

"Yep, he passed out." The blacksmith rubbed his large forearms. A frown marred his normally smiling face.

Hank shook his head. "Poor guy. That had to have hurt."

"I thought he was going to bite right through the belt," Dan added.

Rebecca's gaze moved to the shut bedroom door. "What's Doc doing now?"

"Cleaning up the wound. He had to cut deep and wide for that bullet. Good thing the reverend found him when he did, otherwise he might have bled out."

Bile rose in her throat as she pictured Seth's bleeding body and the doctor working over him to dig out the bullet. She forced it back down, telling herself she couldn't throw up. Soon she'd need to take care of Seth and she'd have to be strong.

Hank rubbed his booted toe against the hardwood floor. "I best be getting back to the livery." He walked to the front door.

"Me, too." Dan followed the other man outside. Just before closing the door, he offered, "If you need any help, Miss Ramsey, give me a holler."

A few minutes later, the doctor stepped out of the room. "Miss Ramsey, he woke up for a few moments and asked that you stay with him."

"I wasn't going anywhere, Doctor." Rebecca wanted to go to where Seth lay but knew she needed to wait to hear what else the doctor had to say.

"Good. He should sleep the night through. I have several other patients I need to check on. Sally Rutherford's baby is due any minute and I'm going to drive out to their farm, but I'll be back in plenty of time to spend the night with Seth." He snapped his bag shut and turned to leave.

"Is there anything special I need to do?" Rebecca followed him to the door. A light breeze lifted her hair.

"Naw, like I said, I gave him a dose of laudanum, he'll probably sleep until morning. Just keep an eye on him in case he comes down with a fever." He patted her hand before leaving.

Rebecca nodded. She watched him climb into his buggy and then turned to the quiet house. She slipped into Seth's room, gathered up the bowl and towels the doctor had used and carried them to the kitchen to scrub clean. Once that was done, she checked on Seth again. He still slept peacefully.

With nothing else to do, Rebecca returned to the sitting room and took down the Bible. She began to read the book of Exodus. The stories of Moses, Pharaoh and the Israelites carried her away to the days of old and the teachings of God.

Several hours later, she stood and stretched, and then she checked on Seth. His pale face matched the clean pillow case. Rebecca said a silent prayer of thanks that he was alive and then returned to the sitting room. A look at the clock told her the doctor would be back soon. She decided he might like a light supper so she headed to the kitchen.

As she moved about, Rebecca began to dream of married life. What would it be like to have her own kitchen? To have babies crawling about her feet? And a man who loved her more than anyone else?

How long had she dreamed of having her own family? Having someone who would love her? The sad truth came to her. It was the day her father married her stepmother. Since the age of fifteen, Rebecca had wanted to be part of a loving family again.

She pushed the sad thoughts away. God had led her to Cottonwood Springs. Her stepmother had forced the issue, but nothing happens without a reason, so Rebecca decided God had brought her here just as He'd led the children of Israel to the Promised Land.

She went for the Bible and checked on Seth. True to the doctor's word, the marshal continued to sleep. Rebecca carried the Bible to the kitchen table and waited for Doctor Clark to return.

At midnight, Rebecca realized he wouldn't be returning. She knew the town gossips would have a field day with the knowledge that she'd spent the night at the marshal's house. She prayed, "I won't leave him, Lord. He needs someone here with him."

The sound of light tapping pulled her from her prayers. She closed Seth's bedroom door and then walked to the front door. In a lowered voice she called out, "Who's there?"

"It's me, Eliza."

Rebecca jerked the door open and allowed her friend inside. "I'm so glad you are here." She pulled her to the couch, where they both sat.

"I began to worry when you didn't come home. Mrs. Tucker said the marshal has been shot. Is it true?" She continued to hold Rebecca's hands in hers.

Eliza must have known it was the truth since Mrs. Tucker's husband, Dan, had helped to hold Seth down while the doctor dug out the bullet, but Rebecca nodded anyway. "It's true."

"Lord, have mercy. Is he going to be all right?" Eliza asked, squeezing her hands.

Rebecca removed her hands from Eliza's. "I believe so. The doctor was supposed to be back by now but he hasn't returned."

Eliza looked over her shoulder at the shut door. "We won't disturb him, will we?"

"No, the doctor gave him something to help him sleep. Would you like a cup of coffee? I don't have any tea here." Rebecca stood and headed to the kitchen.

Eliza followed just as Rebecca had known she would. "Coffee is fine."

A smile pulled at her lips. Eliza wasn't like the town gossips but she did enjoy hearing the details, even though she'd never repeat them. "Do you know what happened?" Eliza asked.

There it was. The question Rebecca had known was coming. She poured two cups of the strong brew. "No, only that Reverend Griffin found him."

Eliza took a sip of her coffee and crinkled her nose.

Rebecca passed the sugar bowl and a teaspoon to her. "Try that. It helps."

"I know, but can the Marshal afford the amount I'll need?" Eliza laughed as she spooned sugar into her cup. She took another sip and sighed. "Much better. Now, did the reverend say anything about what he found?"

Rebecca shook her head. "No, as a matter of fact, I never even saw the reverend today." Why hadn't he come with them to bring Seth home? Maybe he had other business to take care of and would come tomorrow to check on him. She hoped so. Rebecca had questions to ask him, too. Like did he think the Evans gang had been behind this attack? Or was someone else gunning for the marshal? Such as, the same person who had killed Janie's parents. A shiver ran down her spine.

The next morning, Eliza headed back to her house to get dressed and open her shop. Thankfully, her friend had agreed to spend the night. Rebecca made Seth a light breakfast that he never woke up to eat. She waited for the doctor to arrive.

Someone knocked on the door and she went to answer it. Mr. Tucker stood with his hat in his hands. "Good Morning, Miss Ramsey. The doctor sent me over to tell you he's busy bringing another Rutherford into the world this morning. He'll come by as soon as he can."

Rebecca smiled at him. "Thank you, Mr. Tucker, for stopping by and letting me know."

He nodded. "'Welcome. If you need anything, send word and I'll come arunnin'."

Rebecca saw Mrs. Miller huffing up the walkway. She pushed past Mr. Tucker and came right on inside the house. "That's mighty nice of you, Mr. Tucker, but I've already made arrangements for Miss Ramsey to have help."

Rebecca's jaw dropped. "Mrs. Miller?"

"What? You thought we'd let an unmarried woman stay alone here with the marshal? No, ma'am. I've arranged for Mrs. Brown to come stay here for a few days with you and the marshal." She came into the sitting room and dropped onto the couch.

"Well. Then I'll be on my way," Mr. Tucker said.

Rebecca hurried to the door and called after the blacksmith. "Thank you for your help."

Then she turned to Mrs. Miller. Anger flowed from her like honey from a beehive. "Why would you do such a thing without talking to me first?" she demanded.

"I care a great deal about you." She met Rebecca's gaze with gentle eyes.

Rebecca shook her head. "I don't understand."

Mrs. Miller patted the cushion beside her. "Please sit down for a few minutes." When Rebecca sat, Mrs. Miller continued, "The gossips have already started talking. They know you spent the night here last night and want to make you look bad. So I talked to Mrs. Brown. She's fond of Janie and you, so we decided that as long as you have to stay here with the marshal, she'll stay, too, as a chaperone."

"I wasn't alone last night, Mrs. Miller. Eliza Kelly stayed with me." Rebecca wanted to shout that it was no one's business but her own if she stayed to take care of Seth, but knew she'd just go hoarse and the ladies' tongues would continue to wag.

Mrs. Miller sighed. "I'm glad to hear that. We can set them straight now and no harm will be done."

* * *

Seth woke up. Heat traveled up his thigh and seemed to burn into his brain. He remembered waking earlier to find the good doctor digging for the bullet and seeing Hank and Dan, who both had firm grips on his body. The pain had been so intense that he had quickly fallen back into the black abyss of no pain.

His gaze moved to the lantern beside the bed and landed on Rebecca, sitting in the rocker he'd bought for her and Janie. She was slumped to the side and her golden hair reflected in the lamplight. She looked beautiful, he thought, before once more drifting into the sweet chasm of sleep.

The next time he awoke, morning light shone through the window. He tried to sit up but felt as if he were on fire. His throat rasped out Rebecca's name. Just as her sweet face came into view, he passed out again. *Lord, help me.* The prayer never left his lips.

Why couldn't he open his eyes? Seth tried to swim to the surface of the black sea that held him under. Cool moisture touched his brow only to evaporate in a wisp of air. If only he could swim to the surface of the inky blackness, he'd be fine. At least that's what he told himself.

A sweet voice called his name and Seth stopped his movements to listen. Was that Clare? Had he died and gone to heaven?

"Seth, can you hear me?"

He tried to answer, but no sound came from his parched mouth. If only the sweet voice would give him a drink of water, then he would be able to talk. Had he spoken the request aloud? A trickle of sweet, cool water crossed his lips. But no sound exited his throat.

He inhaled the fragrance of vanilla. The woman was

not Clare, but Rebecca. Her voice whispered. "Seth, don't fight it. Try to sleep. You have a fever and I'm working to get your temperature down. Please relax and let me cool you off." Her sweet breath caressed his tired mind. He continued to listen. Seth knew that he would do as she asked.

"I think he's sleeping again," Rebecca said.

Next he heard Mrs. Brown. "That's good, child. Keep sponging him off. The doctor should be here soon."

A cold shiver crawl up his spine. *Oh, please not the doctor,* he prayed. The tremor continued to shake his body. He couldn't stop the movement. Seth reached out a hand and grasped something cool, and then Rebecca's reassuring voice came to him again. A baby cried.

"Stay with him. I'll tend to Miss Janie."

Rebecca's voice filled his ear again. The soft whisper sounded on the verge of begging. "Seth, let me keep sponging you off. We're fighting a fever. You and me, you're not alone."

Had she meant you and me as if they were a couple? Or a team battling his sickness? Seth groaned. He prayed it was the latter. The last thing he wanted was for Rebecca to start going soft on him.

"Seth, can you hear me?"

He tried to nod. That action cost him as a flash of light blew into his brain and then Seth sank into the bitter darkness once more.

Chapter Eighteen

Rebecca tiptoed into his room. She'd heard Seth thrash about on his bed and went to him. She carried a fresh glass of cold water from the well. Thankfully his fever had broken earlier in the day. Three days of a high fever were three days too many. The doctor had said not to be surprised if Seth awoke but didn't make sense. He wasn't sure how having a high fever for that many days would affect Seth mentally.

She had remained by his side all three days and nights. Rebecca felt as if her eyelids were full of sand, but she couldn't go to sleep, not until she was sure that Seth would be all right.

His gruff voice pulled to her in the darkness. "I'm awake."

Rebecca set the glass on the table and lit the kerosene lantern. Seth's pale face glowed in the light. "How are you feeling?"

He barked, "How do you think I'm feeling?"

A laugh made its way up her throat and between her lips. "Like your old self. Grumpy."

She was surprised when he chuckled, too. "Not very grateful-sounding, huh?"

"No, but I didn't expect grateful. I'm just glad you are alive." She moved closer to the bed. "Would you like a drink?"

Seth tried to sit up.

Compassion for him led her to bend down and gently lift his shoulders, while holding the glass to his lips. She watched his throat move with each drink. When she felt him move his shoulders, Rebecca pulled the glass away and laid him back down.

"I feel as weak as a newborn calf." His cheeks filled with color at the admission.

She put the glass back onto the table. "I'm sure you do. You ran a fever for three days. Doc and I were getting very worried."

He moved his arm and winced. Then his hand moved to the bandage on his head. "How bad am I?"

"Not as bad as you feel." Rebecca prayed she was telling him the truth. "Doc says you need to stay in bed for at least a week. He's making you a cane to get around with, too."

"A cane?" Seth looked both frightened and angry.

Rebecca eased into the rocker that still sat beside his bed. "Yes, a cane. You won't be able to walk on your own for a few weeks yet."

Seth yawned. "I don't know about that. I've got outlaws to catch and a town to take care of."

"Maybe so, but Doc appointed Mr. Miller as acting sheriff until you get better or until Sheriff James gets back." She pushed her feet and set the rocker into motion.

He chuckled. "You mean Bob." Seth closed his eyes.

Rebecca stopped rocking. She'd expected him to get angry and say that he was well enough to do his job. But Seth hadn't. Was something wrong with his brain?

The marshal she knew would not want to lie in bed while someone else did his job. She opened her mouth to ask if he was feeling all right, but a soft snore rose from his chest.

Mrs. Brown looked up from her sewing when Rebecca entered the sitting room. "How is he doing?"

Rebecca sat on the couch. "I'm not sure. He seems all right, but when I told him that the doctor appointed Mr. Miller as acting sheriff, he didn't react the way I thought he would."

"What were you expecting?" Mrs. Brown worked the needle back and forth through the fabric.

Rebecca laid her head back on the cushion of the couch. "I thought he'd put up a fuss."

"And he didn't?"

She closed her eyes. "No."

The clock ticked, filling the quiet between the two women. At any moment she'd be lulled into a deep sleep. She couldn't allow that. Forcing her eyes to open, she stood. "I'll go start dinner."

"Already done."

She stopped midstep. "Oh, then I'll go check on Janie."

"Done."

Rebecca yawned. "I guess I could take a broom after these floors."

"Or you could go take a nap." Mrs. Brown looked up from her needlework. "Now that you know he's going to be all right, it's time you started taking care of yourself again, young lady." She shook the needle in Rebecca's direction.

Her gaze moved to the guest-bedroom door. "What if he wakes up again?" Rebecca heard the weariness in her own voice.

"Then I'll come wake you." She bent her head back to the fabric.

Rebecca looked down at Janie. In the past few days, she hadn't devoted much time to the little girl. "Maybe I'll stay up and play with Janie when she wakes." Janie slept in her basket. Rebecca gently swiped hair off the baby's forehead. Her heart swelled with love and she leaned over and kissed her soft cheek.

Mrs. Brown shook her head. "I'll call you when she wakes up. Rebecca, go to bed."

There was no mistaking the no-nonsense tone of the older woman. A yawn overtook her and she made the decision to obey Mrs. Brown. She opened the guest-room door and walked into the room.

The quiet of the room and the gentle ticking of the clock on the side table encouraged her body to relax. With Seth on the mend, the baby sleeping peacefully and Mrs. Brown on watch, Rebecca finally let her guard down.

She turned to the bed. It looked inviting with a light blue and white quilt that reminded her of fluffy clouds in the deep blue sky. She sat down on the edge and sighed. Rebecca took her shoes off and leaned back on the soft mattress. Her tired body sunk into the warmth of the covers. She pulled a lightweight quilt over her and closed her eyes.

"No!" The roar of Seth's voice pulled Rebecca from a deep sleep. Again he yelled, "No!" She jerked herself off the bed.

Rebecca passed a wide-eyed Mrs. Brown as she walked into the sitting room. Janie howled her fear. "Take care of the baby," she ordered as she moved to Seth's door. Rebecca paused long enough to watch the older woman snap out of her fright and scoop up a screaming Janie. Within moments the little one quieted.

Seth thrashed about the bed. Sweat poured from his body. Had his fever come back? *Oh, Lord, please don't let that be the case.* She moved to his bedside and laid her hand on his shoulder. "Seth?"

"Stop!" he yelled, jerking away from her hand.

Fear threatened to choke Rebecca. Her eyes filled with tears. She moved away from the bed as he punched into the air, fighting invisible villains. Then he quieted. In his sleep, he spoke. "Oh, Clare, I am so sorry. So sorry." A sob broke from his throat and Seth rolled to his side. His shoulders shook with unshed sobs.

Rebecca approached the bed again. Her hand moved to his cool forehead. No fever. He didn't flinch away. His breathing had returned to normal.

She sank into the chair. As her heart rate slowed down, she watched him sleep. What had she just witnessed? A nightmare? Who was Clare? And what did Seth have to be so sorrowful for?

Confident she could stand again, she returned to the sitting room. Mrs. Brown was just opening the door for Doctor Clark.

"What's going on here?" With his bag in his hand, he entered the house.

His eyes trained on Rebecca.

How did the doctor know something was going on? Her gaze moved to Mrs. Brown. "Young Josiah was passing by. I sent him to get Doc," Mrs. Brown said.

Rebecca nodded. She returned her attention to the doctor. "I think he had a nightmare." She held out her arms to Mrs. Brown, who placed Janie into them. While hugging the baby close, she explained what she'd witnessed. But held back what Seth had said.

The doctor patted her on the shoulder. "I'll go examine my patient now. Hopefully he didn't pull any of my fancy stitchwork." He offered her a soft smile. "Stop worrying—he'll be fine. Why don't you sit down for a spell?"

She nodded and then watched the doctor hurry to Seth's room and shut the door.

"I'll go check on supper," Mrs. Brown said, shuffling from the room.

Janie cooed up at her. Rebecca smiled down at the baby. Seth's loud voice had awoken her, but she now looked no worse for wear.

Who was Clare? Was she Seth's wife? No, someone would have mentioned a wife. And if Clare was his wife, then she wouldn't allow another woman to take care of him. No, not his wife, but who?

Rebecca realized that she'd been relying on God but had decided His plan for Him. First, she'd thought God had wanted her to marry Jesse. Then after his death, Seth had taken an interest in her well-being, so she'd assumed God was leaning in that direction for her—a husband and family. Now she didn't know what to think. Clare, whoever she was, held a part of Seth that Rebecca had never seen before. She sighed. *Lord, I don't know what Your plans are, but I sure wish I did.*

Seth wanted freedom. Freedom from his bed, freedom from the house, and most importantly freedom from too many people coming to visit. Didn't they understand that when a man was down the last thing he wanted was people coming and going out of his room as if it was a church social? The one person he wanted to see only came in when he needed something.

Over the past few days, something had changed in

Rebecca. What was it? She helped him when he called, brought food for him and made sure his dressings were clean. But she didn't stay and talk. She acted as if she couldn't get out of his room fast enough.

Somewhere in the house he heard Janie cry. Seth pushed back the covers with his good arm and decided he would not lie in bed for one more day. He didn't care what Doctor Clark said. Enough was enough.

He set his feet on the floor. Its coolness felt good. This wasn't going to be so hard. Careful not to push off with his bandaged arm, Seth pushed upward. He stood. His vision blurred. Pain shot through his side and leg. Darkness came faster than a racing stallion.

"Seth Billings! What are you doing?" A blurry Rebecca hurried into the room.

Sweat broke out on his forehead. He gritted one word out between clenched teeth: "Standing."

She squealed. "You are falling."

And she was right. One moment he'd been standing; the next he was toppling over. The sensation of fire exploded within his side and he gasped. The soft mattress wasn't as giving as he'd hoped and he felt as if he'd just landed on a board.

He instinctively grasped his side. Sticky warmth covered his fingers.

"Oh, Seth, look what you've done."

"Woman! I don't have to look, I can feel it. Get Doc."

Rebecca didn't leave the room. She pulled him upright and then swung him around into a lying position. Next she helped him get his feet up onto the bed. "Here, hold this against the wound until I get back." She thrust a towel into his good hand.

Anger radiated from her every pore. What had he done to create so much emotion in one woman? Seth grinned. He kind of liked this little spitfire.

Chapter Nineteen

Seth flinched under the old man's hands. He gritted his teeth and silently prayed his side would be stitched up soon. He growled through gritted teeth, "Can't you do that any faster, Doc?"

"It wouldn't take as long, if you'd be still." The doctor pushed his needle into the flesh once more. "'Course, if you hadn't tried to get up before the doctor ordered, this wouldn't be necessary. Now, would it?"

He chose to ignore the old man and focused instead on Rebecca's worried face. She hovered in the doorway and chewed on her lower lip. Her blue eyes looked as if they sparkled with unshed tears. He couldn't stand that look.

"Miss Ramsey, would you get me a dipper of water please?" the doctor asked.

She nodded and turned away.

Doctor Clark looked to the open doorway. "That little gal cares for you, you know."

"Not in the way you think, Doc."

He laughed and tied a knot in the string. "I've seen that look before, son, and I'm telling you, she cares."

Seth didn't want to believe Rebecca cared for him in the way the doctor was insinuating. "Miss Ramsey is a caring person. She'd be upset to see an old dog getting stitched up, Doc. Don't make too much out of it."

Rebecca came into the room carrying a glass of water. She handed it to Doc and then left the room.

He finished the last stitch and stood. "Try to follow orders, Seth. I can't keep coming over here and stitching you up." Doctor Clark cleaned up his tools and laid the blanket across Seth's lap. "I'm not sure what kind of damage you might have done to your leg. Is it paining you any?"

Seth refused to admit that his leg burned as if a red-hot poker were being plunged into the flesh. "I'm sure it is fine."

Doc raised an eyebrow. "I think I need to take a look." He removed the blanket and felt of Seth's leg above the bandage. "It's hot to the touch."

The desire to protest turned into a moan of pain as the doctor removed the bandage.

"You are a lucky young man. My stitches held here. But, I'm not sure if you didn't pull those muscles." He rewrapped the wound and then patted the blanket back into place. "I suggest you stay in bed awhile longer."

Seth opened his mouth to protest, but Doc's hand came up. "Don't even think about getting out of bed or arguing with me. If you tear the muscles in that leg any more, you may not walk for a month."

Seth's gaze went to the doorway. Rebecca was nowhere in sight. "Would you look to see where Miss Ramsey is?"

Doc Clark raised an eyebrow.

"Please." Seth hated begging but needed to tell the doctor something important. Something he didn't want Rebecca overhearing.

He nodded and then left the room. A few moments

later he returned. "She's in the kitchen feeding the baby."

"Good. Doc, the Evans gang is going to come after Rebecca. If I'm not up and about to stop them, they will take her. I need to be able to protect her."

The doctor put his instruments into his bag. "Why are the Evans boys after Miss Ramsey?"

"She was Jesse's girl." Mentally Seth groaned. Now he was calling her Jesse's girl. The doctor stared at him as if more was required of his story. Seth pressed on. "Jesse stole a large sum of money from them. Before he died he asked me to protect her. At first, I didn't really think Maxwell Evans would come after her, but I was wrong."

The doctor shut his bag and sat in the rocker. "What's happened to change your mind?"

Seth sighed. "Twice he has sent men after her. Luckily the reverend was here the first time, and I stopped the second man."

"I see." The doctor templed his fingers and touched them to his chin in thought. "You know, I really don't want you left alone and I'd rather Miss Ramsey stay with you at all times. She's young and can help you up, if you were to fall again." The doctor shot him a sharp look. "I don't expect that to happen, but I will mention to her that I'd like for her to stay here at all times, and if she needs to run any errands, she should ask young Grace or Mrs. Brown. Will that be helpful?"

Seth chuckled. "I believe that will keep her safe and inside the house. Thank you."

The doctor nodded. "Good. Now that that is settled, I have other patients to go see."

"Thanks, Doc." Rebecca showed the doctor to the door. She fumed at the fact that he'd made her as housebound as he had Seth. His words had been kind and almost flowery in the way he'd praised her care of Seth, but it hadn't taken away their meaning. She wasn't to leave the house until Seth could. Why did she allow it? Why hadn't she said, "No, I'll come and go as I please"? The simple truth was her father had taught her to respect her elders. Even though he hadn't stood up for her when she'd been asked to leave home, she still respected his wishes.

"Miss Rebecca, I don't mind running errands for you after school." Grace held a little red ball that she and Janie had been playing with. She held it down for the baby to slap at.

Rebecca put a smile on her face. "Thank you, Grace. I know you don't mind."

"During the rest of the day, it won't hurt me none to get out for some fresh air so I'll be happy to run any errands that might crop up," Mrs. Brown said, using a ribbon to mark her place in the book she'd been reading.

"I appreciate that, as well, Mrs. Brown."

"Rebecca, why don't you start calling me Edna?" Her eyes bore into Rebecca's as she waited for an answer.

Just a few days earlier, Mrs. Brown had offered her friendship. Now she was making it clear she thought they were good enough friends they could drop the formality and use each other's given names. The older woman needed a friend. "Thank you, Edna."

Edna pushed herself out of her chair. "Good, I'm glad we are done with that."

"Can I call you Miss Edna, too?" Grace looked up at the older woman.

A smile tugged at Edna's lips. "I don't see why not.

Being called Miss Edna makes me feel younger somehow." She tested her leg before walking to the kitchen.

"Miss Edna, why do you walk like that?" Grace set the ball down and followed her newest friend into the kitchen.

Rebecca picked up Janie and walked into Seth's room. She found him propped up with a pillow and rubbing his leg. "Can I get you anything from the kitchen?"

His chocolate gaze met hers. "Would you mind coming in for just a few minutes?"

She moved farther into the room and stood a few feet away from the bed.

"I know you don't like being stuck in the house and I really am sorry to put you in this position." His Adam's apple worked up and down his throat.

Rebecca could tell him it was all right, but she didn't want to. She didn't want to stay in this house for who knew how long. Why hadn't he just stayed in bed like the doctor had told him to?

"I guess I should have followed Doc Clark's orders and stayed in bed." He tugged on a thread in his quilt.

"You guess?" She wasn't letting him off that easily.

A grin tugged at his mouth. "All right, I should have done as I was told."

Her heart wanted to melt as the dimple in his left cheek winked. "Yes, you should have. Now, we are stuck together for who knows how long. So, I'll ask again. Do you need anything from the kitchen?"

He licked his lips and a boyish grin crossed his face. "A cold glass of milk would be nice, and chocolate-chip cookies, if we have any left."

Rebecca nodded. "I'll be right back." When she got to the door, she turned and looked back at him.

He'd rested his head against the headboard of the

bed and closed his eyes. His hand had returned to his leg and he was rubbing it once more. *You didn't say no to Doc about staying because you wanted to be with Seth,* she thought, wishing she could ease his pain.

She walked into the kitchen. Edna and Grace sat at the table with glasses of milk and a plate of cookies on the table between them. "Looks like you two had the same idea as the marshal." She handed the baby to Edna.

"Actually it was Miss Grace's idea." Edna tickled the baby under the chin. "Would you like some milk, too, little one?"

Rebecca gathered up a few cookies and put them on a dessert plate. Then she filled two glasses with milk. She placed them on a tray with the small bottle of laudanum and a spoon. "I'll be back in a moment to get Janie's bottle." She started to walk out of the kitchen.

Edna's voice stopped her. "Don't worry about the baby. We'll fix her up, won't we, Miss Grace?"

Grace answered with a giggle. "We sure will, Miss Edna."

"Thank you both. I don't know what I'd do without the two of you." And she didn't either. Thanks to both of them, Janie hadn't been neglected while she fussed over the marshal.

What was she going to do? Her heart melted each time he smiled. She knew there would never be any chance of them becoming a family so she needed to put distance between them. But now, well, she couldn't. Just before reentering his room, Rebecca silently prayed. *Lord, please help me.*

A knock at the door stopped her silent prayer. Rebecca set the tray down and moved to answer it. She pulled it open to find Reverend Griffin waiting on the other side.

"Good afternoon, Miss Ramsey. How are you today?" He leaned on a cane and smiled.

She pulled the door open and took a step back to allow him entrance. "I'm well, thank you."

He took off his hat as he passed over the threshold and held it in his hand. "I was wondering if the marshal is up for visitors."

"Let's go ask him." Rebecca shut the door and then, picking up the tray, led him to Seth's room. "You have a visitor," she said as they entered.

Seth sat up straighter. "Hello, Reverend."

Rebecca indicated that the reverend sit down in the rocker and then she turned to Seth. She placed the tray on his lap, poured half a teaspoon of the medicine, and held it out for him to take.

Seth arched a brow. He frowned at it but didn't say anything.

"Doc said to give you a small dose." She answered his unspoken question.

Seth took the laudanum and then grabbed one of the two glasses of milk and took a long drink. "That stuff taste horrible." He set the half-empty glass back down on the tray.

"Then eat some cookies to get the taste out of your mouth," Rebecca ordered. She handed the second glass of milk, the one she'd poured for herself, to the minister. "You better hang on to this. He'll drink yours, too, if you aren't careful." She smiled to show him she was teasing.

"Hey," Seth protested, and then he took a big bite of one of the cookies.

"I believe you, Miss Ramsey." The reverend ac-

cepted the glass and took a deep drink of the cold milk.
"That is mighty tasty. Thank you."

"You're welcome. I'll leave you men to chat." Rebecca picked up the spoon and medicine bottle. She started to leave and then turned back around to Seth. "Share those cookies, Seth Billings."

A startled look passed over his features and he pulled his hand away from the cookies. Seth extended the plate in the reverend's direction and asked, "Would you like a cookie?"

The reverend chuckled and took two. "The rest are yours, son."

Seth nodded and picked up another cookie, his gaze met Rebecca's and then in mock hunger he shoved the whole thing in his mouth.

Rebecca ignored him. She turned to the reverend and gave him what she hoped was her sweetest smile. "Lucky for you, Reverend, he's going to get groggy in just a little while."

The preacher laughed. "I'll be sure not to overtire him, ma'am." He turned his attention to Seth. "Doc sent me over with this new cane. He said you can get out of bed in a few days as long as you use the cane to lean on."

Rebecca left the room and closed the door behind her. She leaned her head on the wood and sighed. Thanks to the reverend's visit she put off spending any more time with Seth until this evening. Was the reverend's arrival God's way of answering her prayer? And if so, did that mean that once more He was leading her in a new direction? Sadness enveloped her at the thought.

Chapter Twenty

Seth was sick of it.

Over the past week he'd watched Rebecca create a routine. While Edna fixed breakfast, she made her bed, and then both ladies helped him get up and into the kitchen. While he and Edna chattered with Grace, Rebecca made his bed.

After breakfast Rebecca started dinner while Edna entertained him with several rounds of checkers. Rebecca didn't seem to mind that they were playing games while she worked.

His gaze moved to her back as she washed up their supper dishes. "Miss Ramsey, do you ever just relax?"

Rebecca glanced over her shoulder at him. "Well, of course I do. I play with Janie all the time, I sew in the evenings and listen to you read the Bible."

That was true, but he missed the times they'd chatted over breakfast, dinner and during their walks home. She'd pulled away from him and Seth couldn't help but wonder why.

He looked to Edna. The older woman sipped her evening coffee and shook her head. Seth waited until she looked up and then nodded at her. He prayed she understood that he wanted her to agree with him. "How about we all go on a picnic tomorrow? Get out of the house for a while."

Edna grinned. "I think that is a good idea."

Rebecca dried her hands and turned to face them. "It is a wonderful idea." Her eyes lit up but then faded. "But I'm not sure Doc would agree with us." She stepped closer to the table.

"Why not? It's not like I'm going to do any work."

Edna pushed away from the table and carried her cup to the dishpan. She dipped it into the water and washed it.

Rebecca handed her the dish towel. "No, but didn't he say you had to stay in the house for a full week?"

Seth laughed. "Well, yes, but he also gave me this cane because he knew I wouldn't stay in bed for a week."

Edna rejoined them at the table. "You and I could do all the work, Rebecca. All Seth has to do is ride in the wagon to the riverbank."

"I don't know, Edna."

Seth watched the women stare at each other. "We don't have to go to the river. How about we have it in the backyard?"

They both turned to him and frowned. He laughed. "All right, maybe not the backyard."

Rebecca sat down at the table.

Inwardly Seth grinned. She was joining them, just what he wanted.

"Maybe we could have it beside the church. That way we aren't stuck here, but we won't be far from the house if Seth gets tired."

He saw Edna's head jerk to the side and her mouth gape open. It was obvious the older woman had never heard Rebecca refer to him with his given name. "That sounds good to me. And it would be close enough that if you ladies forgot something you could come to the house and get it," he said.

Edna nodded and her gaping mouth turned into a smile. "I like this idea."

Rebecca stood and returned to the dish tub. "I do, too, but if the doctor comes by this evening, we'll tell him our plans. I don't like doing anything behind his back."

"Fair enough," Seth agreed. He pushed away from the table and headed to his cushioned chair in the sitting room. For the first time in days, he had a real reason to smile.

Doctor Clark showed up just as Seth closed his Bible for the night. Rebecca opened the door for him.

"I'm sorry I'm running late this evening. Mrs. Clark is getting tired of these late nights." He crossed the room and sat. "I'm seriously thinking of looking for another doctor to take over my practice. Then the missus and I can relax for a spell."

Edna laid her sewing to the side. "You mean for the rest of your lives."

"That, too." Doc looked to Seth. "How's the old body feeling?"

Seth laid his Bible on the table. "I'm getting stronger every day."

The doctor looked to Rebecca. "He wants something. What is it?"

Edna laughed. "He knows you well, Seth Billings."

Rebecca set her sewing aside. "A picnic."

Seth explained, "We want to go on a picnic tomorrow but Miss Ramsey thinks we need your permission."

Doc winked at Rebecca. "Smart woman."

Edna put her sewing into a basket beside the couch. "Why don't you and Mrs. Clark join us?"

Rebecca nodded. "That's a great idea. I have lots of ham and bread made up."

The doctor stood. "What time are you ladies planning and where?" He walked toward the door.

"Noon at the church." Edna answered.

Rebecca picked up Janie and walked with the doctor to the door. "Tell Mrs. Clark she doesn't have to bring a thing."

"If I know my wife, she'll bring dessert, anyway."

"That will be nice, but she doesn't have to." Rebecca held the door open.

The doctor looked at each of them. "Thank you for inviting us. Sometimes we forget how to play, since I work all the time."

"You're welcome. It will be fun."

The doctor said goodbye and Rebecca shut the door. She smiled at Seth. "I'm glad you thought of this. It's going to be fun."

Edna started toward the bedroom she shared with Rebecca. "I'll see you two in the morning. I'm going to get up early and make deviled eggs."

"I'm right behind you, Edna. I'll need to make a big potato salad, too." Rebecca followed Edna into their room and shut the door.

With the doctor and his wife coming to the picnic, too, would Seth have any time alone with Rebecca?

Rebecca placed her potato salad in the basket. "I hope this is plenty."

"I think it will be." Edna packed a second basket. "We really have enough food to feed an army."

Laughter spilled from Rebecca's throat. "I'm still amazed at the crowd that is coming."

"What is the count up to now?"

Rebecca held up one hand. "The Clarks, Eliza, Hannah and Grace." She held up her other hand. "You, the marshal, Janie and myself. I think that's all, so nine."

"You forgot about Mrs. Miller and Reverend Griffin," Edna reminded her.

"Oh, that's right. They bring the number up to eleven." Rebecca loved that they'd been able to invite so many people. She'd been worried Seth would have needed her to sit with him. Now with the doctor and reverend coming, she could be free to talk to her friends.

What she looked forward to the most was the sunshine. They'd been cooped up in the house for a week and the only times she'd gone outside were to gather water or hang up and take down the laundry.

A knock sounded on the front door. Rebecca and Edna hurried to see who had arrived as Seth opened the door.

"Hello, Seth. I thought I'd bring the wagon by to pick up you and Janie," the doctor said.

Mrs. Clark climbed out of the doctor's small black canvas-covered buggy. She came to stand beside her husband. "I thought I'd walk up the hill with you ladies, if that's all right?"

Rebecca motioned for her to come inside. "We'd love for you to come with us. I'll go get Janie." She hurried into the bedroom. Janie played in the small corral she and Edna had created out of overstuffed pillows. The baby was growing and needed more space to move about.

She gathered up toys, diapers and a fresh dress. Then Rebecca picked up Janie. She hugged the baby to her chest and enjoyed her fresh scent.

"Come on, you little darling. Seth is taking you to the picnic." Janie grabbed a fistful of hair and giggled. Rebecca scooped up her things and walked back to the sitting room. The baby lurched for Seth, but Rebecca held her back and gave her to the doctor instead. Janie looked confused. Rebecca kissed her on the cheek. "Seth can hold you in the buggy."

Doc took the rest of Janie's things. "Do you ladies need us to take anything else?"

Rebecca smiled. "Yes, that would be very nice."

The ladies quickly loaded the buggy with their baskets and bags. Once it was all in place, Rebecca smiled. "All done."

"Then we will see you there in a little while."

Seth followed the doctor out the door. He took the steps slowly and held on to the porch rail. Was this day out going to be too much for him? Rebecca chewed her lower lip as she watched him make his way to the wagon.

Doc laid the baby down on the floor of the buggy and then came back to help Seth up. Rebecca shut the door, leaving a crack big enough that she could see Seth but he couldn't see her. The last thing she wanted to do was embarrass him.

As soon as he was in the wagon, he turned toward the house. Could he tell she was watching him? He turned to take the baby from Doc. She noticed that he clutched the baby in his right arm. Just as they started to leave, Seth raised his hand and waved to her.

So he had been able to see her. She felt heat fill her cheeks but returned his wave. Seth smiled, and then he leaned down and kissed the baby on the forehead. Her heart lurched at the memory of his lips on hers. Why did those precious moments have to haunt her every thought?

Chapter Twenty-One

❧

Seth hated to admit, even to himself, that he was worn-out. He sat at a table that Hannah and Eliza had pulled from the schoolhouse. The minister had also donated several tables and chairs from the church for the picnic. Janie lay in her basket beside him, napping. A cool breeze blew across the small group of people; the scent of apple pie teased his senses. The sound of his stomach growling filled the air.

He yawned. His gaze searched for and landed on Rebecca.

Today she wore a pretty green dress with little white flowers on it. She laughed at something Mrs. Miller said. The sound drifted to him like feathers on the wind. Her blue eyes met his and she ducked her head. Eliza caught his eye and smiled knowingly.

Seth frowned. How had things gone so wrong? His plan had been to have Rebecca, Janie, Edna and himself on a blanket, eating a simple meal and talking. He'd thought Rebecca wouldn't be able to move away and avoid him. They'd finally chat again, like they had before he'd gotten shot. Was that why she avoided him? Because he'd been hurt while tracking down the Evans gang?

"This has turned into a nice get-together, wouldn't you agree?" The reverend slid into a chair on his right.

Seth nodded.

"I, for one, am glad you thought of it, Marshal." Doc dropped into the chair to his left. "This is just what my Elsie needed."

Elsie Clark stood with Mrs. Miller, who was stirring a pot. Rebecca and Eliza had moved on to another table laden with bowls and plates. Seth wondered what could be in the pot Mrs. Miller stirred, but didn't ask. Mrs. Miller and Mrs. Clark had brought several dishes each. There was probably enough food on the tables to feed the whole town of Cottonwood Springs.

"You're mighty quiet, Marshal. Something eating at you?" Doc turned to face him. "Or have you done too much today?" His trained eye studied Seth's face.

"Nope. Just enjoying being out in the sunshine." Seth reached down and covered Janie's legs with her blanket. He didn't want to give the doctor an excuse to lock him indoors again.

Reverend Griffin smiled. "I don't know how you've managed to stay cooped up for so long. By now I would have been climbing the walls."

"Me, too," Mr. Miller said, joining them.

"Well, hello, Carl. How did you get away from the store?" Doc asked, turning to look up at the newcomer.

Carl Miller pulled a chair out and sat. "I put Josiah in charge. He can handle whatever comes along."

While the men talked, Seth's gaze searched out Rebecca again. She and Grace were carrying pies to one of the tables. The woman fluttered from table to table much like a beautiful butterfly.

Rebecca stopped and looked in his direction. For a

moment her face softened. Then just as quickly her jaw set and she turned away. What was wrong with her?

Rebecca was asking herself the same question. How much longer could she live under Seth Billings's roof without falling for him? How long would she need to remain in the same house with him? Maybe she should talk to the doctor.

Janie's cry filled the afternoon air. Rebecca didn't want to go where Seth was entertaining the men, but Janie's cries grew louder. Seth scooped the baby up and held her in his right arm and she settled down. Rebecca realized the baby was probably wet so she squared her shoulders and walked toward where the men sat. When she stepped up to the table all four of them turned to look at her.

"This was a really great idea, Miss Ramsey."

She smiled at the reverend. "It was the Marshal's idea, Reverend, and I agree it was a good one." Rebecca looked to Seth. "I'll take the baby for a while, Marshal." She extended her arms.

Seth allowed her to take the baby. "She's almost back to sleep."

"Yes, but I would like for her to sleep some tonight, too. Plus, she needs to be changed. I'm going to take her to Grace to play."

The doctor laughed. "Smart woman."

Rebecca turned her attention away from Seth. "Thank you, Doctor. I'd like to talk to you for a few moments when you have the time."

He pushed away from the table. "I have time now, Miss Ramsey."

"Thank you. Please excuse us, gentlemen."

Seth cocked his head to the side and narrowed his eyes. Was he aware she wanted to discuss him?

Rebecca walked with the doctor a few feet away from the rest of the crowd. *Lord, please let my words come out correctly.* They walked beside the church, where honeysuckle was beginning to show signs of new growth. "Doctor Clark, I feel that the marshal is able to take care of himself now. Do you think it will be all right for Mrs. Brown, Janie and I to move back to our own homes? I'll still come in the mornings and take care of breakfast, lunch and supper, but I really think the marshal is doing well and I'd like to move back into my own house. I'm sure Edna feels the same."

He rubbed his chin. "I see. Would you mind answering a couple of questions for me?"

She nodded.

"Can Seth get out of the bed with no assistance?"

Her cheeks heated. "Yes."

"Good. And can he make a pot of coffee on his own?" He studied her.

Rebecca felt like a schoolgirl being questioned by the teacher. "I believe so."

"But you don't know for certain." It was more of a statement than a question.

"No, he hasn't had to do anything for himself. So I don't know for sure." Rebecca hated admitting that Seth might not be able to take care of himself.

"Does he walk slowly and use his cane?"

"Yes." She rocked back and forth with the baby. Moisture was beginning to seep through the baby's diaper.

The doctor turned and studied Seth. "Does he look a little pale and tired to you, Miss Ramsey?"

Rebecca turned to study the marshal. His face did

appear drawn. He seemed paler than he had that morning. Had they overextended him today? Was this outing too much for him? "Yes, he does." She looked back down at the drowsy baby and sighed.

"I know it is an imposition for you and Mrs. Brown to stay with him, but as his doctor, I would prefer that you remain for at least another week. Of course, you don't have to. I can always check around and see if someone else would be willing to take care of him and move in for a while." His gaze remained on the marshal.

Rebecca found herself looking back at the man in question. Selena Martinez had just sashayed to his table. She handed him a glass of something and smiled. He smiled up at her. When had she arrived? Surely she couldn't be any older than sixteen. Only nine years younger than Seth, her inner voice taunted. "No, that won't be necessary, Doctor. Mrs. Brown and I will be fine for another week."

He patted her on the shoulder. "That a girl." And then he was gone.

Rebecca swallowed the lump in her throat. Selena continued to linger at the men's table. Unable to watch, she turned her back on them. Rebecca wanted to be close to Seth but also didn't want her heart broken. Her gaze moved to the cloudless sky. *Lord, I need help. What am I going to do? I can't keep working for Seth and allow myself to fall for him. Can I?*

Trust in the Lord with all your heart and lean not upon your own understandings—that was the general gist of the scripture that came to mind. Peace enveloped her like a warm blanket and she smiled down at the sleeping infant. For now, she had to trust that she was right where God wanted her.

Movement on Main Street drew her attention. A covered wagon ambled down the road and stopped in front of the Millers' store. Rebecca rocked the baby as she continued watching. A man jumped from the covered wagon and entered the store. A woman sat on the seat waiting for him. Several children stuck their heads out of the wagon. A few moments later, the man climbed back onto the seat and headed up the hill toward the picnic.

Assuming he was coming to see Mr. Miller, Rebecca headed back to the tables to tell the other women she'd be back as soon as she changed Janie's diaper. She wondered if the family would be staying. There was plenty of food and the family would be welcome. If she'd learned one thing about Cottonwood Springs, it was that the people were friendly.

A giggle sounded off to her right. Selena had just rejoined her friends, Millie, Charlotte and Elizabeth. *Well, most of the town is friendly,* she mentally amended.

After telling Edna and Mrs. Miller she was going to change the baby, Rebecca slipped into the schoolhouse and took a few minutes to control her jealous feelings toward Selena. She talked to the baby as she changed the wet diaper.

"I have no reason to be jealous. Selena is a child and I doubt Seth would give her the time of day. Besides, jealousy is one of those ugly emotions I try to avoid." Even as she spoke, Rebecca wished that there was a future for her and the marshal. Would she be able to live in the same town as Seth, should he decide to marry?

She closed the last pin and hugged the baby to her. Rebecca returned to the picnic. She moved to the dessert, where Eliza was working. As soon as she was within hearing, Eliza asked, "Did you notice the wagon that just pulled up?" She picked up a knife and cut into a peach cobbler.

Rebecca smiled. "Yes, I saw them coming up the hill. Looks like a big family. Maybe they'll stay for lunch and tell us about their travels."

"Maybe they are settling here." Eliza moved to the loaf of banana-nut bread and started cutting it into slices.

Janie's big blue eyes looked up at Rebecca. A sleepy smile crossed the little girl's face. She reached up and tugged on the ribbons on Rebecca's green bonnet.

"You need to wake up, sleepy head." Rebecca bent over and kissed the baby on the forehead.

"Excuse me, ladies. Miss Ramsey, would you bring Janie and join us over here?" She turned to find the doctor standing at her elbow.

Rebecca looked over his shoulder at the group of people gathered around the men's table. She saw the man and woman from the covered wagon. Another, older woman stood beside them. Both of the ladies looked as if they were crying into white handkerchiefs. The man's arms were crossed over his chest and his head was held high.

Seth leaned against his cane—his brown gaze seemed to bore into Rebecca's.

Eliza stepped forward. "What's this about, Doc?" She planted both hands on her hips.

"The marshal would like to be the one to explain."

Rebecca looked into the kind doctor's eyes. Sympathy reflected there. She nodded and walked beside him back to the group of people that were watching her every step. She stopped in front of Seth. "Marshal?"

The older woman looked up, gasped and reached for

Janie. "She's beautiful. She has Sadie's eyes and Ben's hair." A new sob tore from her throat.

Janie jerked away from the older woman's hand. Rebecca took a step back. What was happening? Who were these people? Her breath came quicker and her heart felt as if someone were squeezing it.

"Seth?" She didn't care who heard the panic in her voice. For the first time in a long time, Rebecca needed a protector. Janie burrowed her tiny face into Rebecca's neck.

Seth stepped forward. "Mrs. Shepherd, please step back."

The older woman moved back and lowered her hand. She wiped at her nose. "I'm sorry, dear." Her gaze never left Janie. "I just want to hold my grandchild."

Seth pulled Rebecca to his side.

"Grandchild?" Rebecca knew she sounded as shrill as an exotic bird but couldn't stop the word from flowing from her lips. She clutched Janie tighter, aware that Seth leaned into her.

"Yes." Both the older woman and the younger nodded. So far the younger of the two hadn't said anything. She simply stared at Janie.

Seth spoke in a soft voice. "It seems Mrs. Shepherd and the Reynoldses have been looking for their family. That search led them to Cottonwood Springs."

The doctor stepped forward. "Let's sit down and discuss the situation." He motioned for the crowd around them to disperse. "Go have lunch, everyone." His no-nonsense voice sent the group returning to the food-laden tables.

Seth turned Rebecca toward the table he and the men had just left. "Please sit down, Rebecca."

She did as he said but kept Janie pressed to her

heart. Rebecca looked from one face to the other. Deep down, she knew they were Janie's family. A family who wanted to rip the baby from her heart and home. She whispered, "I don't want to just give her up, Seth."

He leaned over and answered for her ears only. "We may not have to, Rebecca. At least not until we are positive these folks are her family." Seth leaned back a little and made eye contact with her. His brown gaze searched hers. It seemed as if he was asking her to trust him. To show she understood, Rebecca nodded. "All right."

Had he said "we"? Would he fight for Janie to remain with her? Was this fair to Janie's family? Was it fair to make her give up the child she'd begun to think of as her own? Tears burned the backs of her eyes, but Rebecca vowed to be strong and not allow them to flow.

The man's voice growled at them like a mighty grizzly growls at the hunter. "What happened to Benjamin and Sadie?"

Rebecca narrowed her eyes at him. She didn't like his tone or the way he crossed his arms over his chest as if he alone owned the world. Her gaze moved to the young woman beside him. Did he bully her around?

"We've been through this, Mr. Reynolds. Miss Ramsey and I found a young couple at the stop-off point between here and Farmington. We're not sure if they were your Benjamin and Sadie." Seth placed both hands on the table and laced his fingers.

Mr. Reynolds huffed, "I know that. Where are they buried?"

"Where we found them." Seth spoke softly as if talking to a child.

"Now, why in tarnation didn't you bring them back

here? Or take them to Farmington to be buried like decent folks?" Black eyes clashed with chocolate ones.

Seth sighed. "How can you be sure the man and woman we found are your family? After all, I didn't find anything in the wagon or on their bodies to tell me who they were."

The younger of the two women stepped forward. "My sister had hair the color of dirty sand. Her eyes were blue and she had three dresses. A light blue solid one, a pink one with green leaves on it and a dark yellow one with white dots."

Seth turned to the women. "The couple's wagon is in the barn behind my house. Would you like to look in it to see if you recognize any of their belongings?"

"That would be very nice, Marshal," the older woman said. The younger nodded her agreement.

As if he'd changed his mind, Mr. Reynolds shook his head. "Cora, Ruthann, you aren't going to find anything in there. We should just be on our way."

The older lady turned to face him. "Now, see here, Jack. My daughter is missing and I want to prove that that woman is holding my granddaughter."

He shook his head. "I've already told you, Ruthann, even if she is, we are not taking the baby with us."

Hope grew in Rebecca's heart. Maybe Mr. Reynolds would drive these women out of her life and Janie would never have to leave her side.

"And I have already said that if she is, I say we are taking her with us."

The two of them faced off. Cora, the younger woman, moved to stand between them. "Mom, Jack, let's not do this here. I want to see if the wagon belongs to Ben and Sadie. If it does then we can talk about what to do next."

So this was the voice of reason, Rebecca thought bitterly.

Her mother nodded at Cora. "Agreed, daughter."

Jack nodded. "Agreed."

The doctor stood up. "Seth, why don't you and I lead the way in my buggy?"

No, no, no. This couldn't be happening. Rebecca didn't want them looking in the wagon. Janie sniffled into her neck.

Seth pushed away from the table. "Much obliged, Doc." He looked to Mr. Reynolds. "You're all welcome to ride down with us."

Mr. Reynolds nodded and walked away with the men.

The young woman turned to Rebecca with tear-filled eyes and called out, "I want her to go with us." All three men turned to look at Rebecca.

Rebecca stood. "I'll be happy to go." She walked over and extended her hand. "My name is Rebecca Ramsey and this is Janie."

"It's nice to meet you, Miss Ramsey. I'm Cora Reynolds and this is my mother, Ruthann Shepherd." Both Cora and Ruthann shook her hand.

Janie shied away from the strangers.

"We'll meet you at the house." The doctor led the way while the other two men followed at a slower pace. Seth spoke in low tones to the newcomer.

Rebecca wished she could make out what he was saying, but since she couldn't she turned to Eliza, who stood off to the side with Hannah. "Eliza, I'm going to take these ladies down to the marshal's. Will you be so good as to let Mrs. Brown know where we've gone?"

Eliza nodded.

"Ladies, if you will walk this way we can go on down to the house."

"Wait." Cora looked over her shoulder at the wagon and stopped. Eight small faces peeked out the back. She motioned for them to come to her.

As the eight little children climbed from the wagon bed, the older ones helping the younger, Hannah stepped forward. "Mrs. Reynolds, I'm Miss Hannah Young, the schoolteacher here. Don't worry about the children, I'll take care of them and see that they get some lunch."

The young woman's eyes filled with tears once more. "Are you sure they won't be a bother?"

"I'm sure."

Rebecca marveled at the confidence in her friend's voice. She smiled her thanks.

Cora waited until her children were standing in front of them and then made introductions. She started with the oldest and made her way down. "Miss Young, I'd like you to meet Mary, Martha, Abraham, Sari, Daniel, Samuel, Abigail and the baby is Naomi. Children, this is Miss Young. She is the schoolteacher here."

Hannah smiled at them each in turn. "It's nice to meet you, children."

Cora continued, "You all behave yourself and do what Miss Young says. Ya hear?"

All eight little heads bobbed up and down.

"If they give you an ounce of trouble, you let me know."

Mary looked up at her mother. "We'll be good, Ma."

The girl couldn't be more than twelve. Rebecca couldn't believe that this woman had eight children— she looked so young.

Janie had taken an interest in what was going on when she'd heard the kids arrive. She raised her head and twisted her hand into the neck of Rebecca's dress. The baby studied the children and strange women and then stuck her thumb in her mouth and sucked.

"I think we're ready now," Cora said, pulling Rebecca from her musings.

She nodded and started back down the hill to Seth's home. The doctor's wagon already sat in front of the house. A chant began in Rebecca's ears. *Please don't let the wagon be their family's, please don't let the wagon be their family's, please don't let the wagon be their family's. Please let me keep Janie, Lord.*

Chapter Twenty-Two

Seth sat on a bale of hay beside the open barn door. Normally the sweet scent of alfalfa grass and dust filled him with contentment, but not today. Rebecca's world was being turned upside down and all he could do was sit by and watch. So far she'd put up a brave front, but when the women started crying again as they found Sadie's dresses, Rebecca had hurried to the house to change Janie's diaper.

"Marshal, I'd like to show you something," Mr. Reynolds called from the wagon.

He pushed himself up and leaned against his cane. This day had about worn him out. Seth found himself taking smaller and smaller steps to get to Mr. Reynolds's side. When he stood beside him, Mr. Reynolds pushed on a board on the side of the wagon. Seth heard a soft click and then a small panel opened.

"Well, I'll be. I looked for a hidden compartment but couldn't find it," Seth declared for the whole barn to hear.

Mr. Reynolds pulled out several pieces of paper, a bag of money and a small case. "I think you will find my brother and sister-in-law's marriage license in those papers." He handed the papers to Seth. "I didn't want to show them to you in front of your woman."

Seth took the papers. "She's not my woman." No matter how badly he wished it, Rebecca would never be his woman.

He turned back to the wall of the wagon and shut the secret compartment. "I see."

How much did he see? Could he tell that Rebecca Ramsey was slowly but surely taking over his heart? Seth sighed as he opened the papers. If only he hadn't killed her fiancé…but he had and when Rebecca found out, she would hate him. He hated himself for it so didn't expect any better from her.

One of the papers was the licenses just as Mr. Reynolds had predicted, another was a letter from Ruthann to her daughter and the last one was the receipt for the wagon and horses. Rebecca reentered the barn. Her eyes were red rimmed and Seth wanted to pull her into his arms and spare her the heartache that was soon to come.

Mr. Reynolds cleared his throat. "Since the papers prove this was Ben's wagon and supplies, I'll go get our wagon and pull it up here to transfer the things we want to take with us."

Seth nodded. He folded the papers back up and sighed. How could he protect Rebecca and still do what was right? Janie belonged to Mrs. Shepherd and the Reynolds family.

Rebecca moved out of the big man's way and hugged Janie to her. Her eyes filled with unshed tears. She came to stand in front of Seth. "They have proof that Janie is theirs?"

"I'm afraid so." Seth leaned against a stable door. His leg hurt but not as much as his heart ached for

Rebecca, Janie and himself. He'd grown to love the baby, too.

Mrs. Shepherd stepped down from the wagon. "May I hold her?"

Rebecca swallowed. "If she will go to you."

He watched the older woman hold out her arms to Janie. The baby stared at Ruthann for several long moments. She smiled and then willingly went to her grandmother.

Ruthann buried her face in the baby's neck. She closed her eyes, and tears slipped from between her lashes. "Thank You, Lord, for protecting Sadie's baby." She opened her eyes and smiled at Rebecca through her tears. "Thank you for taking care of her."

Seth stood and put his arm around Rebecca's shaking shoulders. She turned and buried her face in his chest. He wrapped his arms around her. The left one screamed in protest but Seth ignored the pain. Rebecca needed him. She was all that mattered at the moment.

Janie wiggled in Ruthann's arms. She protested being held so tightly with a scream. Ruthann laughed. "I'm sorry, little one. I didn't mean to hold you so tight."

"Ma, may I hold her now?"

"Of course." Janie was passed to Cora.

"I can't get over how much she looks like Sadie." Cora cradled Janie in her arms.

Ruthann looked up at Seth. Compassion laced the other woman's eyes as she watched Rebecca sob into his shirt. "We never meant to hurt you." She laid her hand on Rebecca's shoulder.

Rebecca took a deep breath, stood back a little from Seth and wiped her eyes. She turned to Ruthann. "I know you didn't."

Seth handed her his handkerchief.

"Thank you." She wiped her eyes and face. "I'm sorry I fell apart like that." Her sniffle tore at his already rended heart.

The sound of another wagon pulling up in front of the barn drew their attention. All eight of the children raced inside and circled their mother, who still held Janie. Seth listened as they asked questions and patted or touched the baby.

"Why do you suppose Aunt Sadie named her Janie?" Martha asked, touching one of Janie's curls.

Cora shook her head. "I'm not sure. Last time she wrote, she'd planned on naming her Elizabeth."

Seth remembered the day he and Rebecca had named the baby Jane Beatrix Ramsey. He looked to Rebecca and saw that she remembered, as well. "I named her Jane, but her full name is Jane Beatrix." He left off Ramsey.

The women and children stared at him. Cora laughed. "Well, Jane Mayne will not do, but I do like the name Beatrix. We'll call her Elizabeth Beatrix Mayne."

Rebecca ran from the barn. Mr. Reynolds barely missed colliding with her. "Is she all right?" the man asked Seth.

Seth shook his head. "No, she isn't." He wanted to run after her, but his leg burned so badly now that all he could do was lean against the stall door and pray. And pray he did.

"Why is she upset?" Jack Reynolds asked.

Was the man dense? Didn't he realize that by taking Janie they were ripping Rebecca's heart out? Seth decided to let one of the ladies answer him. He was too tired. He shut his eyes and leaned his head back against the wood.

Cora cooed down at the baby before answering. "Because Janie is coming with us."

"No, she isn't." Jack's firm voice left no room for arguments.

Seth's eyes popped open. Had he heard right?

The silent barn suddenly burst with noise. Cora and Ruthann were both talking at the same time and Jack was shaking his head.

"Enough!" The big man finally brought silence to the barn once more.

He turned to his children. "Kids, go outside and play. Mary, Martha, keep an eye on them and keep them away from this barn until I call you."

"Yes, Papa." The older girls herded the younger children from the barn.

Once they were gone he turned back to the two women. His voice was low but firm. "We will not be ripping this baby from the only home she's known."

"But, Jack, this is my niece. She's all I have left of Sadie." Cora hugged Janie too tightly once more and the baby cried out.

Ruthann took Janie from Cora. "And this is my granddaughter, Jack Reynolds. If you think for one moment I am leaving her, you have another think coming."

The big man sat down on a bale of hay. Seth wished there was one close enough to him for him to ease onto, but there wasn't. He'd learned a long time ago that if you remained still, people forgot you were in the room. This was one time he wanted to be forgotten, so Seth remained pressed against the stall door. He wanted to hear this out to the end.

Jack held up a hand. "Look, we already have eight children to feed, clothe and educate."

Cora interrupted, "One more isn't going to make a difference."

Ruthann stood beside her daughter. Her gaze moved to Seth. Whatever she saw in his face seemed to have changed her mind. "Maybe not to you, Cora, but one is all that Miss Ramsey has. Isn't that right, Marshal?"

So much for blending into the wood. Seth nodded. "Rebecca loves Janie with all her heart."

Janie turned her head in Seth's direction, gave a little squeal and tried to lunge out of Ruthann's arms and into his. He jerked forward and felt his leg and shoulder protest the action. His side felt as if a white-hot poker had just been rammed into it.

Ruthann walked over to him and placed the baby in his arms. "Would you please take Janie inside to Rebecca, while we discuss this as a family?"

Seth shifted the baby into his right arm and then hobbled toward the barn door. Just before he stepped over the threshold he turned back to them. "Jane Beatrix Ramsey is her full name. Rebecca and I named her together on the day that Rebecca found her. Beatrix is Rebecca's middle name." He studied the three faces in front of him. Ruthann nodded her understanding, Cora's mouth opened in shock and Jack grinned. "I just thought you should know." As he hobbled toward the house, Seth prayed, "Lord, let Your will be done."

Rebecca's head hurt. Her eyes burned and she felt like a complete and utter fool. She'd allowed her emotions to get the better of her. How could she have done that? She hadn't cried this hard since her mother's funeral. How was she going to face those people? How was she going to be able to watch them ride away with her baby? If she'd had any more tears to shed, they would have been flowing again, but Rebecca was spent.

She heard the front door open and close.

"Rebecca, I need help."

Seth never asked for help, and for him to do so now meant he was desperate. She jerked the bedroom door open and hurried into the sitting room. He leaned against the door with his eyes shut and Janie clutched in his good arm.

She hurried to his side and took the baby. "Oh, Seth, I am so sorry. I shouldn't have left like that. Stay here." Rebecca hurried back to the bedroom and put Janie down. She handed the baby a cloth book to chew on and rushed back to Seth.

His white face and gritted teeth told her he was in a lot of pain. "Seth, what happened?" She moved under his right arm and pulled him against her. "Lean on me and we'll get you into bed."

Even his voice sounded weak. "No, just get me to the couch."

Rebecca felt his weight against her side and shoulders. "You need to lie down," she argued even as she lowered him onto the couch.

"I will as soon as the Reynoldses come to a decision."

Decision? Rebecca hurried to his bedroom and pulled the pillow off his bed. She forced herself to walk back to Seth. "What decision?" she asked, pushing the pillow behind his back.

"Jack said the baby isn't going with them. Cora said she is, and I think Ruthann is on your side." Seth closed his eyes. "Do we have any of those powders left that Doc gave me?"

Rebecca sank onto the couch beside him. "I might get to keep Janie?"

"They are discussing that right now, out in the barn."

She couldn't believe her ears. Why didn't Jack want Janie? She was the sweetest baby alive. "What do you mean Ruthann is on my side?"

"Maybe a little of the powder might take the edge off this pain," Seth hinted.

Rebecca stared at him as if he'd grown two horns. "What?"

He sighed. "My leg, shoulder and side hurt."

"Oh!" She leaped from the couch and headed to the kitchen. Within a few minutes she came back with medicine for him. "Here, I'm sorry. My mind is wrapped up in Janie."

Seth took the medicine. "Ruthann seemed to be leaning toward letting you keep the baby."

"Why would she do that?"

His voice sounded tired. "I don't know. What does it matter why?"

Rebecca chewed the inside of her lower lip. Did it matter? If they left without Janie, it didn't matter in the least. But, if Ruthann was trying to trick her, it meant a lot. She needed to hold her baby. Rebecca went to the bedroom and scooped up Janie. Cuddling her close, she returned to the sitting room. "I wonder, why doesn't Jack want Janie?"

"He says they already have eight children to take care of." While she was gone he'd laid his head back on the pillow.

Janie pushed away from her. Rebecca sighed and set the baby on the floor. She placed several toys around her. "That's true. But one more wouldn't make that big of a difference."

"That was Cora's argument, too."

"What did Jack say?"

Seth grunted. "After that, the family pretty much kicked me out of my own barn." A frown marred his handsome face.

A knock sounded at the kitchen door. Rebecca stood. "Can you keep an eye on Janie for a few minutes?"

He opened one eye and smiled. "Can do."

Rebecca headed for the kitchen as a second, more insistent knock sounded. "Very funny, Seth Billings."

She listened to him talk to Janie. "I thought so. Don't you agree, Janie girl?" Rebecca shook her head. It felt good to talk to Seth like a friend again. She took a deep breath before opening the door. The thought that it might be Cora Reynolds waiting to take Janie, on the other side stilled her hand.

"Maybe we should go to the front door," Rebecca heard Eliza say through the wood.

The sound of Mrs. Brown's huff came next with the words, "Nonsense. You two step over so I can open the door. I live here now, too, you know."

Rebecca opened the door and smiled. "That's true, Edna, so why are you knocking?" she asked the startled woman, who appeared to have just reached for the door.

Mrs. Brown frowned at her. "This basket's heavy. Move or take it."

Rebecca reached out and took the wicker basket from the older woman. It was indeed very heavy. "What did you pack in here, an icebox?" Rebecca turned and walked to the table.

Eliza and Hannah followed the other two women inside. "She tried. I think Mrs. Brown can out-pack any woman I know." Eliza set another basket on the table.

"I saw the Reynolds wagon parked out by the barn. It looks like they are loading it up. Does that mean they are Janie's family?"

Rebecca didn't trust her voice as a knot the size of an apple formed in her throat. She nodded and opened the top of the basket. Fresh tears stung her eyes and closed her throat.

Mrs. Brown rested a hand on her shoulder. "Are you going to let them take the baby?"

Chapter Twenty-Three

"Marshal, we'd like permission to camp beside your house for a few days. The women and I can't seem to agree on what should be done about the babe," Jack Reynolds said, twisting his worn brown hat in his hands as he stood outside the front door.

Seth looked to Rebecca. How much more of this indecisiveness could she take? He nodded. "On one condition."

Jack stood taller. "What would that be?"

"Rebecca keeps Janie until your family decides what you will do." He felt Rebecca's shocked gaze upon him.

The tall man visibly relaxed. "I think that would be for the best, as well." He turned to face Rebecca. "But, ma'am, I can't promise my women folk won't bug you about holding the baby."

She gave him a watery smile. It seemed as if she were battling within to speak. "If I were in their shoes, I'd feel the same way."

"Thank you. You're a very kind woman, Miss Ramsey." He nodded to them both and then left.

Seth hobbled over to her. He placed his arm around

her shoulder and gave her a gentle squeeze. "He's right, you know. You really are a very kind woman."

"I only spoke the truth, Marshal. If the shoe were on the other foot, I'd feel the same way they do." She pulled away from his embrace. "I want to keep Janie, but I'm also a Christian and I'm trying my best to do the right thing."

He walked over to the couch and sat. "Then in that case, you are doing a good job, *Miss Ramsey*." He'd added emphasis to her name to catch her attention. Did she realize she'd reverted to calling him Marshal? Or had it simply happened from habit?

Her head came up and she searched his face. "Miss Ramsey?" Confusion laced her eyes and her brow furrowed.

Seth smiled. "If you are calling me Marshal again, I suppose I should be calling you Miss Ramsey. But—" he lowered his voice as if telling her a secret "—I'd rather you call me by my Christian name. It comes out sounding ever so sweet."

Her features relaxed. A graceful blush climbed into her cheeks. Rebecca walked to her bedroom door. He watched the gentle sway of her hips as she glided across the room. Just before entering she said, "Janie will be waking up early in the morning. Good night, Seth."

His name sounded like soft music on her lips. "Good night, Rebecca." Did she notice that his voice sounded husky?

Seth waited until her door clicked shut and then made his way out the front door. A question had nagged at him since the Reynoldses had arrived and he wanted the answer tonight.

Jack stood under one of the cottonwood trees, smoking. "Evening," he said as Seth joined him.

Seth nodded. They stood in comfortable silence for several moments. Crickets chirped and fireflies teased their vision.

"Is there something I can do for you, Marshal?" Jack tossed his cigarette down and crushed it beneath his boot.

Nothing like getting straight to the point, Seth thought. He turned to face the man. "How did you know to come to Cottonwood Springs to find your family?"

Jake lit another hand-rolled cigarette, inhaled and released the smoke from his lungs. Sadness filled his voice. "We'd already checked in Durango. The banker said he'd talked to Ben and was told they were going to stop in Farmington. Just to be certain, I came here to see if they'd stopped for a spell. Now I wish I hadn't. Sometimes, I think it would be better for the women-folk not to know. But, then again…" He let the remainder of his thoughts hang in the evening air between them.

Seth understood. Pain and sorrow filled the Reynolds women's eyes. He hated to see it there. It might have been easier on them not knowing, but, like Jack Reynolds, he pushed that thought aside. Now they knew and he worried at the pain and sorrow he might soon see in Rebecca's eyes.

Rebecca shut the door. Edna's soft snores filled the room. She walked to the window and looked out into the moonlit yard. The way Seth had said her name caused her stomach to flutter like hummingbird wings.

Since the Reynoldses' arrival, things had changed again between her and Seth. He'd tried to protect her and even tonight had taken a stand for her and Janie.

Her gaze moved to the twinkling stars and a yawn escaped her lips. Today had been exhausting. Rebecca should go to bed but didn't want to. She looked over at Janie's sleeping form. The urge to pick the baby up and cuddle her almost overwhelmed her.

Instead she decided to take a moonlit walk. Rebecca pulled her shawl from the hook, draped it about her shoulders and quietly left the house through the kitchen door. She didn't know where she was going but knew it had to be someplace quiet.

The Reynolds wagon sat beside the house. Rebecca picked up her skirt and inched past. She could hear the sounds of children and adults preparing for bed. How did they all sleep in that wagon? She could only imagine how cramped they were.

Rebecca walked farther up the hill and sat down in the grass. With the stars and moon shining so bright, she could almost make out the town below. The chirping of crickets and the gentle breeze slowly eased the tension in her shoulders. She looked up into the heavens and tried to imagine God looking down on her. What did He think about her dilemma?

He'd known what would happen today even before it had occurred. So it stood to reason God knew what all her tomorrows held, too. Looking up at the thousands and millions of stars, Rebecca poured her heart out to her Heavenly Father.

Peace covered her like a warm blanket and she smiled. God was in control. No matter what happened, Rebecca knew she would survive because He was her strength. She pulled her shawl tighter around her shoulders.

"May I join you?"

The softly spoken words came from behind her. Rebecca turned to find Ruthann standing a few feet away. She smiled at the older woman. "Please do."

Ruthann spread her skirt out on the ground and leaned back on her elbows. "The heavens are beautiful out here."

"Yes, they are." Rebecca leaned back to enjoy the view with her. "I find it peaceful when I lie out under them."

The older woman glanced across at her. "Do you do this often?"

Rebecca grinned. "Not as much as I'd like, but sometimes, like tonight, I just need to get away from the house and pray."

Ruthann looked toward the house and where her family's wagon sat. "I imagine our arrival has given you much to pray about tonight, hasn't it?"

"Yes." Rebecca inhaled the sweet smell of grass and night air. She wondered what had brought Ruthann to her but didn't ask. The other woman would tell her when she was ready. Until then, she'd enjoy the peace God had hung about her shoulders like a warm shawl.

Ruthann sighed. "You and I are a lot alike."

Rebecca turned to study her face. She still felt as if now was the time to remain silent and so said nothing.

"I came up here to pray, also. You see, I love my daughter and her family, but I don't feel like I belong with them. I agreed to travel to California, but I've never felt as if I'd make the complete journey with them." She sat up and hugged her knees. "I should have come with Sadie, but I thought Cora needed me more."

"Because of the children?" Rebecca asked.

Ruthann nodded. "Yes. I wish I had gone with Sadie and Benjamin." She lowered her head to her knees.

Lord, give me the right words to comfort Ruthann.

Rebecca laid her hand on Ruthann's shoulders. "If you had gone with them, you wouldn't be alive today to see Janie or your other grandchildren grow up."

She raised her head. Tears rolled down her cheeks and her voice quivered. "The only way I will see all my grandchildren grow up is if we take Janie on to California with us."

So that was it. Ruthann wanted her to see how important it was for them to have Janie. How important it was for the little girl to grow up with her family. Rebecca looked to the heavens.

"But I don't want Janie to go on to California. I want her to stay here, with you." Ruthann's words shocked Rebecca. How could she say that? Knowing she might never see the baby again?

Ruthann wiped at the tears and tried to laugh. The sound came out choppy and broken. "I know that doesn't make sense, but I've seen the love in your eyes."

"I do love her, but I also see the reasoning in keeping her with her family." Rebecca's voice cracked.

The older woman nodded. "See, you and I are a lot alike. We can see both sides and we want what's best for my granddaughter."

They sat in silence. Rebecca watched Jack climb down from the wagon and spread a blanket under it. A few minutes later the boys joined him, each carrying a blanket.

"That man loves my daughter too much." Ruthann sighed.

Puzzled, Rebecca asked, "How can a man love a woman too much?"

Ruthann smiled at her. "He didn't want me to come along. Mary hears everything and told me how her mother threatened not to move on to California if Jack didn't see to it that I came, too. The child is young and doesn't know how it broke my heart to hear those words."

How could Jack not want his mother-in-law to go with them? It seemed cruel to want to leave her behind.

"Before you start judging Jack, remember I'm here. Jack is a sensible man. He knew the journey would be hard for me. Jack also knew that he and the boys would end up sleeping on the ground. And, he was wise enough to know I didn't want to come."

Rebecca frowned. "And yet, you are here."

"Because Cora is spoiled and we have given her her way for too long."

They watched as Jack tucked each of his sons in and kissed them on the head. "I'm staying here, Miss Ramsey. That man deserves to sleep in the wagon and so do my grandsons."

"Please, call me Rebecca. If you are staying, I'd like to be friends." She meant it, too. This woman seemed to be a God-fearing woman, a sister in Christ.

"Thank you, Rebecca." She looked up into the heavens and closed her eyes.

Rebecca started to get up and leave her to what she thought were Ruthann's prayers.

Ruthann's hand grabbed her arm. "Please stay. I would like to discuss something else with you."

She eased back onto the grass. "All right."

"I know this is none of my business, but I have to say it."

Rebecca looked into the woman's face. She looked to be in her early sixties, the same age as Mrs. Walker and her fellow gossips. Had the women spoken to Ruthann about her? Given her reasons to send Janie on with

Cora and Jack? "Please, go on." The words tasted bitter in her mouth, but she felt God easing her onward.

"I've been approached by a group of women who have shared your story with me. I'm not proud to say I listened. Come to think of it, I'm not proud of my scolding lecture that I gave them on gossip either, but I digress." Ruthann brushed a wayward strand of light brown hair from her face. "I understand you are a mail-order bride whose groom died suddenly."

Rebecca nodded. "It's true."

"Is it true that you are living with the marshal?"

Rebecca felt heat fill her face. "Yes, but not in the way I'm sure they led you to believe. Mrs. Brown— Edna—is staying there as well until the marshal gets better."

Ruthann patted her leg. "Yes, I knew that, too."

Rebecca didn't understand why she'd even asked then. She waited, sensing Ruthann wasn't finished talking.

"They also tell me that you used to reside with Mrs. Kelly, the owner of the hat and dress shop in town."

Rebecca sighed. "That is true, too, and as soon as the marshal is able to walk without the cane, I will be moving back in with Eliza."

"I thought as much." Ruthann glanced back down at the wagon. "This may sound crazy to you, but I think I know how we can both be happy."

"I'm listening."

Ruthann patted her leg again. "Thank you. I have money of my own. I'd planned on buying a house once we got settled in California, but now I want to settle here. Mrs. Porter told me her husband has a small house on the edge of town for sale. I asked how much he wanted for it and bought it."

Rebecca came fully awake. Her voice squeaked out. "You bought it already?"

The older woman grinned and nodded. "I've been thinking on this all day and it just made sense, so while Cora fed the children and Jack was inside talking to you and the marshal, I bought the Porter place."

Didn't Ruthann realize her whole family was leaving for California? They might even be taking Janie. What would she do for money? Had she used all her savings to buy the place?

"Oh, dear. I can see by the expression on your face that you think I've done the wrong thing." Her gaze returned to the wagon. "And if you think so, I can only imagine Cora's expression tomorrow when I tell her that Janie and I are staying right here."

Chapter Twenty-Four

Two mornings later, Seth groaned as the child again ran from the kitchen, out the front door and then back through the kitchen. At least he thought it was the same child. Who knew for sure? There were so many of them.

His stomach growled at the tantalizing aromas of bacon, sausage, eggs and fried potatoes that filled his house. Children's laughter and squeals were becoming a part of life in the Billings home. How much longer would it last?

"Here, Marshal." Jack Reynolds handed him a plate. "I'm sorry we've taken over your house, but Cora's insisting the children sit at the table for their meals. Thankfully, she still allows me to say the blessing."

Seth chuckled at Jack's pun. "Much obliged." Seth looked down at the eggs, sausage, potatoes and biscuits on his plate. He had two of everything.

Rebecca carried a cup of coffee to him. The rich aroma preceded her. She set the cup down on the end table and smiled. "Can I get you anything else?"

She was up to something. Rebecca had her old bounce in her step and her eyes twinkled. As far as he knew, the Reynolds family still hadn't made a decision as to whether they were taking Janie or leaving her. Cora carried the baby around as if she were her own, only giving her up when Rebecca said it was nap- or bedtime.

Ruthann Shepherd also seemed to be up to something. She shared glances and smiles with Rebecca when they thought no one else would notice. The older woman had disappeared several times with the excuse of going shopping, but she never returned with anything. Had the others noticed this? If they had, they weren't saying anything.

Jack smacked his lips. "That young gal can sure cook. If I weren't already married, I'd beg her to marry me quick." He patted his stomach.

"I heard that, Jack Reynolds." Cora stood in the kitchen doorway.

Jack turned to Seth. "You heard her, Marshal. If I'm dead by this evening, you'll know who did it."

Cora shook a spoon at him. "And make myself a widow with this passel of children? I don't think so. You are stuck with my bad cooking for many years to come." The teasing glint in her eyes told everyone that she wasn't truly angry.

"That's why I love you, Cora Beth. You are a sensible woman."

"Ma! Naomi spilled her milk again," Mary cried from the kitchen.

Cora turned back to tend to her children.

Seth looked to Jack. "There for a second I thought you'd done yourself in talking about another woman's cooking like that."

Jack laughed. "Cora knows I'll never look at another woman. She holds my heart."

The sound of Rebecca's laughter drifted from the kitchen. Did she hold his heart? And if so, what about Jesse? What about Clare? Even if she held his heart, would she crush it when she learned he was the cause of both their deaths?

As soon as breakfast was over, Cora sent the children outside to play. Ruthann caught Rebecca's eye. She smiled and nodded. Rebecca's heart picked up a beat. Now was the time. She'd talked Ruthann into waiting to tell the family of her plans until she could get her home ready to show them.

Ruthann wiped her hands dry on the dishcloth. "Ladies, let's go join the men. I have an announcement to make."

Cora's eyes narrowed and she looked to Rebecca. As they followed Ruthann, she hissed to Rebecca, "Do you have something to do with this?"

Rebecca ignored her and entered the sitting room. Seth and Jack were playing a game of checkers. Seth looked up and met her gaze. She looked down. He wasn't going to like Ruthann's announcement, at least not her part in it.

Ruthann moved to the center of the room. She picked up Janie, who had been playing on a blanket. "I have an announcement to make." Her gaze moved about the room as each eye turned in her direction.

"Ma, what is this about?" Cora placed her fisted hands on her hips.

The older woman glared at her daughter. Her sharp voice chastised the young woman. "I raised you to respect your elders and I'll thank you to keep quiet."

Cora dropped her gaze. Her cheeks turned pink and

she dropped her hands to hang limply by her side. "Yes, ma'am."

"If this is a family matter, Rebecca and I can step outside." Seth reached for his cane.

"No need for that, Seth. You and Rebecca are a part of this family."

Cora's head snapped up. She opened her mouth, but Ruthann held up her hand to stop her daughter's protest.

"The day you took Janie in, you became a part of our family. So I want you all to hear my announcement."

Jack leaned back in his chair and crossed his arms. His gaze met his wife's and he shook his head.

"I have decided to stay here in Cottonwood Springs and Janie is staying with me." Ruthann tickled the baby's tummy and kissed her cheek.

"No!" Cora gasped. "Ma, you can't."

Ruthann shook her head. "Yes, I can, Cora."

"How? You don't have a place to stay. And I hate to say this, but you aren't young anymore." Cora shook her head. "No, you are going with us and that's final." She turned to Jack. "Jack, let's get packed up and leave now before these people can put any more silly notions in Ma's head." Cora turned her glare onto Rebecca.

"No, Cora. We're going to hear your mother out."

Cora turned on him. Her face turned a molten red. "Jack! These people have turned her against us. All they want is Janie. As soon as we leave, they will cast Ma out into the cold. I won't let that happen!"

Janie began to fuss and reach for Rebecca. Rebecca walked over to Ruthann and took the baby. "We have no intention of casting Ruthann out into the cold." She smiled. "Besides, she's not staying with us. We're staying with her."

"What?" Seth stood.

"Please sit, Marshal, and let me explain. You, too, Cora." Once they were seated, Ruthann explained. "The other night, Rebecca and I were visiting and we decided the best way to raise Janie is with her family. Rebecca loves Janie like a mother and I am her grandmother. So, I bought the old Porter place and have been working on it off and on to create a home for the three of us."

"But Mother, you know we are leaving in the morning. I can't imagine leaving you here. And, what about the rest of us? We'd like to see Janie grow up, too." Tears filled Cora's eyes. Around a tight-sounding throat, she accused, "You are just being selfish."

Jack stood and walked to his wife. "No, Cora, we are the ones who have been selfish. We've dragged your mother from her home. Asked her to help with a wagon full of children and expected her to be happy." He placed an arm around her. "We need to be happy for your mother."

"Thank you, Jack." Ruthann pulled a handkerchief from her sleeve. She wiped her watery eyes. "I think this is where God wants me to be, Cora. Please, try to understand."

Cora buried her face in Jack's shoulder.

Seth stood. "If you will excuse us, Rebecca and I have some things to discuss, as well." He walked to the door and held it open for Rebecca.

She picked up a blanket and toy for Janie, then stepped outside. The days were turning warmer and she inhaled the sweet smell of the honeysuckle that grew beside the house. Seth closed the door and walked down the steps using his cane.

He put his hand on the small of her back and then directed her to a tall tree. "We need to talk."

Warmth traveled up her back and into her hair; goose bumps popped out on her arms. "What about?" She moved away from him and set Janie on the ground while she spread out the blanket. The sound of the other kids playing on the other side of the house floated on the air.

Seth bent over and picked up Janie. He tickled her belly and made her giggle. Then he set her down on the blanket. "What is this about you and Ruthann living together? Do you even know where the Porter place is?"

"Of course I know where it's at. I've been over there helping with the furniture arranging, setting up the kitchen—and, my favorite part, setting up rooms for Janie and myself." Rebecca sat down beside the baby and handed her a round toy with rattles hanging off the side. It looked a lot like a baby tambourine.

He leaned down and looked into her face. "And just when were you working on the house?"

Seth Billings was about to get very angry. "In the evenings." She stared back into his chocolate eyes. They narrowed.

He growled, "After everyone else was in bed?"

Rebecca swallowed. "That was the only time Ruthann and I could get away."

"Rebecca Ramsey! Have you not listened to a word I've said about the Evans gang? What if one of them had nabbed you? With this cane I couldn't do a thing about it! I can't believe you put yourself in danger like that, and Ruthann, too. What were you thinking?" He jerked away from her and stomped to the tree, where he leaned his back against the trunk.

Who did he think he was? She stood and planted her arms across her chest. "I'll thank you to stop yelling at me, Seth Billings. What I do is none of your business."

He lurched away from the tree and was within a hair's breadth from her before she realized he'd moved. His voice whispered across her face. "What you do is very much my business, Miss Ramsey. I promised Jesse I'd protect you and that's exactly what I've been trying to do."

So that was why he'd taken such an interest in her. She stood up straight and squared her shoulders. "Well, you can stop trying."

"No, I gave Jesse my word and I intend to keep it." His chocolate eyes were almost the color of black licorice now. Anger seeped from him like a visible force. A whiff of coffee floated about her, mixed with the earthy scent that was entirely Seth Billings.

She pulled back. "Look, I'm not Jesse's girl anymore and you are not responsible for me. I release you from your promise to him."

Seth sighed. He ran his hand through his brown hair. "It's not that simple, Rebecca."

"Yes, it is. I became a mail-order bride because my stepmother thrust the ad upon me and then pushed me out of my father's house. All I have wanted since that day was a home, a family. Ruthann and Janie are the answer to prayers I've prayed, Seth." She stared at him, willing him to understand. To take her into his arms and tell her that he was a part of her family.

The door to the house opened. "Children!" Ruthann was the first out, followed by Edna, Cora and then Jack.

Kids tumbled around the corner, pushing, shoving and running at full speed. Mary brought up the rear, holding little Naomi's hand.

"Would you like to come see my new house?" Ruthann continued down the short steps. At their squeals of delight she smiled. "Good." Then she turned in their direction. "Rebecca, why don't you bring Janie and the marshal, too?"

Rebecca looked upon Cora's sad face. Today the young woman had to face the reality that her mother didn't need her as much as she'd thought. Wasn't it the same between her and Seth? He didn't really need her but had hired her to keep a promise. She realized they were all staring at her. "All right, but I'll need to hitch up the wagon first. We'll meet you there."

"You go on ahead. I don't feel like going." Seth walked back to the house and shut the door.

In his own way, Seth had let her know he didn't want to be a part of her family. Rebecca scooped the baby up and bravely walked to where the others waited. "I'm ready."

Chapter Twenty-Five

Later, Rebecca sat at the table with Eliza and Hannah. She sipped her tea and sighed. "I've missed your tea, Eliza."

"I've missed you." Eliza set her cup down and frowned. "The house seems so quiet now with you moved in with Mrs. Shepherd."

Hannah looked into her cup. A frown marred her pretty face.

"I'm sorry, but I've explained why I moved out." Rebecca set her tea down and glanced at Hannah again. Was it her imagination or did Hannah have tears in her eyes?

Eliza dropped a teaspoon of sugar into her cup. "I know but I still miss you." She stirred her cup.

Both of her friends' faces were filled with misery. Eliza was lonely, but what was wrong with Hannah? Rebecca set her cup on the table. "All right, you two, snap out of it. This is my time to have fun and you're spoiling it." Her words had the effect she wanted.

They gasped and looked at each other. Shock filled their surprised faces.

"Good, now that I have your attention. Hannah, what

is bothering you?" Rebecca leaned back in her chair and waited.

Eliza searched Hannah's face. "I'm sorry, Hannah. I've been wallowing in self-pity and didn't realize something was wrong. Please, tell us. Maybe we can fix it."

Hannah looked to Rebecca. Rebecca nodded.

"Well, I've been moved from one student's home to another and I'm sick of it. Not once since we've known each other did you ever think to ask me to live with you, Eliza. Why not? I thought we were friends, too." Hannah studied her hands in her lap.

How long had Hannah been carrying this hurt? Rebecca reached out and placed her hands on top of Hannah's.

Eliza jumped up from her chair and ran around the table. She knelt beside Hannah. "I am so sorry, Hannah! I didn't think you were comfortable around me. I mean, you only come over now when Rebecca comes for tea."

A tear dripped from Hannah's chin. "I didn't think you wanted me around except when Rebecca was here." She covered her face with her hands.

Eliza gently pulled them down. "Hannah, you and I were friends before Rebecca moved to town. I never meant to hurt your feelings and I didn't realize that you were being shuffled from house to house. Normally, I do all the talking and you let me. Since I don't have children in school, I didn't know." She pulled her friend into her arms.

Rebecca watched them hug. Hannah pulled away and wiped at her tears. She tried to smile.

"Not that it's any of my business, but since Eliza is so lonely and you need a place to stay..." Rebecca let her words hang between them.

The squeal had both Hannah and Rebecca grabbing their ears. "Oh! Why didn't I think of that? Hannah, please come live with me!" Eliza clapped her hands.

Rebecca smiled and nodded to Hannah.

Hannah gazed hopefully at Eliza. "Are you sure? I don't want you to feel like you have to let me live with you. Especially since…"

"I'm positive."

Rebecca left a half hour later. Both her friends were smiling and making plans. She enjoyed the walk back to Seth's house. He seemed to be doing much better and very seldom used the cane now.

It had hurt when she realized that Seth only helped her because he'd promised Jesse he'd watch out for her. Rebecca held her head high. She didn't need a protector. No, she'd traveled all the way from Maryland to marry a man she'd never met and had arrived safe and sound. She needed the job and so hadn't quit working for Seth, but she didn't need his ever-present watching eyes.

She entered the house and found Edna and Seth playing a game of checkers.

The older woman looked up and winked at Rebecca. "I've got him cornered." She smiled.

"How was Janie doing?" Seth focused on the board.

Rebecca picked up her dust rag. "I don't know. I went to Eliza's for tea."

His head shot up. "I thought you went home to check on the baby."

"I didn't say that was where I was going."

Edna chuckled. "No, she said she was going out."

"You knew that's what I thought," Seth said.

"Now, how am I supposed to know what you are

thinking, Seth Billings?" She walked to the kitchen door. Just before she entered she heard Edna.

"Are we playing checkers or arguing?" Edna asked.

Rebecca snuck a glance back. Seth had refocused his gaze on the board. "We're playing." He moved his checker.

Edna chuckled. "Not very well, you aren't." She jumped three of his game pieces.

Rebecca couldn't stop the giggle that burst from her lips as she watched his expression go from shock to irritation.

Seth looked at the group of people he'd called together—the doctor, Mr. Hamilton, the reverend, Edna Brown, Dan Tucker, Hank Browning, the Millers, Eliza Kelly and Hannah Young. After Rebecca moved in with Ruthann Shepherd, Seth found his protective instincts toward her even more overbearing. She'd been hurt by a member of the Evans gang before and he couldn't stand the idea that she could be hurt again.

If he couldn't watch Rebecca all the time, he would ask for help. He cleared his throat to get everyone's attention. "I guess you are all wondering why I've called you together."

Some nodded; others simply waited for him to go on.

"The Evans gang is after Miss Ramsey."

Hannah gasped. Mary exchanged looks with Edna. The doctor and the reverend nodded. The rest continued to listen and wait.

Seth hated admitting he was weak, but in this case he had no choice. Rebecca refused to use caution when moving about town. He worried about her safety and even though he was getting better every day, Seth couldn't keep up with her.

"What do you want us to do, Marshal?" Dan asked.

"I want you to keep an eye on her, but don't be obvious. Rebecca won't appreciate us keeping track of her every move."

"How do you suggest we do this?" The reverend leaned forward and studied Seth's face.

"Well, I thought the ladies could offer to go with her places and the men could just kind of keep an eye out for her. That way she'll never be alone. The Evans gang won't try to nab her if she is with someone else or they can see someone else about." Seth stopped and studied their faces. Fear filled the women's eyes.

"Ladies, you will be safe. They only want Rebecca. You being with her will scare them off, but if you are afraid, it's understandable."

Eliza answered, "I'll try to be with her as much as possible in the evenings."

"That will be good." He sighed. This just might work.

"I'll come by after school and walk her to our house for afternoon tea." Hannah sat up a little straighter.

Each lady spoke up with ways they would help spend time with Rebecca and keep her from going anywhere alone. Seth praised them and added to their suggestions.

He noticed the men were sitting quietly, not contributing. Seth rubbed his chin. "Is there a problem, gentlemen? Did I forget something?"

Dan spoke up. "It's easy for the women to keep an eye on her, but I'm thinking Miss Ramsey will notice if we start following her around."

"So will our wives," Hank added.

Seth nodded. "Don't follow her, just watch her until she is out of your sight."

"I could offer to walk her home in the evenings," the reverend volunteered.

Seth looked at the reverend. He'd never mentioned a wife and Seth couldn't help but feel a twinge of jealousy. How old was the reverend? "I think that would work, Reverend, at least until I am up to walking her home again myself." Did the man of God understand what he'd just said? Seth hoped he had.

The reverend nodded and grinned. "Walking pretty ladies home is one of my favorite parts of my job. If it's all right with you, Seth, I'll be coming by each evening. We'll read from the Word and then I'll make my excuses to leave about the same time Miss Ramsey does."

This time Seth nodded.

"If we're done here, I need to be getting home to my family." Dan stood and stretched.

Seth walked to the door with him and held it while each person left. "Thank you all for coming," he called after them.

Edna was the last to leave. She stopped and waited for the rest of them to get out of earshot and then she said, "Seth Billings, I hope you know what you are doing. Because when Rebecca learns what you've done here tonight, I am not sure she will forgive you." Then she walked out onto the porch.

Why wouldn't she forgive him? He was doing this for her own good. Seth closed the door, leaned against the wood and frowned. His home seemed quiet. During the past few weeks he'd gotten used to Edna, Janie and Rebecca being within its walls. He especially missed Rebecca—the way she would sing Janie to sleep at night and the way her laughter made the air about him seem light and carefree.

If only he hadn't killed Jesse. If only he didn't already have to live with Clare's death. If only he could forgive himself. God had forgiven him, but even knowing that, Seth couldn't bring himself to put another woman in harm's way. Besides, when Rebecca learned he'd killed Jesse, she would probably move on to another town. She'd not want to live in the same town as a murderer.

"Why, thank you, I'd be delighted to have you walk me home." Rebecca smiled at the reverend.

"I'd love to see Janie and invite Mrs. Shepherd to church." He stood and gathered up his Bible and hat.

She'd been pleasantly surprised when he'd arrived right before dinner. Seth had seemed happy to see him, as well, so she'd invited him to dinner and while she cleaned the kitchen, the men had visited. She'd listened to them discuss King David and how the shepherd boy had become a king, one of her favorite events from the Bible.

Seth walked them to the door. He no longer needed the cane around the house. "Thanks for stopping by, Reverend. Come back anytime."

"If Miss Rebecca will fix me dinner every night, I might just take you up on that."

Rebecca smiled. "I'll take that as a compliment." She turned to Seth. "Good night, Marshal."

He frowned and nodded. "Good night, Rebecca."

The reverend offered her his arm. She slipped her hand into it and turned her back on Seth. Since she'd learned he was only interested in keeping her safe for

Jesse, she'd reverted back to calling him Marshal. It didn't seem as personal and made her job easier.

The reverend patted her hand. "Dinner was delightful, Miss Rebecca."

A blush filled her cheeks. Rebecca was thankful that the night wasn't as bright as it had been on other days. "Thank you. It was only chicken and dumplings. I would think you've had many dinners that were much better."

A warm chuckle built in his throat. "You'd be surprised at what I've had to choke down."

She laughed. "Well, I'm glad you enjoyed it." Her gaze moved into the cloudy sky. "Janie will probably be asleep when we get there."

He looked up, too. "Then maybe I can walk you home tomorrow night, too. We can start earlier and I can see both Janie and Mrs. Shepherd."

"That will be nice."

They walked on in silence. The sounds of insects and the cool breeze soothed her warm cheeks. The reverend was a nice man with a big heart. She enjoyed his sermons and found his company pleasant.

"Here we are." The reverend released her hand from under his. "Home sweet home."

Rebecca wasn't sure what she was supposed to do. She smiled and walked to the door. "Thank you, Reverend, for walking me home."

"It was my pleasure." He turned and walked away.

She sighed. *Lord, I'm so confused as to what Your plan is but I'm willing to wait until You tell me what to do.* Rebecca opened the door and looked about.

Ruthann sat in the sitting room, waiting for her to come home. "How was your day?" she asked.

Rebecca looked down into Janie's basket, which still

served as her bed. They would need to get the baby a bigger basket soon—she was growing every day. "A little confusing."

"Really? What was confusing about it?"

Janie had kicked off her blanket. Rebecca covered the baby once more and kissed her forehead. "The reverend walked me home tonight."

"That was nice of him." Ruthann laid her book to the side. "Why didn't you invite him in, dear?"

She glanced at Ruthann over her shoulder. Did the reverend walk her home to see Ruthann Shepherd? He had said he wanted to see Janie and invite Ruthann to Sunday service. Relief washed over her at the thought.

"It was late, but he said he'd like to come in tomorrow night. I told him that would be fine, if it's all right with you." Rebecca yawned. She covered her hand with her mouth, but Ruthann had already seen the gesture.

She smiled at Rebecca. "I think that will be nice. Maybe I'll bake a pie tomorrow afternoon and we can have coffee and dessert with him."

Rebecca nodded. "I'll invite him then." She picked up Janie's basket and carried it to the baby's room. Had she seen a sparkle in Ruthann's eyes at the thought of the reverend coming by for dessert? She smiled and decided it might be fun to play matchmaker.

Chapter Twenty-Six

Things were going as planned. Rebecca had constant supervision. The only thing that didn't sit well with Seth was that the reverend and Rebecca had become very good friends. She encouraged him to walk her home and then, from what he'd gathered from their conversations, they'd enjoyed dessert and board games once there.

He was recovering nicely and now Seth felt he could continue hunting down the remainder of the Evans gang. Horace Nance was at the top of his list. The man had shot him and then left him to die.

"You have outdone yourself again, Miss Rebecca." The reverend rubbed his belly and smiled.

"Thank you."

She no longer blushed at his compliments, which verified for Seth that they were becoming very close. Too close. "Reverend, I'll be happy to walk Rebecca home this evening."

"No!" they both answered in unison and then shared a smile.

Seth's blood boiled. They'd answered way too quickly for his taste.

The reverend recovered first. "I enjoy my evening walks with Miss Rebecca."

She smiled. "I'm ready to go now, James."

When had she started calling the reverend by his Christian name? Seth saw red as they walked out the door and onto the porch.

"Good night, Marshal." Rebecca walked down the steps. The reverend extended his arm and she placed her hand within the crook of his elbow.

Seth's heart sank. The only reason they could have for not wanting him along was because they wanted to be alone. He should have been happy that Rebecca was finding someone to love her. To give her the home and family she'd told him she craved.

But he loved her. The thought took him by surprise. He wanted to give her the home and family. Children with blond hair and blue eyes, like Rebecca's.

When had his feelings turned to love? He'd signed on to be Rebecca's protector, not to fall in love with her. Seth pulled the door shut behind him and eased down his stairs. He followed the couple at a safe distance.

They never looked back. The reverend bent his head and listened to her every word. Some protector the reverend was. James had no idea he was being followed. Tomorrow he'd have a talk with the reverend about his lack of awareness of their surroundings. He could have been a member of the Evans gang stalking them.

Seth stopped and leaned against a tree when they got to Rebecca's front door. Would James kiss her goodnight? Seth leaned his head back against the bark, watching but not wanting to see, if the reverend did kiss her.

Rebecca opened the door and stepped inside. The

reverend turned, waved at him, and then followed her inside, closing the door behind them.

So the good preacher had known they were being followed. Relief and irritation battled for controlling emotions. Seth turned and walked back to his own house. She could see whoever she chose to see. Still, his heart warred with his head.

Two hours later, Seth laid his book down and glanced at the ticking clock. Were they still together? What were they doing tonight? The questions continued to swirl in his mind. He looked down at the book. Seth shook his head. He couldn't even remember what he'd read.

A light tap on the door drew his attention. Who would be calling so late? He walked to the door. What kind of trouble lurked on the other side? As a U.S. Marshal, he expected the worst when someone arrived in the middle of the night.

"I hope you don't mind my dropping by so late, Marshal." The reverend stood with his hat in his hand.

Seth pulled the door open farther and moved back to allow him in. "Not at all, Reverend. What can I do for you?"

The reverend laughed. "It's more a matter of what I can do for you."

What did he think Seth needed help with? "Oh?"

"May I sit down?"

"Of course." Seth followed him into the sitting room. The reverend chose a chair and Seth moved to the couch. "What's this about, Reverend?"

"It's about your feelings for Miss Rebecca." He held his hat between his legs and stared into Seth's eyes.

"My feelings or yours?" If this were any other man, he wouldn't be having this conversation.

"I know my feelings are pure friendship. What are yours?"

Had his feelings been out there for everyone to see but himself? It was a relief to know the reverend only felt friendship for Rebecca. "Until tonight, I didn't know I had any feelings for her."

"Well, now that you know, what are you going to do about it?"

He sobered. "I don't know. Probably nothing."

"So you're not going to tell her?"

Seth stood. "No. I've just discovered how deep my love for her runs and I can't bear the thought of losing her forever."

"You aren't making any sense, Seth. Why don't you sit back down and tell me what's eating at you? Maybe with God's help, we can work though it together."

Seth had never talked about what had happened to Clare or Jesse with anyone. He looked into the reverend's kind eyes. Maybe this was the man to tell. Maybe the reverend could help him overcome the guilt he harbored within his heart. He sat back down.

The two men sat in silence for several minutes. Seth didn't know where to start. Should he tell Clare's story first? Or Jesse's? Would talking about them make any difference?

He cleared his throat. "I gave Clare my heart when we were teenagers. Three years ago we were planning on getting married." Seth stopped and pictured her face. Instead of the pain that normally swept through him at her loss, he simply enjoyed the beauty of who she had been.

The reverend asked in a soft voice, "What happened?"

Seth focused on the far wall as the memories flowed.

"Clare was a quiet young woman, timid with most people. I arrested a man named Copper. His brothers, Josh and Jasper wanted him out of jail. They abducted Clare and took her to their hideout. Then they threatened to kill her if I didn't release their brother." Seth swallowed the lump in his throat. "I refused and they killed her."

"You are not responsible for her death."

Seth met the reverend's gaze. "How can you say that? I didn't protect her. I didn't rescue her in time." He ran his hand through his hair. "I let Clare down. What if I do the same thing with Rebecca?"

James leaned back in his chair. "The person responsible for Clare's death is the man that killed her. You tried to protect her. You tried to rescue her, but in the end it was her time to die. We all have to die at some time and none of us know when God will call us home."

"Are you saying I couldn't have saved her no matter what?" Seth wanted to believe that God had called her home and Clare hadn't died before her time.

He nodded. "Seth, do you feel God led you to the life of a U.S. Marshal?"

"Yes, I do." If there was anything in Seth's life that he was a hundred percent sure of, it was that he was supposed to protect others.

"And a marshal's job is to protect others and uphold the law, right?"

Seth nodded.

"Can you protect everyone from the evil of this world?"

"No, only God can do that."

"Then why are you beating yourself up for Clare's death?"

For three years he'd dealt with the guilt of losing

Clare. He had blamed himself because she had trusted him to rescue her. But, he had never thought to put God into the equation. God didn't want his children to live feeling guilt-ridden. Seth had no control over what God did or didn't do, but he could choose not to punish himself because of something he couldn't control. "I see what you mean."

"Good. Now are you going to tell Miss Rebecca how you feel?"

Seth grinned. "Not yet. I still have unfinished business with the Evans gang and then I'll tell her everything, including that I'm the one who shot Jesse and that I love her. Satisfied, Reverend?"

James grunted. "Not really, but that's good enough for now, I suppose." He grinned.

Half an hour later, the reverend said good-night and Seth returned to his chair. His thoughts never strayed far from Rebecca. How was she going to react to the news that he'd shot Jesse?

He'd half expected the reverend to be shocked that his bullet was the one that had ended Jesse's life, but the reverend had accepted the fact as if it were nothing. Seth didn't think Rebecca would be as forgiving. Jesse was to be her husband—the man that she could have started a family with—but with one shot he'd taken Jesse's life. Would that be an unforgiveable sin in Rebecca's eyes?

Rebecca slipped into the house. She didn't want to disturb Ruthann and the rest of the quilters. Their laughter filled the house and for a brief moment, Rebecca was afraid they'd wake Janie. She laid the baby in her crib, waited for her to begin sucking on her thumb again and then decided to go make a cup of tea.

With Seth gone, this week she'd had extra time at home. As she avoided the sitting room and made her way to the kitchen, Rebecca thanked the Lord again for such a nice house. It was large with four bedrooms, two sitting rooms, a formal dining area and a comfortable kitchen that felt cozy and warm.

Voices came from the kitchen. "The way I heard it, the marshal thinks she has the money."

Rebecca stopped just outside the doorway. The person speaking had spoken so softly, she felt sure the woman didn't want to be overheard.

"I heard that, too. It's sad really to think that she'd keep stolen money."

Rebecca recognized Mrs. Walker's familiar hiss. When had she started attending Ruthann's weekly quilting bee? Not wanting anything to do with gossip, she turned to leave. But Mrs. Walker's next words stopped her. "But I knew when she showed up here announcing she was Jesse Cole's mail-order bride she was no good. It's a disgrace, that's what it is."

They were talking about her. Rebecca squared her shoulders and walked into the kitchen. "I think you ladies should know that I don't have anyone's stolen money." The shocked looks on their faces at having been caught gossiping about her should have brought a smile to Rebecca's face, but they didn't.

Mrs. Walker raised her head. "Well, that bit of news came from the marshal himself. If the law thinks you took it, who am I to doubt them?" She marched out of the room as if she were the queen of the castle.

Rebecca wanted to tell her she was a hate-filled woman who needed a good thrashing, but decided that would be most unchristian of her and held her tongue.

Instead she turned her gaze on Mrs. Hamilton, the other woman who she'd heard first. "Is that true?"

"Well, I didn't hear the marshal say that, but my husband told me pretty much the same."

So everyone around town thought she had stolen money. "Where did I steal this money from?" Rebecca continued to stare at Mrs. Hamilton.

The older woman swallowed. "Well, the rumor isn't that you stole the money. It's that Jesse stole it from the Evans gang and now, because you are Jesse's girl, they think you have it."

Rebecca felt heat fill her neck and face. "And this is what the marshal believes, too?"

Mrs. Hamilton nodded. "He told Mr. Hamilton to keep an eye on you. The Evans gang thinks you have the money and they are going to try and kidnap you to get it back."

"But that makes no sense at all. When I got here Jesse was already dead. How did he give me the money?" Rebecca leaned against the sideboard.

Mrs. Hamilton inched toward the door. "I don't know, dear, I didn't start the rumor."

Rebecca pinned her with a gaze. "No, but you are keeping it alive, aren't you? Do you have any idea how much gossip hurts others? Or is it that you just don't care?"

The older woman gasped and then fled the room.

Bitterness laced Rebecca's thoughts. So the marshal not only kept an eye on her because of his promise to Jesse, but he thought she was a common criminal who just might slip and lead him to a pile of stolen money?

She didn't want to stay where she wasn't trusted. A plan began to form in her mind. Maybe now was the time to leave Cottonwood Springs.

Chapter Twenty-Seven

Horace Nance loved to hear the sound of his own voice. After two hours of listening to him go on and on about nothing important, Seth was tempted to stop their horses and gag his prisoner. But maybe he could get the villain to talk about something besides himself.

"Hey, Nance, instead of talking about yourself, why don't you tell me where Maxwell Evans is hiding out?" Seth could almost feel the daggers Horace's eyes bore into his back. He didn't doubt that Horace would love to throw a real blade at him right now, but since his hands and feet were tied around the beast he rode upon, Seth wasn't too worried about that happening.

Horace barked, "Where's the fun in that?"

"The judge just might shorten your sentence some, if you do." He glanced over his shoulder.

"Yeah." Horace nodded. "And Maxwell just might kill me when he catches up with me, too."

Seth turned back around. "I might kill you if you don't." The threat hung heavy between them.

Horace forced a laugh. "Not likely."

Seth turned in his saddle. "No? What makes you so sure?"

The outlaw leaned back in his saddle. "I've learned to read people, Marshal. You wouldn't kill anyone unless it's in self-defense. It isn't in your nature."

Seth faced forward again. Horace was right. Never would he gun down a man, just because he could. Jesse had been an accident.

"But, Maxwell, he's another story. I thought I knew him, but after he got his first taste of killin' a few months ago, he hasn't been the same. He shot a boy, just because he could. Then a few weeks ago, we stumbled upon this couple with a babe. While Maxwell forced them deeper into the woods, I hid that baby." Horace grew silent. "Never could stomach killin' for the sake of killin', and I couldn't allow him to kill that pretty little girl."

Maxwell had killed Janie's parents? Had he meant for the law to think the local Indians had done such a thing? Probably, but Seth had never thought the Indians were responsible.

"You know he's goin' after Jesse's girl, don't you?"

A cold chill ran down Seth's spine. He steeled his voice and asked, "Why?"

Horace rocked in the saddle from side to side. "He thinks she's pretty and he thinks Jesse told her where the rest of our money is hidden."

"Doesn't he know that she hadn't even arrived when Jesse was killed?" Seth led the horses down to the riverbank, the same one Horace had ambushed him at weeks earlier.

"Oh, he knows. But to his way of thinkin', Jesse told her in a letter or somethin' like that."

Seth rubbed his aching thigh. Hadn't he had the same thoughts? But he'd seen the letters and knew it wasn't so. He held the canteen for Horace to drink out of.

After he'd had his fill, Horace frowned. "I guess since you caught me, he'll have to go after Jesse's girl on his own."

Seth acted uninterested. He took a swig of water and sloshed it around in his mouth. "I'm surprised he doesn't send one of his men after her."

"Ain't got no more men. It's just me and him now. You best watch out. He's waitin' for me in Durango, Marshal." Horace's gaze jerked to him. "That's just what you wanted to hear, ain't it, Marshal?"

Seth grinned up at him. "Didn't hurt my ears hearing it, Horace."

Rebecca finished the dishes and then dried her hands. She was tired. Her nights had been restless waiting for Seth's return. The longer he was gone the madder and more hurt she became. Rebecca didn't know how much longer she could stay in a town where she was constantly referred to as Jesse's girl and where everyone talked about her behind her back.

"Dinner was delicious." The reverend smiled at her as she passed his chair.

"Thank you, but don't forget Ruthann lives here, too, and tonight she cooked the meal."

He smiled. "I know."

Rebecca shook her head. "Oh, I'm sorry. I thought you were complimenting me. I guess I wasn't paying very good attention."

"That's all right, dear," he assured her.

Ruthann joined the conversation. "I've noticed you've been distracted over the past two or three days.

Is there anything I can do to help?" She motioned for Rebecca to sit in the vacant chair at the table.

"Or, any counsel I might give?" the reverend asked as he handed Ruthann the red checkers.

Rebecca smiled. She would miss both of them when she left. Then the thought came to her: Had the reverend been keeping an eye on her, too? She'd almost confided in him. Rebecca stood. "No, I'm fine. Thank you both."

As the reverend laid out his game pieces, he said, "On my way over here, I saw the marshal heading for his house."

So he was home. "Maybe I should take him a plate, in case he hasn't had dinner yet." Rebecca started to leave the room.

"Oh, that won't be necessary. When I saw him, he'd just left the diner."

Rebecca eased back into her chair.

"Did he have a new prisoner with him?" Ruthann made the first move.

The reverend looked across at her and grinned. "No, normally they drop prisoners off at the jailhouse and then go eat."

Ruthann nibbled on the inside of her bottom lip as she studied the board. "I wonder if he got his man this time, then." She didn't notice the teasing glint in Reverend Griffin's eyes.

Rebecca wondered the same thing. It was no secret Seth had been gathering up the Evans gang. Most of them he took straight to Durango, but some he brought with him here and then in the morning they'd head on out.

"Yep, he got him. He's all locked up in the jail."

He'd be leaving at first light to get him to Durango.

Rebecca stood. "If you will excuse me, I think I'll turn in."

"Good night, Rebecca. I hope you sleep well tonight." Ruthann jumped two of the reverend's game pieces.

"Good night." Rebecca hurried to Janie's room and checked on the baby. Janie looked up at her and grinned.

Rebecca groaned. She'd hoped the baby would be sleeping so she could sneak out and see if Seth had caught another member of the Evans gang. Since Janie was awake, Rebecca changed her diaper and then picked her up. She carried the baby to the rocker and sat down.

If she left Cottonwood Springs, would she have to leave the baby with Ruthann? She ran her finger over the baby's forehead. Janie's eyes drifted closed. Rebecca had learned early that rubbing Janie's forehead put the baby right to sleep.

She laid her head back and closed her eyes. With a will of their own, her feet continued rocking them back and forth. No, if she left it would be in the still of the night. She couldn't leave Janie. The baby was hers and she was taking her.

The next morning, Rebecca woke with a crick in her neck and a headache. She groaned as she sat up in the rocker. Moisture coated her arm and she looked down at a smiling Janie. "I see we've spent the night in this rocker again."

Janie tugged at a strand of Rebecca's blond hair.

Ruthann called as she passed the bedroom, "Good morning. Coffee's already made, if you'd like a cup."

Rebecca grinned at the baby. "Grandma is very chipper this morning. Do you think you'll soon have a grandpa with the last name Griffin?" She tickled the baby's tummy and then stood to change her and get ready for the day.

Today was the day she was going to quit her job. She'd saved up enough money to keep her and Janie fed for a while. She carried the baby in to Ruthann. "Would you mind watching Janie for a few hours this morning?"

Ruthann took the squirming baby. "Of course not. She and I can bake cookies today. How does that sound, Miss Janie?"

"Thank you." Rebecca poured a cup of coffee. "I'm going to get dressed for work."

"That's fine." Ruthann set the baby in a chair and strapped her in with an old belt. "That should hold you."

Rebecca hurried to her room and changed her dress. She pinned her hair up and then worked the buttons on her shoes. A quick glance at the clock told her she needed to hurry if she were going to make it to Seth's house before he left with the prisoner. Rebecca grabbed her apron from its hook and tied it about her waist.

Her heart pounded in her chest. "Ruthann, I'm leaving now."

"Wait for me!" Grace raced from the kitchen with two apples in her hands.

How had Grace known she'd be walking to the marshal's house today? "Good morning, Grace. I didn't expect to see you this morning."

The little girl stopped. "Why not? I've been walking with you to the marshal's house ever since you started working for him." She handed Rebecca one of the red apples.

Rebecca took the fruit. "Thank you. How did you

know that I'd be going to the marshal's house today?" She opened the door and Grace went out in front of her.

"Oh, that's easy. Ma told me that he was home and to get over here so I could walk with you." Grace took a big bite from her apple.

"I thought school was out right now. Doesn't your Ma need you at the store?" Rebecca looked at the fruit in her hand. She wasn't hungry so slipped it into her apron pocket.

Grace giggled. "Nope, I'm lucky my new job is to walk you to the marshal's house every morning."

Rebecca stopped walking. "What do you mean your new job?"

"My old job was to sweep the store before it opened, but now I get to walk to the marshal's with you." Grace skipped a few feet ahead then stopped. "Aren't you coming?" The little girl waited for her to catch up.

She felt a headache coming on. "I don't understand, Grace. Why is it your job?" Maybe this was just Mrs. Miller's way of getting her daughter out of the house for a little while.

Grace shook her head. "I don't know, but I heard Pa tell Ma that nothing would happen to me. All the marshal wants is for someone to keep an eye on you at all times. Isn't that sweet, Miss Rebecca?"

Sweet, her Aunt Annie! Not only was he telling everyone that she stole money, but now he had little children watching her every move. Was the whole town watching her? Rebecca turned and looked toward downtown.

Mr. Tucker waved from the blacksmith shop. Come to think of it, he stood in the doorway of the smithy a lot. Was he watching her? Had he been watching her all along? She felt both angry and sick at the same time. Did the town hate her so much, just because she'd arrived as a mail-order bride?

"Wait for me!" Grace called, running to keep up. "Are you mad, Miss Rebecca?" she panted.

"No, Grace, dogs get mad. I'm angrier than a big bull."

"But why?"

Rebecca stopped in front of Seth's house. She turned to Grace. "Go home, Grace. As you can see, you've done your job because I'm here."

"Yes, Miss Rebecca." She turned to go, her shoulders slumped and head down.

She couldn't let the little girl go like this. "Grace. Wait." Rebecca walked to her and knelt to her level. "Sweetheart, I'm not angry with you. I'm sorry that I sounded so harsh. I just need to talk to the marshal alone. All right?"

Grace nodded.

"Good." She gently tugged the little girl's braid. "Thank you for walking with me this morning." Rebecca offered her a smile. The last thing she wanted was for Grace to go home upset. If that happened, the town would start to call her a child hater on top of all the other things they were calling her and saying behind her back.

"You're welcome." Grace hugged her and then skipped away.

Rebecca started up the stairs just as the front door opened. Seth stepped out onto the porch. "Good morning, Rebecca."

His face was freshly shaven and he smelled of soap. An easy smile brought out the winking dimple in his cheek. Why did he have to be so handsome? Why couldn't he have just trusted her? Asked about the money instead of having her watched like a common criminal?

She needed courage and her anger to help her stand up to this man. "Marshal, I quit. You have told everyone in town that I know where Jesse kept the stolen money. You've had the whole town watching me like a common thief. I can no longer be in your employment." Rebecca spun on her heel and headed back down the stairs.

"Rebecca, wait!" He grabbed her arm and spun her around to face him. "I never said you knew where the stolen money was."

"Then why is the whole town talking about me and saying you did?" She glared at him trying to ignore the warm sensation of his hand on her arm.

Seth dropped her arm and ran a hand through his hair. "I don't know."

"Did you know that I am being watched? By everybody?" Rebecca looked into his warm brown eyes. She had missed him while he was gone.

He nodded.

"So you do think I know where the money is hidden." Rebecca's emotions were all over the place. One moment she wanted to slap him, the next she wanted to melt in his arms. Then he admitted the truth of her suspicions and she was back to wanting to slap him again.

"When I first met you, I thought there was a chance Jesse might have told you where the money is hidden. But not anymore."

Rebecca fought the allure of his eyes. He didn't trust her, not then and not now. "You've never trusted me. I'm Jesse's girl, remember? He had a bad past so I must have been just as bad."

Hurt filled his eyes. "I'm a lawman, Rebecca. I had to follow my hunch."

"Well, I hope you are happy with yourself, Marshal. No one in this town trusts me."

Seth took a deep breath and stood to his full height. "I am sorry about that."

"So am I." A tear slipped from her stinging eyes.

He turned away. "I have a prisoner to take to Durango. When I get back, we'll talk."

Her voice broke. "Goodbye, Seth." And then Rebecca turned toward home. She noticed that Eliza stood on her front porch sweeping. Or was her friend watching her, too? Tears streaming down her face, Rebecca ran.

I may not be here, Seth Billings, when you get back.

Chapter Twenty-Eight

Seth swayed in the saddle. Why hadn't he pulled Rebecca inside and explained everything? Instead he'd walked away like a coward. No, pulling her inside the house and closing the door would have only added fuel to the gossipers. Thanks to him, everyone in town watched her every move.

"What's the matter, Marshal? Afraid ol' Maxwell is gunning for you?" Horace called from his horse.

Seth ignored him.

Horace waited a few moments more. "He's not going to jump you on the trail."

"No?" Seth's senses came to full alert. It had been his experience that outlaws were liars, most of the time.

"Why don't you gag him, Marshal?" Jason Cook, a young man who had approached Seth about learning the ropes as a sheriff and about helping to find the Evans gang, trailed behind Horace.

"You wanted to learn how to be a Sheriff. Well, this is part of it." He glanced over his shoulder at both men. "If you let them talk, they'll eventually tell you what you want to hear. Isn't that right, Horace?"

Horace snarled an ugly grin and spit on the ground.

"Yep, just what you want to hear. Told ya what ya wanted to hear yesterday, didn't I?"

The gleam in Horace's eyes set Seth on edge. "And why won't Maxwell be gunning for us on the trail?"

"That's for me to know and you to find out." Horace sounded like a schoolboy taunting his friends. But they weren't friends and never would be.

Seth looked to Jason.

Jason gave a slight nod of his head. "Aw, don't listen to him. Maxwell is the big boss. This one's just his crony. He'll do and say anything to be able to lick old Maxwell's boots, won't ya, Horace? He has no idea what's really going on."

Seth faced forward once more. He'd let the boys behind him argue for a few minutes. Maybe Jason could get something useful out of Horace. The young man seemed to instinctively know how to get Horace riled up.

His thoughts returned to Rebecca. It seemed they never strayed far from her. Her voice had cracked when she'd said goodbye and then she'd run. His heart broke. He'd make it up to her once he captured Maxwell.

"I may not be as bright as Maxwell, but I can tell you this. He didn't come up with his latest plan on his own. Nope, I helped," Horace bragged.

Seth shook his head and brought his thoughts back to Rebecca. She'd sounded so hurt, and the way she'd said the whole town didn't trust her had broken his heart. He sat straighter in the saddle. If she thought no one cared about her in Cottonwood Springs, would she leave?

No, she'd never leave Janie. But what was stopping her from taking the baby with her? He wasn't there to stop her. Ruthann would try, but only if she knew of Rebecca's plans. His only comfort was knowing that if she did leave, Maxwell was nowhere near Cottonwood Springs.

"You think you are so smart. I can lie, too, you know?" Horace said.

"Well, sure you can lie, Horace. That's what bad guys do." Jason continued to taunt the prisoner.

Horace laughed. "Yeah, well, while you and the marshal are planning on capturing Maxwell in Durango, he's back there in Cottonwood Springs taking care of Jesse's girl."

Seth turned to look at the outlaw. His blood ran cold. *Please, Lord, let him be lying.* He pulled his horse to a stop and jumped down. His legs felt stiff as he walked back to Horace. "Why should we believe you now?"

Happy to have upset the marshal, Horace laughed. "I might be telling the truth and then again, maybe I'm not."

Jason rode his horse up beside Horace and smashed his fist into the outlaw's cheekbone. "Are you?" he demanded.

Horace spit blood in Seth's direction. Seth jumped back, avoiding the splatter. The outlaw turned to face Jason. "Wouldn't you like to know?" He smiled, revealing bloodstained teeth.

Jason pulled his gun. His words came out sounding as cold as the steel that now rested between Horace's eyes. "I'll shoot you where you sit."

"You can't shoot me, can he, Marshal?"

Seth shook his head at Jason but answered Horace. "He's not a real sheriff or marshal yet, Horace, so I guess he hasn't learned that rule yet."

Fear filled Horace's voice now. "You won't let him shoot me, will you, Marshal?"

"As I'm standing over here and he's sitting over there

on a horse, I'm not sure I can stop him." Seth hated using tactics such as this, but he needed to know Maxwell's whereabouts. If the outlaw really was in Cottonwood Springs, then Rebecca was in real danger.

Rebecca sipped her tea. She hated feeling as if her friends were no longer her friends. Eliza had invited her to dinner, but the meal had felt strained, as if everyone had something to say, but no one knew how to say it. She set her cup down.

Eliza sighed. "You know, don't you?"

Hannah gasped. "Eliza, don't."

"Don't what, Hannah?" Rebecca asked. "Tell me that the marshal suspects I know where Jesse stashed his money or that you all have been watching me for weeks to make sure I lead you or him to said money?" All Rebecca's pent-up hurt and anger came through loud and clear. As soon as the words were out, she wished she could take them back.

"Oh, you don't know anything." Eliza laughed. "That wasn't what I was talking about."

Hannah frowned. "It wasn't?"

"No, silly. I thought she knew we'd been watching her because the marshal wanted her protected from the Evans gang. Remember, he told us all that he didn't believe she had the money or that she knew where it was but that the Evans gang did believe that and that since he couldn't watch over her, he needed our help." Eliza smiled and poured them all fresh tea. "So you see, she had it all wrong."

Hannah and Rebecca shared glances. Hannah was the first to laugh. "She's right, you know. You did say it all wrong."

Rebecca felt instant relief and couldn't stop laughing.

She'd been so afraid that her friends didn't trust or care about her, and the man she loved thought she was a thief and had turned the others against her, that her insides had been turned into knots. She sobered. Maybe Eliza was wrong. "He doesn't still believe I know where the money is?"

Eliza patted her hand. "Honestly, I don't think he ever did, but he had to follow that lead. He is a lawman, after all."

She should have listened to him. "That's what he said." The look in Seth's eyes should have caused her to believe him, but her anger had prevented her from seeing that he was telling the truth.

Hannah sighed. "You love him, don't you?"

"With all my heart, but it's complicated."

Eliza stared at her. "When is love not complicated?"

Rebecca shook her head. "I mean we have trust issues."

"You don't trust him? Or he doesn't trust you?" Hannah asked.

"Both, I think. I know he doesn't trust me fully or he would have told me what was going on. Instead, he told the whole town." Rebecca tried to smile.

Eliza threw her hands in the air. "Rebecca, he is trying to protect you! Men don't think like women do. If they did the world would be a much happier place."

Once more they all broke into laughter. Rebecca's laugh wasn't as full and sweet as the other two women's, but she could see the humor in Eliza's words.

The sound of shattering glass interrupted the women's laughter.

Hannah was the first to speak. "What was that?"

"It sounded like glass breaking." Eliza pushed out of her chair.

A growl came from the dark hallway. "Sit back down, pretty lady." Light reflected off a gun barrel.

When the man stepped into the light, Eliza spoke. "Maxwell Evans, don't you 'pretty lady' me."

He shook the gun in her direction. "You always were too sassy for your own good, Eliza Kelly. Sit down before I shoot you in the leg and set you down."

"If you shoot her in the leg, someone will hear the noise and call the marshal." Rebecca couldn't believe the words were coming from her mouth.

Maxwell laughed. His black eyes bore into Rebecca's. "I don't think so. The marshal is out of town, and since you've been in here for over an hour, don't reckon anyone is looking out for you right now." He chewed on a dirty thumbnail.

"What do you want?" Eliza ground the words through her teeth.

He walked over to Eliza and slapped her across the mouth, causing her to fall to the floor and Hannah to gasp. "I told you to sit down."

Hannah helped Eliza into her chair. Eliza wiped a trickle of blood from her cut lip.

Maxwell looked at Rebecca. "I want Jesse's girl to tell me all she knows about the gold he stole from us." He pointed the gun at Hannah and Eliza. "And fast, this gun just might go off if I don't hear real quicklike."

"Mr. Maxwell..." His bark of laughter stopped Rebecca from finishing her sentence.

The stench of his breath carried across the table. Cheap whisky and chewing tobacco filled the small eating area. The urge to gag had Rebecca swallowing hard. She half expected the large vase of fresh flowers that sat in the center of the table to wilt and die under the siege of odors.

He waved the gun around. "See, Eliza, you could take a lesson from this here gal. She has some good manners. I ain't never been called Mr. Maxwell."

Eliza scolded. "Since your name isn't Mr. Maxwell, I can see why not."

"Hush your mouth." He turned back to Rebecca. "Now what were you going to say, darlin'?"

The urge to hold her breath had already seized Rebecca's lungs. His body odor filled the room, as well as his bad breath. "I was going to say, I don't know where Jesse hid the gold."

His laughing face turned rock hard. "That's not what I came to hear."

Rebecca bravely stood. "It's the truth." There was something in his eyes that scared her more than the gun he waved about. She refused to give in to her fear. And thanked the Lord above that Janie was home with Ruthann.

He walked over to where Eliza and Hannah sat. Maxwell stood between them. "Look, I came here for the money and I intend to leave here with it. Where is it?" He smashed the gun against the table.

Eliza's jaw tightened and her eyes flashed. "That's my good china. You best not break one cup, Maxwell Evans."

Maxwell scowled at Eliza. He leaned close to her face and growled, "You might be my ma's age but you aren't my ma. I'm going to enjoy shooting you."

She turned her face away from him. But not before he heard her mutter, "I'm closer to your age, you lunatic."

His eyes narrowed. "Lunatic? You think I'm a lunatic." He raised his hand back to hit Eliza again.

Hannah spoke up. "I'm sure she didn't mean that."

Rebecca's mind worked. What were they going to do? She didn't know where the money was and even if she did, he would still kill them.

Maxwell swiveled around on Hannah. His dark eyes bore into her frightened face. "No?"

Hannah shook her head in fear.

Rebecca cleared her throat. "Excuse me, Mr. Evans."

He looked at her.

"If I take you to the money, will you leave my friends alone?" She gripped the front of her dress and prayed she could lure him away.

Hannah gasped.

Maxwell turned to the schoolteacher. He ran the back of his hand down the side of her face. "I'd rather not."

Hannah jerked her face away from him.

"Then I guess we'll stay here and you can kill us." Rebecca's chest hurt from the pounding her heart was giving it.

Maxwell straightened. "I said I'd rather not, not that I wouldn't. But I can't leave them here to tell the marshal what they know when he gets back." He scratched the side of his head with the gun.

"I could tie them up and gag them," Rebecca suggested as a plan began to take form in her mind. She would not let him scare and kill them as he willed.

"Yeah, you can do that." He came to stand in front of her. Maxwell leaned forward and breathed into her face. "But, if you try anything, I will kill your friends right before your eyes. Then, I'll do the same to you."

Rebecca swallowed and nodded. "We'll need some rope."

Maxwell waved his gun at Eliza. "We need rope," he barked.

Eliza's voice shook and she stared at Rebecca in disbelief. "The only rope I have is my clothesline out back."

He marched over to her and jerked her upright. "Let's go get it." Maxwell turned his glare on Rebecca and Hannah. He shoved Rebecca back into her chair. "You two stay put and be quiet. If either of you run or make any noise, this old hag is going to get a bullet in her head. Understand?"

"I'm not old." Eliza glared at him, but he ignored the look and shoved her back toward the kitchen.

As soon as they were out of sight, Rebecca leaned toward Hannah. "I'm going to tie you really loose. As soon as he starts shoving me to the back door, shake off the rope and grab this vase. You are going to have to hit him in the back of the head as hard as you can. Can you do that, Hannah?"

"I don't know." Hannah looked at the vase. "I'm scared."

"So am I, but if we don't fight him, he's going to kill all three of us. I don't want to die. Do you?" Rebecca hissed back.

Hannah shook her head. "No."

They waited for Maxwell and Eliza to return. It seemed to be taking forever.

"What's taking them so long?" Hannah whispered in a tight voice.

Rebecca looked over her shoulder at the empty doorway. "I don't know. Maybe they are having trouble getting the rope down." Deep in her heart she feared that Eliza had attempted to run and Maxwell was taking his wrath out on her. She silently prayed for Eliza's protection.

"Should we go check on them?" Hannah asked.

Maxwell shoved Eliza into the room. "What are you two whispering about?" he demanded.

"She's scared," Rebecca answered for both of them as Hannah looked to the floor.

Lord, please let my plan work. I want to tell Seth I love him. I want Janie to grow up with a mother. And Lord, I want this man locked away forever.

Chapter Twenty-Nine

Seth whipped his horse into a full-out run. If what Horace said was true, Rebecca was in danger. What would Maxwell do to her when he discovered she had no clue where the money was hidden? He should never have left her alone.

Lord, please protect her.

He arrived in Cottonwood Springs just as the sun went down. Seth slid off the saddle and ran to the front door of Ruthann's house.

Ruthann answered the door with a frown. "Marshal, I just got the baby down. Your banging is going to wake her up."

He ignored her scolding. "Where's Rebecca?" Seth stood on his toes and looked over Ruthann's head.

"She's having dinner at Eliza's. Is something wrong?" Her brow creased in worry.

Seth spun on his heel. "I hope not."

He stayed in the shadows as he darted toward Eliza's house. The hair on the back of his neck rose. A sure sign of danger. Seth inched his way to the back of the house. A big black stallion snorted a greeting and bobbed his head.

Then he saw them. Maxwell had just pushed Rebecca out the back door and followed her. The sleeve of her dress was torn at the shoulder. The sight of Maxwell's pistol pressed into her back stilled Seth's own gun hand.

A loud crash sounded and Rebecca's body went into action. She stepped back hard on the outlaw's foot and her elbow thrust into Maxwell's ribs. She jerked out of his grasp as his head came down. She twisted around and slammed her palm into his face and then leaped out of his range.

Hannah stood a few feet behind them holding a broken vase. She had a cut on her cheek but didn't look as if she was in pain.

Rage burned in the depths of the outlaw's eyes. He raised his gun and pointed it toward Rebecca.

Hannah's scream filled the night air.

Seth rushed forward and grabbed Maxwell's gun arm, forcing it upward. "Get in the house!" he yelled to the women as he struggled with Maxwell to keep his weapon pointing toward the night sky.

Rebecca ran to Hannah and pushed her inside. He prayed Rebecca followed her as he'd told her to do but he didn't have time to watch to make certain she had.

Both men grunted as they struck out at each other. The gun flew across the dark yard. Fists continued to connect with flesh.

Thanks to Hannah's scream, a group of men came running forward. The sounds of guns being cocked stopped both men.

"We've got him covered, Marshal," Doc's voice announced.

Maxwell snarled at the doctor. "You won't kill me."

A woman's voice filled the night air. "He might not, Maxwell, but I sure will."

Ruthann stepped from the shadows. Her hand shook. Seth stepped away from the outlaw. He didn't want Ruthann to kill him but saw the rage in her eyes and knew he didn't want to take a bullet for the outlaw, should she miss.

The back door opened and closed. Rebecca walked out. "Ruthann, he's not worth it."

"He's a killer, Rebecca." The older woman's eyes filled with tears. "Just like the man who killed my Sadie."

Rebecca slowly walked toward her. "Let Seth do his job and lower the gun. Maxwell isn't going anywhere."

Maxwell's fists clenched as Rebecca placed herself between him and Ruthann. Seth moved forward and grabbed the outlaw once again.

He didn't need the citizens of Cottonwood Springs taking matters into their own hands. He yanked Maxwell's hands behind his back and wished he had his handcuffs, but unfortunately he'd left them with his horse.

Hannah hurried from the house and handed him some rope. "Here you go, Marshal. This is what he made Rebecca tie Eliza and myself up with."

Seth smiled at her. "Thanks." He quickly tied the outlaw's hands.

He looked about and found not only the doctor, but Dan and a couple of other town men, standing within the shadows. Their guns were still trained on Maxwell. "Gentlemen, thank you for coming out and assisting, but we're done here. Go on home to your wives. I'm sure they are wondering what has happened to you."

As the men departed, Seth jerked Maxwell to a tree.

When he refused to sit, Seth hit him in the jaw as hard as he could. Hours of pent-up anger went into the hit and Maxwell slumped against the tree.

Rebecca's eyes met his over Ruthann's head. She held the older woman sobbing against her shoulder. Ruthann still held her gun in her right hand. Rebecca stood strong and tall, offering comfort.

Eliza exited the house. "I missed everything. Rebecca, what were you thinking tying me up so tight?" She touched her split lip.

"I don't know. I guess I just wanted you to stay put. For some reason, Maxwell Evans doesn't like you much." Rebecca grinned at her friend.

Seth wanted to pull Rebecca into his arms and hug her tight. Her earlier bravery had made him proud of her. He realized that unlike Clare, Rebecca had fought back.

The doctor gently pulled Ruthann from Rebecca's grasp. "Come with me." He gently tugged her along.

Rebecca held her arm in front of them, stopping them. "Ruthann? Where is Janie?" Panic filled her voice as she realized her daughter wasn't with her grandmother.

Ruthann hiccuped and wiped her tears. "I left her with Edna."

Blue eyes so brave earlier now took in their surroundings and the man at Seth's feet. Rebecca's gaze came up and met his and she offered Seth a wobbly smile.

Thank you, Lord, that she can still smile.

"Rebecca, I'll take Ruthann home and check on the baby," the doctor offered.

At her nod, he spoke softly to Ruthann and the pair turned in the direction of home.

Rebecca joined her friends on the back porch. She allowed them to hug her. Eliza's voice drifted on the evening breeze as she relived the events of the night. Hannah simply stood silently twisting her hands. Rebecca held Seth's gaze over the heads of her friends.

His love for her pounded through his veins with the speed of a raging river. Seth prayed that when he told her of that love that she'd return it.

What about Jesse? his inner voice taunted. Would she be able to forgive him for his part in Jesse's death? That question haunted him night and day. Seth silently prayed. *Lord, please help her understand I never meant for Jesse to die. I know You understand and don't blame me, but my own feelings of guilt will not go away overnight. I also know that if I continue to lean on You, someday forgiveness will come.*

God didn't blame him, but would Rebecca?

Rebecca forced herself not to run after Seth as he pulled a now semiconscious Maxwell off to jail. When she'd first seen him, her instinct had been to run to Seth, throw herself into his arms and let his warmth comfort her.

Hannah sniffled and wiped at her nose, drawing her gaze from Seth's receding back. Rebecca put an arm around her waist and said, "I'm very proud of both of you. You stood up to that bully."

"We did, didn't we?" Hannah wiped tears from her cheeks.

Rebecca smiled at her. "Yes, we did. You waylaid him with that vase."

Hannah stood a little taller and her head came up. "I did, even though I was scared." Her shoulders drooped again. "But it didn't stop him."

"No, it didn't stop him, but it slowed him down and we're all safe now." Rebecca hugged Hannah again and then turned her gaze on Eliza.

Eliza opened the door and the women went inside. The room no longer felt warm and welcoming.

Rebecca felt the adrenaline ease from her body only to be replaced with a thick tiredness that threatened to overtake her. "I'm sorry I put you both in danger," she offered as she picked up a chair and set it upright.

"Nonsense. You didn't put us in danger. Maxwell Evans did, and now that Seth has him, I don't think that man will ever hurt anyone again." Eliza scurried about the room, putting everything back in place.

Rebecca turned her eyes upon Hannah. The cut on her cheek was swelling and turning colors. "I'm sorry you got hit, too."

Hannah stared across at her. "Maxwell didn't hit me."

"He didn't?"

"No." Hannah reached up and touched her cheek. "When the vase broke, it shattered and a piece of glass did this."

Rebecca sat up straighter. "I'm sorry. I hadn't thought about the glass hitting you." She sat down, leaned forward and placed her elbows on her knees. Her head felt extremely heavy now.

Thanks to her, both Hannah and Eliza had been hurt. If only she'd taken the threat of Maxwell and the Evans gang more seriously. Why hadn't she listened to Seth's warnings? Were there more of the Evans gang out there looking to torture her and anyone she was close to?

Hannah smiled at her. "It's all right. It wasn't your fault Maxwell raised his ugly head this evening."

"It was my fault. If he hadn't thought I knew where

Jesse hid the money, Maxwell wouldn't have come after me and therefore put you in danger." Rebecca sat up.

Hannah moved her chair closer to Rebecca's. She took on her schoolteacher's serious voice. "Look, Eliza and I would go through this evening again if we thought it would keep you safe. We're friends, and that's what friends do for each other."

Eliza moved to stand beside them. "That's right. So don't you give this evening a second thought."

Tears stung Rebecca's eyes. "Thank you."

Hannah reached out and the women clung to each other. Rebecca cried for her friends' pain and the other two women's tears joined hers. They comforted each other with pats and soft words of friendship.

After a few moments, Hannah asked, "What do you think the marshal will do with him?"

Rebbeca's voice sounded weary. "I don't know."

"I hope that they lock him up for the rest of his life for what he's done." Bitterness dripped from Eliza's tongue.

Would any of them be the same after tonight? Rebecca sighed.

She'd realized tonight that her love for Seth ran deep and that no matter what happened she had to tell him. But would telling him only cause her more heartache?

Chapter Thirty

The next morning, Seth wasn't at his house, so Rebecca walked to the sheriff's office. The sun was shining and birds were singing. What was Seth's reaction going to be to her declaration of love?

She stepped up onto the wooden sidewalk and entered the sheriff's office. It took a moment for her eyes to adjust to the lighting. The smell of leather and wood filled her nostrils. Mr. Walker sat at Seth's desk.

The Walkers hadn't been the kindest to her so Rebecca decided to get straight to the point. "Good morning, Mr. Walker. I'm here to see the marshal this morning. Is he in the back with the prisoner?"

"He left for Durango this morning, Miss Ramsey." Mr. Walker continued to straighten the papers on Seth's desk.

Seth was gone.

Rebecca took a deep breath. "Do you know how long he'll be gone?"

"No, now that the Evans gang has been rounded up, I'm not sure when he'll come back this way." He walked around the desk and pinned a Wanted poster up on the bulletin board that hung on the far wall. "The marshal said to tell you not to leave town."

Seth didn't want her leaving town. Was it because she might have to be a witness against Maxwell? Or because he cared?

"Thank you, Mr. Walker." Rebecca turned to leave. She breathed a sigh of relief knowing that Maxwell had been the last of the gang to be arrested.

She stood on the porch trying to decide what to do next. It seemed like weeks ago that she'd told Seth she quit, but in reality it had only been a few days. Would he be upset if she continued cleaning his house? How long would he be gone this time?

"Good morning, Miss Ramsey."

Rebecca turned to see Mrs. Walker and Mrs. Hamilton standing behind her. "Good morning, ladies." She stepped back to allow them to pass.

Mrs. Hamilton stepped forward. "Miss Ramsey, we owe you an apology."

Was this a joke? Were they looking for gossip to spread? Had they heard of the events of the night before? Rebecca didn't know what to say.

Mrs. Walker sighed. "I don't blame you for not believing us. We've acted dreadful toward you and we are asking your forgiveness."

Rebecca nodded. "Thank you. If you don't mind my asking, what changed your minds about me?"

The two women smiled at her. Mrs. Walker answered, "Everyone is talking about how you saved Mrs. Kelly and Miss Young from that horrible outlaw. Anyone who would fight for their friends like that can't be all bad."

"But I didn't…"

Mrs. Shepherd came down the sidewalk. "Rebecca!"

she called. Janie was crying and kicking her little arms and legs in a fitful manner.

"We'll let you get to your child, Miss Ramsey. Have a good day." They crossed the street and entered the Walkers' general store.

Rebecca stared after them. Only a few days ago the women had treated her as an enemy. Today, she was treated as a friend. Rebecca hoped they would continue to be friends.

Seth was saddle sore. He unsaddled his horse, gave him fresh grain and water and then brushed him down. He'd been gone a month, making sure that Maxwell Evans was hung for the deaths of Janie's parents and that the rest of the Evans gang would be in prison for a long time. Now Rebecca was safe.

He rubbed the stubble on his chin. Tomorrow morning he'd go get a shave and a haircut. His thoughts turned to the woman he loved. Had Rebecca ignored his request that she stay in town? Had she taken Janie and left?

Seth pushed the kitchen door open. The scent of fresh baked bread greeted him. He stepped into the room and looked about. A covered plate sat on the back of the stove. The sound of humming came from the living area. He followed the sound.

Rebecca had her back to him. She was sweeping the floor and humming to herself. Her hair was fixed in a loose fashion that swung about her shoulders. His fingers itched to touch it.

He didn't know whether to say something or not. It might scare her. But letting her turn around and see him might scare her, too. After her ordeal with Maxwell, Seth wouldn't blame her if she was jumpy.

She turned around and stopped humming. Her eyes grew wide and then she smiled. "Welcome home, Seth."

Her soft voice washed over him like a warm summer rain. She stood staring with those big blue eyes, eyes that could see into his soul. He wanted to take her into his arms and kiss her pretty face. "Thank you."

"Dinner is on the stove, if you are hungry." She swept the dirt out the front door.

He cleared his throat. "Let me wash up."

Rebecca nodded. "While you do that I'll slice the bread and ham. Do you want milk or coffee with your meal?"

Seth couldn't believe they were having this conversation. She'd told him she quit, but here she stood in his home acting as if they were married or she still worked for him. He realized he was staring. "Cold milk would be nice. Thank you."

He spun on his heel to go wash up. Fresh water stood in the basin in his bedroom. Rebecca had thought of everything. This was the woman he wanted by his side for the rest of his life. *Lord, please let her understand I killed Jesse thinking he was armed. Help her to find it in her heart to love and forgive me.* He dried his hands and face, then walked into the kitchen, where she waited.

Rebecca sat at the table. She looked up and gave him a tense smile.

Did she have something she wanted to tell him? Something bad? Was she angry he'd told her to stay in town? Seth mentally shook himself and sat. "This smells wonderful. How did you know I'd be coming home this afternoon?"

"I didn't." She played with a loose string on the tablecloth.

Seth took a sip of the cold milk. His gaze moved about the kitchen. When had she bought an icebox? He didn't remember it being there before. "I see I have a new icebox." He smiled to soften the words.

Rebecca blushed. "Yes. I asked Mrs. Miller to order it a couple of months ago. It came in while you were away."

"I'm glad you did. Milk tastes much better cold." Seth set the glass down. He wanted to tell her he loved her. He needed to tell her he'd shot and killed Jesse. But how?

She cleared her throat. "Seth Billings, I think you should know that I love you."

A soft pink color filled her cheeks after she said the words.

He sputtered. Had he heard her right? Rebecca loved him?

Before he could say anything, she pressed on. "It was my love for you that gave me the will and strength to fight off Maxwell Evans. I'll understand if you don't love me, too, but I want you to know that I'll fight for you."

Seth didn't know whether to laugh with joy or ask questions. "What do you mean 'fight for me'? Who are you going to fight?"

She pulled at the loose string. Rebecca whispered, "Clare."

How had she known about Clare? What did it matter? Since the day he'd confided in Reverend Griffin, he'd made peace with the memory of Clare. "You can't fight a ghost, Rebecca."

"A ghost?"

"Yes, a ghost. How did you learn about Clare?" He wiped his mouth and leaned on his arms. His gaze held hers and he felt as if he could drown in the blue pools of her eyes.

The blush in her cheeks deepened to a deep red. "When you were sick, you had dreams."

Seth smiled. "And I talk in my sleep."

Rebecca nodded.

"Clare is dead, Rebecca." He reached out for her hand. Its warmth and softness filled his palm. "She and I were to marry, but she died before we could."

Her stricken eyes met his. "I'm so sorry, Seth."

Seth rubbed the back of her hand with his thumb. The skin felt silky smooth under his. Someday he'd tell her about Clare and how she died, but for the moment, he just wanted to continue holding Rebecca's hand. "That was three years ago, I've made my peace with Clare's death."

"So you are free to love me?" Rebecca's question tore at his heart.

He released her hand. "Yes, but I'm not sure you will love me when you learn what I've done." Now that the time had come to confess his part in Jesse's death, Seth didn't know if he could do it. His palms began to sweat.

Rebecca reached across the table and took back the hand he'd pulled away. "Tell me."

Seth fought for the right words. He searched his mind and decided to start at the beginning. "Remember the day you arrived here in Cottonwood Springs?" At her nod, he continued. "I had just returned from Durango. The First National Bank had been robbed a few days before and one of the outlaws had been shot."

"Yes, that was the same day Jesse got caught in the cross fire. Right?" Rebecca turned his palm over and began drawing circles within its center.

He pulled his hand away. At her hurt look, he admitted, "I'm sorry, I can't think straight with you doing that." What had her question been? Seth played it over in his mind. "Oh, yes, but Jesse wasn't just caught in the cross fire, Rebecca."

"He wasn't? What happened?" She stared into his eyes.

Seth took a deep breath. "At the time I didn't know this, but Horace Nance, one of the members of the Evans gang, likes to talk. He said the day of the robbery, Maxwell and his boys came across Jesse. They forced him to help them rob the bank in Durango. Jesse gathered the money while they held everyone at gunpoint."

Confusion laced her beautiful blue eyes. "Why did they make him do that?" she asked.

"The way Horace tells it, Jesse took a large sum of money from them when he left the gang and they wanted it back. When Jesse continued to refuse, they forced him to help do their dirty work."

"Oh, I see." Rebecca nodded for him to continue. "I still don't understand what you mean by 'he wasn't killed in the cross fire.'"

Seth's mouth went dry. "I saw Jesse holding the bag of money. When Maxwell began shooting, I returned fire. I'm not sure how it happened, but my bullet found Jesse." He choked as he said the last words.

Rebecca didn't say anything. Tears filled her eyes.

He had to press on. Seth knew he had to tell her everything before he chickened out. "Jesse didn't have a gun, Rebecca. I killed him in cold blood."

A tear escaped and ran down her face. Pain filled her eyes, Seth couldn't take hurting her like this. The chair scraped against the wood as he pushed out of it.

His heart felt as if it were being shattered into a million pieces.

She didn't love him anymore.

How could she?

Rebecca's chest hurt. Tears eased from her eyes as deep down she ached for this man. The pain in his gaze and voice cut deeper than a two-edged sword. Had this been the reason he'd been moody whenever they got too close? Had guilt caused Seth to fight his feelings for her? She watched as he pushed from his chair and walked to the door.

"Seth?"

His shoulders dropped and he waited.

Lord, please give me the right words to ease his pain. Rebecca inhaled and released the breath she'd been holding in. "Seth, I never knew Jesse Cole other than a few letters. But you I know. I've seen your heart, your pain and the guilt you carry around with you over Jesse's death."

When he didn't respond, she pressed on. "I know that you would never deliberately kill an unarmed man. It was an accident." She stressed her next words. "Seth, you had no way of knowing that Jesse didn't have a gun." He still didn't speak.

Rebecca tried to reach him again. "You were doing your duty to uphold the law. And I know that you tried to keep his dying wish. To take care of me."

Rebecca pushed away from the table and walked toward him. The need to reach out and comfort him pulled at her, but a still-small voice told her to wait. "I love you, Seth Billings, and when you decide what you want to do, I'll still be in town." She turned around to leave. Seth needed time to let her words sink in. Rebecca prayed he'd do so soon.

Her heart clenched as she walked back through the living area. Just as she reached to open the door, Seth grabbed her by the arm and swung her around to face him. She searched his warm chocolate eyes. The love within melted away all her fears.

"Rebecca Ramsey, I love you, too, and if you'll have this foolish man, I want you to be my wife." Seth reached out and moved a strand of hair so he could see her eyes.

"I've been waiting a month to hear those words." Rebecca reached up and pulled his face down to hers. When she could feel his breath against her lips, she whispered, "Yes, I will marry you, Marshal."

His kiss was warm and full of love. He held her close and Rebecca could hear his heartbeat as it joined hers. Seth broke the kiss with a soft moan.

She missed his closeness when he set her away from him. He still held her arms and pressed his forehead to hers. "You might have been Jesse's girl when you arrived, but after tomorrow, everyone will know that you are, now and forever, the marshal's bride."

Epilogue

Marriage agreed with Rebecca Billings. She found it hard to believe that she'd been married four months. The summer sun beat down on her as she walked to Eliza's for afternoon tea.

She'd just told Seth about her visit to Dr. Clark and now she couldn't wait to tell her best friends that she and Seth were going to have a baby.

Cottonwood Springs had turned out to be the most wonderful place on earth. Rebecca found herself thanking God daily for bringing her to this part of the New Mexico Territory.

She entered Eliza's dress shop and stopped inside the doorway. The little bell over the door dinged. The scent of cinnamon filled her nostrils and her stomach growled. Had Eliza baked sweet rolls again? Rebecca hoped she'd serve them with the afternoon tea.

Eliza stepped around the corner. "Come on in, Rebecca."

Rebecca followed her into the small kitchen. Since Maxwell's attack, Eliza had moved the table into the kitchen. She no longer took her meals in what she used to call the eating area.

"Hello, Rebecca." Hannah sat at the table sipping her tea. A plate of freshly baked cinnamon rolls decorated the center of a pretty blue tablecloth.

Rebecca walked to the chair closest to the stove and sat down. "Hello, Hannah. How are you today?"

Hannah poured Rebecca a cup of tea. "I'm well. I could ask you the same question. Eliza said she saw you go into the doctor's house earlier."

"I did go see the doctor today." Rebecca spooned sugar into her tea. She glanced at the rolls and wondered if she should have held off on the added sugar.

"Are you feeling all right?" Eliza put her cup back onto the table. She passed Hannah and Rebecca dessert plates with a cinnamon roll on each one.

Rebecca took her plate and smiled. "Yes, and the doctor said that I'm healthy for a woman who is going to have a baby in six short months."

"A baby!" Eliza jumped up and hugged her.

Hannah also hugged her and declared, "Janie's going to be a big sister."

"Yes, she is." The three women smiled at each other.

As soon as the other two returned to their seats, Rebecca forked a large bit of sweet roll into her mouth. She closed her eyes and chewed, savoring the taste of cinnamon and sugar on her tongue.

Eliza gushed, "That is wonderful news, Rebecca. Have you told Seth yet?"

Rebecca nodded and swallowed. "He's as happy as I am."

"Two babies. You are going to have your hands full." Hannah smiled. "Someday I'm going to get married and have a houseful of children, too." She sipped her tea. A dreamy look passed over her face.

"Oh, I can't wait to start making her dresses. I think

the first one should be pink or yellow. Maybe I'll add matching bonnets and little ribbons for her hair." Eliza smiled and nodded. "Yes, that's what I'll do."

"She might have a boy," Hannah, the voice of reason, butted in before Eliza could press on.

Eliza clapped her hands. "Even better. I'll make little shirts and trousers. And—" The bell over the dress-shop door dinged, cutting off Eliza's sentence.

"That will be Seth—he's picking me up here," Rebecca told them as she wiped at the stickiness that coated her mouth, and stood.

Eliza protested, "But we haven't had any time to talk and plan for the baby."

Rebecca laughed as she pushed away from the table. "That's probably why he's here early."

Hannah smiled. "We have six months to plan and talk, Eliza. Let her go to her husband."

Eliza blushed. "Well, all right, but be sure and come over tomorrow afternoon. I'll do some sketches of dresses and you can tell me if you like them."

The three friends hugged and then Rebecca hurried to the front door where her husband waited. Her heart beat a little faster when she saw him.

The other two followed her to the door and hugged her again. Rebecca stood back and smiled at her two best friends. She mentally thanked God for bringing these women into her life.

Seth tipped his hat to the ladies. "Ladies." Then he pulled Rebecca to his side. He slipped her hand into the crook of his arm.

As he turned her to leave, the other two women waved and offered congratulations. Rebecca laughed and waved back.

A few minutes later she walked on the wooden sidewalk with her handsome husband. God had brought her to Cottonwood Springs as a mail-order bride, so that she could meet Seth and live happily ever after.

"I love you, Seth Billings." She snuggled against his side.

He laughed. "I love you, too, Mrs. Billings."

As they continued to walk she asked, "Do you ever regret I came to town as someone else's mail-order bride?" She looked up into his chocolate eyes.

Seth stopped and turned her so that they faced each other. "No. My life is perfect with you in it. If you hadn't answered Jesse Cole's ad, I wouldn't have the most beautiful wife in all of the New Mexico Territory."

Those were the words Rebecca needed to hear. She rose on tiptoe to kiss his mouth. She didn't care who saw them. When he pulled her closer and leaned into her, Rebecca thanked the Lord for her handsome marshal and his love.

* * * * *

Dear Reader,

Thank you for picking up a copy of *The Marshal's Promise*. Rebecca and Seth's story started with a basic idea my husband had. He suggested that Rebecca answer a mail-order-bride ad from an outlaw. My brain immediately went to what if said outlaw was killed while trying to rob a bank? And then what would happen if he asked the man who shot him to take care of his mail-order bride? From there, *The Marshal's Promise* was born and Seth Billings became a bigger-than-life hero. I hope you enjoyed reading Seth and Rebecca's story as much as I enjoyed writing it.

Feel free to visit me on my website and blog and www.rhondagibson.com.

Warmly,
Rhonda Gibson

Questions for Discussion

1. When Rebecca learns that her fiancé Jesse Cole was killed and won't be marrying her, she decides to stay in Cottonwood Springs. Would you have stayed if you were her? Why or why not?

2. How do you think Rebecca's life would have been different if Jesse had lived?

3. Seth offered Rebecca money to go home, but she didn't take it and decided to stay. Do you think he was a little hasty in offering her a job? Why or why not?

4. Hannah and Eliza helped Rebecca begin a new life. Have you ever moved to a new place and met friends who have helped you?

5. Seth was dealing with guilt over the deaths of Clare and Jesse. Have you ever felt a deep guilt that has changed your life?

6. It took Seth a long time to realize that God didn't blame him for the deaths of Clare and Jesse. Have you been able to accept God's love and forgiveness? Is there a time that you realized that God didn't blame you for things that you blamed yourself for?

7. Rebecca had to deal with gossip and speculation regarding her past. Have you ever had to deal with gossips? How did you handle the situation?

8. All Rebecca wanted was someone to love her unconditionally. She felt Janie would be that person and so adopted her. Rebecca almost lost Janie to her birth family. Have you ever adopted a child? Were you afraid the birth family would come and take him/her away from you?

9. Do you have people in your life who feel like family but aren't blood relations? If so, who are they? And what makes them so special?

10. Which character in this book did you most connect with? And why?

INSPIRATIONAL

Love Inspired.

HISTORICAL

celebrating
15
YEARS

COMING NEXT MONTH
AVAILABLE JUNE 12, 2012

A BABY BETWEEN THEM
Irish Brides
Winnie Griggs

THE BARON'S GOVERNESS BRIDE
Glass Slipper Brides
Deborah Hale

A PROPER COMPANION
Ladies in Waiting
Louise M. Gouge

WINNING THE WIDOW'S HEART
Sherri Shackelford

REQUEST YOUR FREE BOOKS!

2 FREE INSPIRATIONAL NOVELS
PLUS 2
FREE
MYSTERY GIFTS

Love Inspired.
HISTORICAL
INSPIRATIONAL HISTORICAL ROMANCE

YES! Please send me 2 FREE Love Inspired® Historical novels and my 2 FREE mystery gifts (gifts are worth about $10). After receiving them, if I don't wish to receive any more books, I can return the shipping statement marked "cancel". If I don't cancel, I will receive 4 brand-new novels every month and be billed just $4.49 per book in the U.S. or $4.99 per book in Canada. That's a saving of at least 22% off the cover price. It's quite a bargain! Shipping and handling is just 50¢ per book in the U.S. and 75¢ per book in Canada.* I understand that accepting the 2 free books and gifts places me under no obligation to buy anything. I can always return a shipment and cancel at any time. Even if I never buy another book, the two free books and gifts are mine to keep forever.

102/302 IDN FEHF

Name	(PLEASE PRINT)	
Address		Apt. #
City	State/Prov.	Zip/Postal Code

Signature (if under 18, a parent or guardian must sign)

Mail to the **Reader Service:**
IN U.S.A.: P.O. Box 1867, Buffalo, NY 14240-1867
IN CANADA: P.O. Box 609, Fort Erie, Ontario L2A 5X3

Not valid for current subscribers to Love Inspired Historical books.

Want to try two free books from another series?
Call 1-800-873-8635 or visit www.ReaderService.com.

* Terms and prices subject to change without notice. Prices do not include applicable taxes. Sales tax applicable in N.Y. Canadian residents will be charged applicable taxes. Offer not valid in Quebec. This offer is limited to one order per household. All orders subject to credit approval. Credit or debit balances in a customer's account(s) may be offset by any other outstanding balance owed by or to the customer. Please allow 4 to 6 weeks for delivery. Offer available while quantities last.

Your Privacy—The Reader Service is committed to protecting your privacy. Our Privacy Policy is available online at www.ReaderService.com or upon request from the Reader Service.

We make a portion of our mailing list available to reputable third parties that offer products we believe may interest you. If you prefer that we not exchange your name with third parties, or if you wish to clarify or modify your communication preferences, please visit us at www.ReaderService.com/consumerschoice or write to us at Reader Service Preference Service, P.O. Box 9062, Buffalo, NY 14269. Include your complete name and address.

LIH11B

Love Inspired HISTORICAL

celebrating
15
YEARS

Author

WINNIE GRIGGS

brings you another story from

Irish Brides

For two months, Nora Murphy cared for an abandoned infant she found while on her voyage from Ireland to Boston. Now settled in Faith Glen, Nora tells herself she's happy with little Grace and a good job as housekeeper to Sheriff Cameron Long. A traumatic childhood closed Cam off to any dreams of family life. Yet somehow his lovely housekeeper and her child have opened his heart again. When the unthinkable occurs, it will take all their faith to reach a new future together.

A Baby Between Them

Available June 2012 wherever books are sold.

www.LoveInspiredBooks.com

LIH82919

For a sneak peek at Valerie Hansen's
heart-stopping inspirational romantic suspense
THREAT OF DARKNESS, read on!

If Samantha Rochard hadn't already been so keyed up that she could barely think straight, she might have shrieked when she saw the cop's face. Her jaw did drop and she was pretty sure her gasp was audible. His light brown hair and eyes and his broad shoulders were all too familiar. It couldn't be him, of course. It simply couldn't be. She hadn't had one of these déjà vu moments for months. Maybe years.

Her pulse leaped as reality replaced imagination. She couldn't catch her breath. This was not another bad dream. John Waltham, the man who'd broken her heart so badly she'd wondered if she'd ever recover, was standing right in front of her, big as life.

Before she could decide how to greet him, he set the mood of their reunion. His "What did you think you were *doing?*" was delivered with such force it was practically a growl.

That attitude stiffened her spine and made it easy to answer, "My job."

"You're a nurse, not a cop."

"Oh, so I'm supposed to just stand there while you and your buddies waltz in here and start shooting?"

"If necessary, yes."

"Don't be silly. I knew Bobby Joe wasn't going to hurt me," she insisted, wishing she fully believed her own assertion. When an addict was under the influence, there was no way to predict what he or she might do.

Handling the pistol expertly, John unloaded it and passed

it to one of his fellow officers to bag as evidence before turning back to Samantha.

She noticed that his expression had softened some, but it was too little too late. "What are you doing back in town?" She eyed him from head to toe. "And why are you dressed like a member of our police force?"

"Because that's what I am. I've come home," he said flatly.

Samantha couldn't believe her ears. After all he'd put her through, all the tears she'd shed after he'd left her high and dry, he had the unmitigated gall to return and go back to work as if nothing had changed. How *dare* he!

Pick up THREAT OF DARKNESS
for the rest of Samantha and John's exciting, suspenseful
love story, available in June 2012, only from
Love Inspired® Suspense.